Visit Lucy March online:
www.lucymarch.com
www.facebook.com/LucyMarchBooks
@LucyMarch

Also by Lucy March

A Little Night Magic
That Touch of Magic

LUCY MARCH

piatkus

PIATKUS

First published in the US in 2015 by St Martin's Press
First published in Great Britain in 2015 by Piatkus

1 3 5 7 9 10 8 6 4 2

A CIP catalogue record for this book
is available from the British Library.

ISBN 978-0-349-40293-2

Printed and bound in Great Britain by
Clays Ltd, St Ives plc

Papers used by Piatkus are from well-managed forests
and other responsible sources.

MIX
Paper from
responsible sources
FSC® C104740
www.fsc.org

Piatkus
An imprint of
Little, Brown Book Group
Carmelite House
50 Victoria Embankment
London EC4Y 0DZ

An Hachette UK Company
www.hachette.co.uk

www.piatkus.co.uk

For love
or
Magic

Chapter 1

"Let's be clear about one thing, Seamus," I said, giving the bull mastiff the French fry he had been whining about since I pulled it out of the bag. "Just because I'm feeding you doesn't mean you're my dog."

I wasn't trying to be mean, but I didn't want him to start getting all attached just because I gave him a stupid French fry, either. In truth, there didn't seem to be much danger of that; he inhaled the fry and continued to remain indifferent to me, which was really best for everyone.

It was at that moment that the steering wheel in Judd's tattered old sky-blue Chevy pickup truck began to rattle. I hadn't wanted that stupid truck and I didn't particularly like it, but I'd gotten stuck with it anyway. Much like Seamus.

"C'mon, you stupid—" I banged my fist on the steering wheel, and it stopped rattling.

"Hey," Judd admonished from the spot between me and Seamus where he crouched. "Be gentle with my girl."

"You talking to me or the truck?" I said, giving him deadly side-eye.

He made that answer clear by patting the truck's dash. "This truck is awesome. Perfect to haul home all those garage sale chairs and tables. I'm gonna refinish them, baby, sell 'em at a yuge profit, and we'll be livin' like kings."

"It's *huge,* not *yuge,* and you never did bring home a single piece of furniture. You couldn't keep your word if it was sewn into your underwear, and I hate this stupid truck." To make my point, I downshifted from fifth gear to fourth, letting the gears grind as I deliberately jammed my elbow into Judd's gut.

Not that Judd had a gut anymore. He was dead.

"You do know that, right?" I said. "You're dead. I'm a widow. Move on already, would you?"

"*I've* moved on," he said, his South Boston accent just as thick as ever. Even in death, he talked like he had a mouth full of peanut butter. "I'm dead. It's *you* who's keeping me here."

He pronounced *here* with two syllables. *He-ah.* You'd think if I had to be haunted by the imagined ghost of my dead ex-husband, I'd at least give him a reasonable accent. British, maybe. I shot him a sideways look.

"Say 'jolly good,'" I commanded.

He laughed. "You got a wicked sense of *yumor*, Ellie."

"It's humor. *Hu*-mor. With an *h*." I stuffed a fry in my mouth. Seamus whined again.

"I don't care what you say," Judd said, and shot me a sidelong glance, his eyes glinting with *yumor*. You had to give Judd that; no matter what he was doing, he always had a great time doing it. "You still love me, and you know it."

I glanced in the rearview and saw his cocky smile, the very smile I'd fallen for way back in the day when I was too young and stupid to know better.

"Shut up." I gave Seamus another fry, and he wolfed it down with such enthusiasm that I had to check my hand quickly to be sure all my fingers were still there. They were. They were covered in slobber, but they were still there. With the luck I'd had lately, I guessed I should be grateful. I wiped my hands on my jeans and took the left onto Wildwood Lane, which sounded like it should be really nice, but in reality it looked like the kind of abandoned dirt road where they shoot those *the-missing-girl-was-last-seen-here* pieces for the local news.

"Are you kidding me with this, Judd?" My heart started racing in response to the panic rushing through my veins. "What the hell kind of place did you buy, anyway?"

Judd leaned forward, grinning like the charming asshole he'd been in life. "Wait for it, baby. You're gonna love it."

"I doubt that," I said, but when I looked to Judd, he

was gone, and I was alone in *his* stupid truck with *her* goddamned dog, on my way to the only thing I had left to my name, thanks to him.

I hit my foot to the gas, a move which had little actual effect on how fast that old rust heap moved but which did provide some emotional payoff. While I was distracted, Seamus stuffed his massive nose into the fast-food bag and ripped it to shreds. My burger, wrapper and all, was gone in two bites.

"Son of a bitch."

Seamus, as usual, ignored me.

The mailbox was not "rust-colored" as the real estate paperwork had claimed, but rather rust-*covered*, which I'd like to state for the record, is *different*. I wanted to drive past it, but unfortunately, the number 144 was clearly painted onto the wooden stake the mailbox was impaled upon, and I couldn't pretend I hadn't seen it.

"Home sweet home," I muttered, and turned down the dirt driveway, although calling it a driveway was a little generous. It was more a visible suggestion that once or twice some sort of vehicle had accessed the house this way. The branches and leaves slapped at Judd's stupid truck and eventually cleared away to reveal the glorified shack that turned out to be the only thing my dead husband owned that his debt hadn't eaten.

Well, that, his dumb truck, and his girlfriend's dog.

I stopped the truck, turned it off, and stared at my future, such as it was.

At least you'll have a place to live, the estate law-yer had told me last month as he closed his leather briefcase and lifted it off the table in the diner where we'd met up. *In cases where a husband leaves this kind of debt behind, I've seen widows left without anything. Or worse, with nothing,* and *bills left to pay. Consider-ing how things could have gone, you're actually pretty lucky.*

Yeah, that was me. *Lucky.*

I tightened my grip on the steering wheel, staring through the windshield and thinking.

"You don't suppose . . ." I said to Seamus. "I mean . . . you don't think Judd was running some kind of scam out here, do you?"

The dog, apparently uninterested in the *why* behind Judd's real estate ventures, ignored me, but my mind kept picking at the problem. Judd had traveled a bit, and like most wives of small-time con men, I hadn't asked a lot of questions for fear of getting the truth. Had he been out here, working a scam, during some of those absences? But why? Nodaway Falls, despite the name, had no real falls to boast of; there was little to no tourist traffic, and even less local industry. It was an hour and a half from Buffalo and a whisper away from the Pennsylvania border; the land itself was worth little more than Judd's stupid truck. Not to mention that there were plenty of easy pickins on the one-hour route between Taunton, the small town in southwestern Mas-sachusetts where he'd parked me after we got married, and Boston, where the rich and stupid came to get fleeced by the smart and lazy. The drive to Nodaway Falls, which based on appearances was not a super wealthy community, was eight and a half hours. If Judd had been out here working a scam, it had been for something other than money, because nothing he'd get out here would have covered the gas.

I looked at Seamus and he panted at me, sated and slobbery in the midsummer heat. I wondered if he had eaten the girlfriend's lunches, too.

"Dumb dog," I said, and kicked open the driver's-side door. I stepped out onto a patchy clearing that passed for a front yard, and stared at the run-down shack that was now all mine. It had shutters that were actual shutters, not just decoration, covered in peeling green paint. They might not be terrible with an updated color, maybe. The multipaned front windows were so old that even from what was passing for my front yard, I could see that they hadn't been replaced in at least fifty years. The place was small, about nine hundred square feet, with two bedrooms and one full bath. Not grand by any standards, but hell, it had a roof and a fenced side yard for Seamus, and I wasn't exactly in a position to be picky.

Seamus lumbered out of the truck and stood by my side. His head came up well past my hips. The monstrous canine was a hundred and fifty pounds, more horse than dog. What kind of woman would buy a dog like that, anyway?

Of course, I knew exactly what kind of woman. The Christy McNagle kind of woman, the kind of woman who gets her blond from a bottle and her sexual ya-yas from my husband.

Former husband, I thought. *Dead husband.*

I looked down at Seamus and contemplated him for a bit. It was nicer to think about the stupid dog than it was to think about Christy McNagle and Judd doing whatever it was they were doing together while I was oblivious and stupid.

"Go on, dog." I nudged him with my knee. "Run around. Get some exercise."

He looked up at me and licked his slobbering jaws, retrieving a sesame seed that had stuck to his nose. He let out a little huff of impatience and lay down in the dirt, settling his big dumb boulder of a head on his front paws.

"Yeah," I said on a sigh. "I know how you feel."

I stared at the house. I didn't want to open that door, didn't want to see what was inside, but I didn't want to sleep outside, either. My dusty, used-to-be-white Keds moved forward step by step, and eventually, I found myself putting the key in the lock. Before I turned it, I looked back at Seamus, who was still lying on the dirt, watching me.

"Coward," I said, and turned the knob.

I had taken a chunk out of my dwindling checking account to hire someone to clean the place. I'd started accounts with the gas and electric companies while staying at Judd's sister's house in Providence, so at least there would be lights and hot water. It was dark inside and I hit the ancient push-button switch. To my utter surprise, it didn't set off a fire, and the ceiling dome light actually turned on, if a little reluctantly.

"See, what'd I tell you?" Judd said from over my shoulder. "It's not so bad, right? I got the furniture and appliances included in the deal."

I ignored him. He was dead. And, according to Dr. Fliegel, he was just my imagination anyway, a hallucination I made up to work through the grief. He wasn't even a real ghost. A real ghost could tell you *why,* could explain, could apologize. All fake-ghost Judd did was the same stuff he did when he was alive; smile, charm, and lie.

I turned away from Judd, focusing my attention on the place. It really wasn't that bad. To my right was the living room; it was small, but it had a woodstove in the center of the far wall and what looked like usable, if old, hardwood floors.

"You just buff those up, stain 'em, seal 'em, they're good as new," Judd said.

"Where did you even get that money?" I asked. "You paid a hundred thousand dollars in cash for this place, but can't buy a decent truck. What the hell is that about, Judd?"

He grinned at me, and dodged the question. "I'm a man of mystery, baby."

"Shut up," I said absently as I surveyed the place. To one side of the woodstove was an overstuffed chair next to a standing lamp; a reading area. To the other side was a writing desk. In front was a beige La-Z-Boy that had seen better days, and a floral Victorian couch that made your back hurt just to look at it. No television, but that didn't matter much. As soon as I got the wi-fi hooked up, I could watch movies on my laptop.

"What do you think, Seamus?" I asked the dog. "You think it'll work?"

He ignored me.

I looked to the left; there was an eat-in kitchen, also small, but kind of quaint, separated from the cooking area by a peninsula counter that cut the space in half. The dining half had a small farmhouse table with four wooden chairs, no seat cushions. Lace curtains hung over the windows, unmoving in the stilted summer air. I walked to the window, and with a significant amount of effort and cursing, got it open. It didn't let much fresh air in, but it was a start.

I moved farther into the kitchen. The lumbering yellow appliances looked like they were straight off the set of *I Love Lucy,* with a big double-oven gas stove, and a yellow refrigerator with soft, rounded edges.

"Coldspot," I said, reading the script logo written in metal on the door, and noticed that Seamus was suddenly at my heels. Of course he'd be here now; I was about to open a fridge, and the opportunity to eat more of my food was apparently too big to resist.

"It's an antique," Judd said, leaning one ghostly hip against the counter. "I bet it even works. Go on, open it."

I pulled the large silver lever, half expecting it to fall off in my hand, but the door opened easily. I stuck my hand inside the fridge; it was legitimately cold in there.

The freezer chest—I knew what to call it because it had FREEZER CHEST written in scripty metallic lettering on the plastic door—was a separate compartment tucked away up top, but when I pulled the plastic door down and peered inside, I saw that someone had put in modern ice cube trays, and the cubes were frozen solid.

Huh, I thought, closing the fridge. Must have been the cleaning service. My eyes teared up suddenly, and my throat tightened with emotion. It was a small kindness, but when things were bad, it was the small kindnesses that did you in.

"A little work," Judd said, moving into the living room, "a little elbow grease, a little TLC, and this place is going to be our dream, Ellie."

I wiped my eyes, leaned against the oven, and looked out the front windows. In my imagination, I saw pale yellow curtains flowing in the breeze, and fresh cushions on the chairs.

Yeah, maybe, I thought.

I headed down the hallway. The bathroom had mint-green walls with white ceramic tile halfway up, and was oddly large considering the dimensions of the rest of the house. The floor had white honeycomb tiles with dark blue ones marking out little daisy shapes at regular intervals, and I'll admit it; my breath caught in my throat a little bit.

"Look at that," Judd said over my shoulder. "A claw-foot tub. Just like you always wanted. Do I know you or do I know you, huh?"

Seamus pushed himself past me into the bathroom, hitting the backs of my knees and making them buckle a bit. I checked the faucet and the handheld shower-head that was attached to the side of the tub; they were old, but they worked. It took the hot water a little while to come to the party, but hell, I was grateful there was hot water at all. There was no standing shower, but I liked baths well enough.

I could work with this.

I poked my head into the tiny back bedroom, which was empty except for the built-in bookshelves and the plain metal radiator under the window. I could paint the radiator white, and strip the faded pink floral wall-paper, and it would make a decent office. Emotion bloomed in my chest, so powerful and unfamiliar that I had to lean against the wall to hold myself up as it rippled through my being. I recognized the emotion, but just barely.

It was hope.

"See?" Judd said, grinning like a fool. "I knew you'd like it."

"Yeah, yeah, yeah." I crossed the hallway, put my hand on the old metal doorknob that presumably led to what the paperwork had described as "the big bed-room," and turned. The knob rolled loosely from side to side, but didn't open.

Crap.

I jiggled it; I could hear the metal bits clinking around inside. I yanked at the doorknob, cursing and kicking at the door. No joy. Seamus sat a few feet back, watching me dispassionately. I leaned my forehead against the door and let out a breath, my entire body vibrating with nerves as the thought occurred to me.

The knob is made of metal.

A painful jolt of fear ran through me, and I stepped back from the door. My magic was gone. It was gone-gone, had been gone for sixteen years and it wasn't coming back.

"Then what's it gonna hurt to try?" Judd asked from over my shoulder.

I shot him a sideways glance. "You don't know about the magic. I never told you. So shut up."

He grinned at me, and my heart soared a bit, but I couldn't tell whether the flutter was coming from the memory of Judd's intoxicating smile or the momentary power fantasy of having my magic back and not having to dig through the truck to find my tools.

I shook out my hands, released a sharp breath, and closed my eyes. I could feel the workings inside the knob. I'd locked up my ability to manipulate metal, but I hadn't lost my connection to the element. A piece had broken loose inside the mortise latch; I could turn that knob all day and it wouldn't do a damn thing. It happened sometimes with old lock assemblies. Most likely, the cleaning people had shut the door too hard when they'd left, and the lock had finally broken down in protest. Or maybe the house had already made up its mind about me, and the verdict wasn't good.

But either way, I was going to need my tools. I pushed up from my knees and headed out, Judd calling out after me, "What? You're not even going to try?"

"Six years trying to get the truth out of you taught me not to attempt the impossible," I shot over my shoulder at him.

I went out to the truck, got my beat-up old toolbox from behind the driver's seat, and spent the next fifteen minutes dismantling the lock assembly while Seamus slobbered over my shoulder.

I got the door open, pushed through it, and my breath caught. The room had white beadboard wainscoting and yellow walls and gleaming wood floors and it was . . .

"Beautiful," I breathed.

Right in the middle of the back wall was the refurbished white-painted cast-iron bed I'd had delivered from the local antiques shop. I'd been charmed by the picture on the website, by the shiny exposed metal springs, by the idea that I could love it even after everyone else had abandoned it. I'd spent way more money than I should have on an old-fashioned feather mattress to go with it, which had also been delivered and was leaned up against the wall, still in its plastic wrapping.

I walked over to it and ripped off the plastic in a frenzy, then hauled the mattress over and, with some effort, got it onto the bed.

"What do you think, Seamus?" I said, looking back at the dog who had finally found his way to the room. "It's okay, right?"

Seamus walked over to the bed, sniffed the mattress, and curled up on the floor next to the bed.

"I don't care what you say," I said, "it's gonna be—"

"Great, baby," Judd said from behind me, hijacking the last of my sentence. "You and me, on an adventure, the way it was supposed to be."

I turned and there he was, leaning against the doorjamb, looking sexy as hell, his black hair ruffled and his smile just as crooked and bent as his soul. And stupid me, I wanted him back. I wanted his arms around me and I wanted him in my bed and I wanted to believe in the beautiful lies he spun for me, my own corrupted Rumpelstiltskin spinning gold from bullshit. I missed him so much it hurt, and I hated him so much that I wished he could come back to life just so I could kill him myself.

"You're not allowed in here," I said, and shut the door in his face while his mouth was opening to form a reply. I kicked off my shoes, stepped over Seamus, and settled down onto my new old bed, groaning with exhausted delight before falling into a dead sleep.

The dream started out the way the dream always started out, just a simple reliving of the day that changed my life. I was in the basement of the First Presbyterian church in Lott's Cove, Maine, with twenty-eight other people. My mother. My best friend, Del. Del's parents. My math teacher from the seventh grade. We were packing up tool kits for the Habitat for Humanity volunteers who were taking the bus to

Bangor later that day to help build houses over the summer. It was going to be the first time either Del or I had gone away from home for more than a night or two. We were going to be gone for one full week. We were insanely excited, just the way that day was in real life.

In the dream, though, instead of what really happened, the basement starts to fill with glowing gerbera daisies. It just fills, from bottom to top, and at first everyone thinks it's cute, that the flowers are beautiful. They all play with them, and I try to tell them not to, but no one hears me. Eventually, the flowers cover our heads. It gets dark as they press in on us and people start to panic. That's when it finally occurs to me to open the door and get everyone out, but I'm always too late. I reach for the doorknob, but just as I do, it turns into a daisy, and I touch it before I can stop myself. As soon as I do, electric-blue lightning sparks from my fingers, evaporating the flowers and hopping from person to person, killing them one by one. The door opens and there's my father, smiling wide with his arms outstretched for me, as though he hadn't just used me to kill them all.

Same dream. Every time.

"Babe." I could feel the warmth of Judd's breath on my ear. "Babe. People in the house."

I jolted up in the bed, my heart racing, the instinct to rush to the door setting all my nerves on fire, but then I opened my eyes and slammed back into reality. I reached instinctively for Judd before realizing with a stab of sudden understanding that he wasn't alive and warm in my bed.

He was dead.

I fell back on the pillows and breathed deep, slowly rising out of the dream and into my new reality.

Widowed, broke, and living in Nodaway Falls.

And there were voices coming from the front of the house.

I sat up, rubbing my eyes and trying to process what was happening. The voices belonged to women, and they sounded light and happy, not threatening. It was still light outside, so I hadn't been asleep for that long, but I felt like I'd been out for years.

"Hey," I said, and nudged Seamus gently with my foot. He raised his head and looked at me.

"You hear that? People are *in the house.*" I hurled myself out of bed and tried to smooth out my T-shirt and jeans, which also happened to be covered in dog hair, a thing I'd gotten rather used to over the last eight months. "You are the worst watchdog on the planet. Surely someone has told you this."

Seamus did the dog equivalent of rolling his eyes and lumbered up off the floor to follow me into the living room, where I found an older woman with wild, flowing gray hair showing another woman—younger, blond, and massively pregnant under a red and white polka-dotted dress—where to put the covered glass platter that held a huge chocolate cake. The older woman was wearing a flowing yellow sundress and a big floppy hat with a sunflower on the side, and was so focused on her duties ordering Polka Dots around that she didn't even notice me walking in. Polka Dots, however, saw me right away and instead of reddening with shame for breaking into my home, she grinned and waved. She was uncommonly beautiful, and I swiped at my own unkempt brown mop, hoping neither of the intruders were the judgy type.

"Hi!" she said, disappearing into the kitchen where she put the cake on the counter. "You must be Eliot!"

The woman with the gray hair turned to me, her face bright. "Eliot!" Her arms flew out and she ran to me, pulling me into a big hug.

"Oh, so . . . wow, you guys are huggers," I said as she let me go.

"Such an unusual name for a woman, Eliot," Polka Dots said. "I love it."

"Thanks," I said. "My mother was a George Eliot fan."

She patted her belly. "We're having a girl. Nick— that's my husband, Nick Easter, I'm sure you'll meet him soon—wants to name her Bunny."

"Yeah, that's a bad idea," I said automatically.

Polka Dots made a face and laughed. "I know, right? So now I'm all obsessed with girl names. The little monkey was due three days ago, but she *refuses to come out!*" Polka Dots yelled playfully toward her stomach and laughed.

"Yeah. Good luck with that." A weird silence followed, and I wished not for the first time that I had Judd's gift for charming strangers with meaningless chitchat. "Um, not to be rude but . . . who are you people?"

Polka Dots slapped her hand to her forehead and laughed. "Oh! Wow! We totally forgot to introduce ourselves! You must be like, 'Who are these crazy people in my house?'"

"A little," I said. "Yeah."

She smiled. "I'm Bernadette Easter, but you can call me Peach. Everyone does. And this is Addie Hooper-Higgins. She owns the antiques store. She sold you your bed."

Addie Hooper-Higgins. The name did ring the vaguest of bells.

"Oh, right. Nice to meet you." I held out my hand on instinct, but Addie just pulled me in for another hug. Over Addie's shoulder, Peach smiled and winked at me, as if we were sharing a joke. *That crazy Addie. Always hugs people twice.*

"Um, yeah," I said when Addie released me the second time. "I'm Eliot. Well, you know that. And this big guy is Seamus."

"Oh!" Addie clapped her hands, delighted. "What a beautiful creature!"

"Don't be offended if he's a little standoffish. He's not exactly friendly, but he doesn't bite." I hesitated, deliberating. "That I know of."

The words were barely out of my mouth before Seamus was up on his hind legs, his massive paws on Addie's shoulders as he attempted to lick her face right off her head. I stared in disbelief. The little bastard. For eight months, I've been feeding that dog—and not the cheap stuff, either, freaking *Iams*—and he had yet to lick my face or show any affection for me at all. On a good day, he tolerated my presence. On a bad one, he ate my lunch.

"What a little love!" Addie laughed and patted his shoulders lightly. "Down now, Seamus."

Seamus immediately hopped down. He ambled over to Peach, sniffed her knee and licked her hand.

"Sweet dog!" Peach said, rubbing his head.

"Yeah." I had a sudden hopeful thought. "You want him?"

They both looked at me as though I had just offered them my firstborn or something, and then Addie laughed.

"Oh, you," she said. "You're funny."

I hadn't been kidding but . . . whatever.

"I'm sorry," I said. "I just got here this morning and I wasn't expecting visitors, so I don't have anything to offer you."

"Oh, get the woman a soda, would you, Peach?" Addie said, and Peach went into the kitchen. I followed. Peach opened my fridge, and I was shocked to see that it was full. I could only catch a glimpse of the bounty in the few seconds while Peach grabbed three bottles of soda, but I saw a number of disposable Gladware containers and something that looked like lasagna before Peach closed the door.

"Wow, you filled the fridge. That's . . . uh . . . neighborly." My stomach was growling at the thought of that lasagna, and I hoped they couldn't hear it.

Peach whipped the cap off one of the sodas and handed it to me.

"Thanks," I said, and took a sip.

"I hope you don't mind us just barging in like this," Addie said, without the slightest hint of shame. "We knocked, but the door was unlocked, so we figured we'd drop all the stuff off and surprise you." She shrugged. *Just a little breaking and entering. No big deal.* "Welcome to Nodaway Falls!"

I looked at Peach, who had the good grace to look at least a little abashed.

"It's a thing we do here when someone new moves in," she said. "Everyone contributes a dish, or knits homemade dishcloths . . ." She motioned to a paper grocery sack on the counter which I guessed held the nonperishable items. "You know, whatever we're good at. Everyone throws in something."

Addie beamed. "I made the pecan pie."

I smiled back, and felt a bit of grudging happiness spark inside. These people and their good cheer were apparently contagious.

"Oh, I love pie," I said. "It's literally one of my favorite things."

"Addie's pecan pies are the stuff of legend." Behind Addie's back, Peach gave me a hand signal which I read to mean that I should absolutely under no circumstances eat the pecan pie.

"Okay. Thank you," I said to both of them. There was another long silence and then I realized that, despite their intruder status, I should probably be doing something hostesslike. "I'm sorry. Do you guys want . . . to eat something you brought?" I tried to smile again, but felt like a stiff jack-o'-lantern this time. How did Judd do this so easily, just . . . like . . . *talk* to people? Of course, he wasn't here at the moment to tell me what to do. He tended to only show up when I was alone. God forbid the guy should be actually useful, even in death.

"Oh, is your moving truck late?" Peach said, gracefully corralling the conversation. "When my parents moved to Florida, their moving truck went to Pensacola instead of Sarasota and it took them two weeks to get their stuff."

"Yeah, that sucks," I said. "But, uh, no. Everything I own is out in the truck."

Addie and Peach exchanged a quick glance, and then Addie laughed and clapped her hands. "Starting over fresh! You know, that's such a smart thing to do. Leave the past in the past, right?"

"So, where's your husband?" Peach said, motioning toward my left hand. I glanced down at the wedding set that was still on my finger. It wasn't worth much when Judd bought it new, so selling it wouldn't have helped, and despite everything, I hadn't been able to take it off quite yet.

"I'm widowed," I said in a simple, matter-of-fact tone. "He took his mistress out for a night on the town—in my car, classy as always. He hit some black ice and drove off Route 44 and into the Taunton River, which wasn't easy. Plowed right through the side rail and just . . . *plooosh*." I made a sound of splashing water. "It was pretty cold. The cops said they both died quick, so . . . that's a good thing, I guess."

Silence. Wide eyes. Frozen postures. I had told the story so many times, I forgot how kind of horrifying it was. I swallowed and kept talking because neither of them seemed up to the task.

"Anyway, I had to sell the house and most of our stuff to pay off the debt he didn't tell me about."

More silence. I let it sit for a moment, but it got too uncomfortable, so I opened my mouth and made it worse.

"Yep. All I have left to my name is that crappy truck, this old house, and her dumb dog."

"Wait," Peach said, stepping forward. "You adopted your dead husband's mistress's dog?" Her eyes were wide with what I could only describe as wild admiration, and it made me hellishly uncomfortable.

"I don't know about *adopted*," I said, giving Seamus a dubious look. "Her family wouldn't take him, so I was kinda stuck. I know that, roles reversed, she probably would have hit my dog in the head with a shovel and tossed it off an overpass, but I think I got a superiority buzz off of being a better person than she was, not that *that* was a high bar, but . . ."

You know those moments in the movies when it gets so silent you can hear the clock tick? Yeah. This was something like that. So I kept talking. "I have some of my things still. Clothes, underwear, stuff like that. I pretty much spent my last dime on that bed, so . . . gonna need a job soon."

There was nothing left to report, so we stood there in a heavy, unbroken, tick-tock silence for a while. But somehow, I felt lighter just saying the words. In the kind of town where they brought the new neighbor homemade dinners and pecan pies and hand-knitted dishcloths, word would travel fast. Saying all of this once, to these two, meant I would never, ever have to tell that story again to anyone, and that was a comforting thought.

"Oh, honey," Peach said, her eyes full of tears as she held her arms out and pulled me into yet another hug. Because of her baby-girth, I had to lean into the hug and reach my arms out awkwardly to pat her back as she sniffled on my shoulder. "I'm so sorry about your husband. That's so sad."

"It's okay," I said. "He was really kind of an asshole."

"You poor, poor thing." Peach sniffed as she finally released me, her eyes red. "You've been through so much."

"Ah, you get used to it," I said, shrugging uncomfortably. "What are you gonna do, right? Life hands you lemons, and all that."

Peach put her hands on my shoulders. "You are so strong."

"Bah," I said awkwardly, making a dismissive

gesture. "It's not strength when you don't have a choice. It's just not falling down."

"You know what?" Addie said, clapping me on the shoulder. "I like you."

"Thanks." I smiled, feeling an odd rush of warmth at the compliment. "I like me, too."

She reached into her purse and pulled out two business cards, putting them one by one in my hands. One read GRACE AND ADDIE'S BED AND BREAKFAST, and the other read ADDIE AND GRACE'S ANTIQUES SHOPPE.

"Come by the antiques store tomorrow," she said. "We open at ten. You can bring Seamus."

I looked down at Seamus, then back at Addie. "You really want that big ox of a dog near your antiques?"

Addie waved a hand in the air. "It'll be fine. I know everyone in this town, and if there's a job for you, I'll find it. What is it you do? Do you have any marketable skills?"

I hesitated. "I have a graduate degree in philosophy and spent six years working in a video rental store that finally went belly-up last fall. Unless there's a market for someone who can discuss the themes of Randian objectivism in *The Incredibles*, then no. Not really."

Addie looked at me for a moment, then patted me lightly on the cheek, the way I imagine a mother might. "That's okay. I like a challenge."

"Then you'll like me," I said, and moved toward the door. They both took the hint and followed me. Just as

I put my hand on the knob, I said, "Oh, hey, I have a question. What's the grungiest dive bar in town?"

The two of them answered in unison, without hesitation: "Happy Larry's."

"Why do you ask?" Peach said.

Because if Judd was in this town, he was in that bar. "No reason. Just curious. Thanks so much for coming by. I really appreciate all the stuff."

I followed them out to the porch, surprised to find that next to Judd's beaten-up blue pickup was an almost equally beaten-up green pickup with EASTER LANDSCAPING painted on the driver's-side door. The similarity between the two pieces of crap gave me a brief feeling of belonging, which I appreciated. Peach hurled herself up into the driver's seat and Addie climbed into the passenger side, and they both waved at me as they drove off. I waved until they were out of sight, then looked over to see Seamus lifting his leg to the back tire of Judd's truck. I thought about stopping him, but there was something oddly gratifying about it, so I let it go.

I traipsed down the porch steps and untied the tarp covering the bed of Judd's truck to uncover all of my worldly possessions, which amounted to some clothes, a few basic toiletries, and two boxes of kitchen stuff. Once back in the kitchen, I grabbed a fork from one of the boxes and, out of sheer curiosity, picked into the pecan pie and took a bite.

"Oh, gah, yugh," I said, and spit it into the sink. I

ran the tap and stuck my mouth under it, swishing the
water around and spitting it out, then staring at the of-
fensive pie. "What the hell is that? Flaxseed? Jesus."
Then I popped the lasagna into the oven to cook while
I took a shower to clean up before my visit to Happy
Larry's.

Chapter 2

Happy Larry's definitely earned the title of Grungiest Dive Bar in Nodaway Falls, not that there seemed to be a lot of competition. It was windowless, airless, and underlit. What light fought the good fight to illuminate the place was dusty and yellowed, as if they deliberately bought lightbulbs on the brink of death for the purposes of atmosphere. It sported one aged pool table in a back corner, wood-paneled walls that displayed the scars of many a bar fight, and a big cranky dude with an unconscionable amount of facial hair behind the bar.

Totally Judd's kind of place.

I sat on the worn leather-topped bar stool and slid Judd's picture across the bar to the big guy.

"I'm wondering if this man has ever been to this

town before," I said. "He bought a house here, and I don't know why. Have you seen—"

"Nope," he said without looking at the picture. His voice was deep and rumbly, and I thought I detected a hint of redneck in it. "What'll it be?"

"Nothing. Can you just tell me if you've ever seen him? It probably would have been, I don't know . . ." I thought back to the date Judd had signed on the closing paperwork I'd seen. "About a year ago, maybe?"

Beady dark eyes stared out at me from under the thickest eyebrows I'd ever seen. "Those seats are for paying customers."

"I just want to know if this guy has spent time in this town. It's a simple question."

"And I answered it. Now, what'll it be?"

"You didn't answer it. You didn't even look at the picture."

He leaned over the counter and looked me dead in the eye. "It ain't my job to make sure your man isn't a damn cheat. If I answered that question for every woman looking to catch her man in a lie, I'd be out of business in a heartbeat."

"I appreciate your conundrum, but I promise, he's not going to be giving you any more business either way."

The guy didn't blink. "What'll it be?"

"Nothing." I held the picture up in between us, so he couldn't avoid looking at it. "I just want to know if you've ever seen this man. Did he have any friends here or anything?"

Through the mass of facial hair, I was handed a dead-eyed stare. "I only answer questions for customers."

"*Fine,* I'll have a Coke."

"I make my money on the alcohol."

I lowered the picture of Judd and stared at the bartender. "You kidding me with this? It's barely four o'clock."

"And yet, you're in a bar," he countered.

"Fair enough," I said, conceding the point. "But I don't drink alcohol during daylight hours, so I'm not buying any."

His expression didn't change.

I glanced down at Seamus, who was sitting at my feet. "Go ahead, boy. Sic him."

Seamus gave no indication he'd even heard me. Little asshole. The bartender could launch himself over the bar, wrap his beefy hands around my neck, and throttle the life out of me, and Seamus would only move if one of my twitching limbs disturbed his personal space.

"Hey." The bartender leaned over the bar and looked down at Seamus. "We don't allow dogs in here."

"Yeah, well, you didn't see what he did to my truck the last time I left him in there alone," I muttered.

The bartender stared at me, as though he hadn't heard me.

"He's my service dog," I said, a bit louder. "His name is Seamus."

The bartender didn't miss a beat. "You want to keep the dog in here, it'll be two drinks."

"Look," I said, holding out Judd's picture, "if you want me out, just tell me if you've ever seen this man, and I'm gone."

"I told you, it'll be—"

"Quit being a jerk and answer her questions."

I glanced over to my left, the direction the voice had come from. Two stools down from me, a woman with long, curly brown hair pulled back into a messy ponytail was huddled over a drink. Her jeans and T-shirt were baggy on her, like she'd lost a bit of weight quickly and hadn't exactly noticed yet. I had instant sympathy for her; that was how my clothes had fit in the early weeks after Judd had died.

She raised her head and turned toward us. She was about my age, maybe a little younger, so I put her at late twenties, early thirties. She wore a black T-shirt that read DEPARTMENT OF REDUNDANCY DEPARTMENT in blocky yellow type. She was pretty, but her face was drawn, and her eyes had the hollowed-out look of someone who'd been through it lately. I had no idea what specifically had happened to her, but whatever it was, it was recent, and it wasn't good.

"I can take a look at it if you want," she said, motioning to the picture in my hand without looking directly at me. "I work at the waffle house in town. Pretty much everybody goes through there."

"Does it have a liquor license?"

She shook her head.

"Yeah, in that case, Judd probably wouldn't have paused passing by, but . . ." I set the picture on the bar between us. She picked it up, angling it to hold it in the dim shaft of yellow light that came down from the hanging lamps over the bar.

"I'm not even sure he was ever here," I said, deflating. "I just want to know why I suddenly own a house in this town. That's all."

She stared at the picture for a bit and shook her head, then held the picture out to the bartender. "I don't think I've seen him. How about you, Larry?"

Larry shot me a hard glance. "Two drinks."

"Wait. *You're* Happy Larry?" I said, staring at him. "So it's an irony thing, then?"

"Fine," the woman said to Larry. "Two more drinks. For me. I'm buying." Her words were only slightly slurred, but I could tell she'd been there for a while.

Larry shook his head. "Not for you, Liv. You're cut off."

Liv turned to me. "Honestly. I threw up in this bar *once,* when I was sixteen, and the guy still holds a grudge."

I looked at Larry, and for a moment I caught a hint of something in his eyes, and it wasn't a grudge. He was worried about her. But it was just a flash, and as soon as Liv looked up it was gone.

"I'm not going to barf on your stupid floor, Larry. I'm a paying customer, and I just want—"

"Two drinks," I said to Larry. "I'll have what she's having."

Larry's eyes flitted back and forth between the two of us, and he proceeded to pour what looked to be gin and tonics, hold the tonic. He slid them both in front of me and said, "That'll be fifteen dollars."

"Fine." I pulled my wallet out of my back pocket and peeked inside. "I've got twelve bucks and a stick of Juicy Fruit."

Larry gave me a beady-eyed glare, but held out his hand. I put the money into it, kept the gum, and said, "That sign in the window. You're hiring? For what position?"

"Bartender. Why?"

"Because you just took my last twelve dollars, that's why."

His eyes narrowed. "You want to work here? You got experience?"

"I'm cranky and intransigent," I said. "That pretty much seems to be the vibe here, right?"

He didn't respond. I held up the picture of Judd.

"Do you remember ever seeing this man?" I asked.

Larry took the picture, held it to the light, examined it, and shook his head. "Nope."

I called out a sarcastic, "Thanks so much," to his retreating back and slid the drinks down the bar toward Liv. "Thanks for your help."

She didn't look at me. "Did he run off?"

For a moment, I wasn't sure who she was talking about, but then I connected the dots. "Oh. Judd? No. He's dead. I'm just trying to put some pieces together."

"I'm sorry," she said, empathy on her face. "Was he your boyfriend?"

"No. Husband."

She nodded, staring down into her drink. "Well. At least you were married."

"Huh. Most people say, 'Everything happens for a reason.' Good on you for going in a different direction."

"No, I mean . . ." She paused for a moment, staring into her glass. "If you're married before he runs off, people don't just expect you to get over it and move on."

"Judd didn't run off," I said, beginning to suspect we weren't talking about me anymore. "He's dead."

"Right," she said, not looking at me. "Sorry for your loss."

Unsure how to respond, I let the conversation die there. After a few minutes, the door to Happy Larry's opened, letting in an aggressive shaft of sunlight. When my eyes adjusted, I saw a strikingly gorgeous brunette in jeans, work boots, and a plaid shirt tied in a knot at the waist. She stalked across the bar, beelining for Liv.

"Hey, you." Her voice was soft, even if her expression wasn't. "Time to go home."

"Stace!" Liv swiveled on her stool, sloshing a bit of her drink. "Meet my new friend . . . um . . ." Liv drifted off, looking at me expectantly.

"Oh, um, hi. I'm Eliot Parker." I waved at Liv's friend. The woman smiled stiffly and nodded. I didn't take it personally, since it was obvious her tension had naught to do with me.

"Stacy Easter," she said, and focused on Liv. "We really have to go."

"She's new in town," Liv said, motioning to me. "That's her dog, Shane."

"Seamus," I corrected. "Not that he answers to it. I called him 'little asshole' for a while to see if I could goad some kind of response out of him, but he didn't answer to that, either."

Liv snapped her fingers. "Oh, hey, you're the one who just moved into that place on Wildwood Lane?"

"Yeah, that's me."

Liv looked at Stacy and smiled. "She's the one who just moved to Wildwood Lane. She's asking about her husband. He's dead, but she's just trying to put some pieces together. Is that right, Eliot?"

"Yeah," I said, and smiled. I liked Liv. It was rare I found someone with less social panache than I had, and it made me feel better. Of course, she was drunk, but still. I pulled the picture of Judd out of my back pocket and showed it to Stacy. "Did you ever see him around here?"

Stacy took the picture and looked at it. She was exactly the kind of girl that Judd went for; dark, gorgeous, attitude up to here, trouble with a capital *T*. If he was going to be a memorable nuisance to anyone in this town, it would be her.

"No," she said, shaking her head as she handed the picture back to me.

"Thanks, anyway," I said.

"I'm glad you got that place," Liv said. "It has potential. I knitted you the dishcloths."

"Oh," I said, dizzying a bit as I tried to keep up with Liv's zigzagging conversational style. "Thank you."

She waved a dismissive hand. "I've got a ton of them. I knit at night while watching TV. Something to do." She gave a small, sad smile, then added, "We used to make tiramisu for the Welcome Wagon, but Tobias was the cook and he's not here anymore, so . . ."

Tobias must be the boyfriend who ran off, I thought. And from the way things looked, Liv was not taking it well. I felt a stab of deep sympathy for her. At that moment, two more pieces of my day snapped together, and I looked at Stacy Easter.

"Easter," I said thoughtfully. "You related to Bernadette? I mean, Peach?"

"Yeah, she's married to my brother Nick." Stacy took the glass out of Liv's hand and placed it on the counter. "We've got to go, honey."

"We can't." Liv motioned to the drinks. "These drinks are full, and Eliot doesn't drink, and there's no one else here except . . ."

Liv glanced around. It was me, her, Larry, and some tall, thin, dark-haired guy reading a book in the corner booth. He looked up and locked eyes with Stacy. Something passed between them, and while I couldn't say what it was, I could tell that whoever that guy was, Stacy was not a fan.

"*Desmond* called you to come get me?" Liv said softly, her voice mixing surprise and a little disgust.

The tall, thin guy—I presumed that was Desmond—returned his attention to his book.

"Let's go," Stacy said, tugging on Liv's arm, and Liv picked up her purse and stood without a word of resistance.

"It was nice to meet you, Eliot," Liv said as Stacy herded her out the door.

I waited a moment for my eyes to readjust to the dimness again, then picked up the two gin and tonics and headed over to the booth where Desmond was sitting. Seamus lumbered along behind me.

"Hi," I said, putting the drinks down in front of him. "Larry made me buy these, but I don't drink during the day."

He raised his head, looking up at me with intelligent brown eyes and cheekbones that could cut glass. His hair was wavy and a little unkempt, but he still cut a fine figure in his pressed black shirt and pants. There was something elegant about him, and a little strange, which I liked. I could tell by his clothes alone that he wasn't from around here, where the prevailing fashion seemed to be construction-worker shabby, and there was something about the way he obviously didn't fit in that made me feel more comfortable around him.

"I don't drink much, either." With long, delicate fingers, he motioned toward the full beer in front of him. It had been sitting there so long that the condensation had dribbled down to create a small pool of water at the base of the glass.

"Huh." I sat down across from him in the booth. "What are you doing in a bar, then?"

"I imagine the same thing you're doing." He flashed something that seemed to be an attempt at a polite smile, but really made it clear he was tolerating my intrusion on his solitude out of civility, and not a great desire to talk to me. That made me like him even more.

"And what am I doing here?" I prodded. I didn't care much if he wanted to talk to me, I just didn't want to go back to that house without any answers. Not yet.

"Absorbing the atmosphere." He said it completely deadpan, and even though he came off a bit cold and rude, I felt instantly comfortable around him. It was better to have someone be rude and let you know where you stand than charm you so much you couldn't see the hits coming. Being married to Judd had taught me that, at least.

"How long have you lived here?" I asked.

"About a year," he said, and it was then that I noticed the light touch of aristocratic England in his tone. *He has an accent,* I thought. *Run.*

But instead of leaving, I pulled the picture of Judd out of my back pocket and slid it across the booth table to him.

"Have you ever seen this guy?"

Desmond picked up the picture and held it in the light. He studied it for a while, then shook his head and handed it back to me. "I'm sorry. Is he missing?"

"No." I sighed, dropping the picture on the table. "I know where he is."

"All right." Desmond put his hand back on his book but didn't open it, a polite gesture to let me know that if I wanted to leave, I could do so without offending him, but if I wanted to stay, he'd tolerate my presence a little while longer.

"Being and Nothingness," I said, reading the spine of his book. "Sartre will make you jump off a bridge, you know that, right?"

He smiled, and there was a slight glint of surprise in his eyes, the same surprise I usually see when people discover I've read books. "You're not a fan, I take it."

"Of the books? No," I said. "I like the letters."

One eyebrow rose. "The ones he wrote to Simone de Beauvoir?"

I nodded. "Yeah. They're both so dense and pretentious in their philosophical texts, but the letters they wrote . . ." I smiled, remembering how I'd felt when I'd read the letters, like I was slipping into a cozy, warm robe, fresh from the dryer on a cold day. "They weren't trying so hard, you know? She was one of the world's most kick-you-in-the-balls feminists, and he called her 'My dear little girl,' and she *liked* it. She could just be a woman with him. Don't get me wrong, she was a hot mess, but he knew it and loved her anyway and there's something hopeful in that. A nutty lid for every crazy pot, that kind of thing."

"Hmmm," he said noncommittally. "I haven't read the letters."

"You should. The things they wrote to each other

were more real and meaningful than any other work either of them ever did. I mean, the guy is famous for saying, 'Hell is other people,' and yet the only reason anyone reads *Being and Nothingness* is so that other people will be impressed. What kind of messed-up legacy is that?"

Unfortunately, I didn't realize I was insulting him until I'd finished insulting him. I opened my mouth to say something smooth and charming that could get me out of the hole I'd just dug for myself, but what was I going to say? *I'm sure you're not reading it to show off*? Of course he was, because that's the only reason people read Sartre.

"Unless you're taking a college class," I said slowly.

"I'm sorry?" he said.

"Are you . . . ?" I motioned toward the book with my chin. "Is it, like, an assignment or something?"

"No." His voice was clipped, and I took that as a sign that the conversation was over.

I pushed myself up from the booth and started to walk away, then thought twice and turned around, holding out my hand to him. "Well, thanks for your time. I'm Eliot, by the way. Eliot Parker."

He stood up as well and held out his hand. "Desmond Lamb."

Our hands touched, and I felt it. *The spark.* It was faint, but it was there. My stomach flipped, and I could suddenly feel my lunch sitting in my gut like a brick.

It was just static electricity. It was nothing. Don't get all freaked out over nothing.

But it wasn't just static. I knew that. Desmond had magic. He wasn't a born magical, that was for sure, but if he'd been a conduit, someone a full magical had used to run power through, or maybe if he was a conjurer working with potions all day . . . that could explain it. That slight electrical hint left in his skin, a hint that only someone like me could detect. Even with my power gone, I still had that. I'd used it to avoid getting too close to magicals for the last sixteen years, and it had served me well.

And now, I'd just moved into a town with one.

Desmond moved closer, laying one hand gently on my shoulder. "Are you all right, Ms. Parker? You look rather pale. Would you like to sit down? Can I get you a water?"

"No . . . no. I'm fine." I stepped back from him, stumbling a bit. My muscles felt weak, and my thighs were shaking. My head was spinning and my heart was racing, and I tried to talk myself down.

Magicals are rare, but they're everywhere. It's just a coincidence. Judd just happened to buy a secret house he couldn't afford in a town that has magic in it. That's all.

Just a coincidence.

"Ms. Parker?" Desmond said again. I must have looked like I was gonna wobble, because he reached out for me, and I held out my hand to stop him from touching me.

"I'm fine," I said weakly. I pulled on Seamus's leash

and somehow managed to lead him outside and drive home without getting us both killed.

I kicked the front door open and headed straight for the fridge, hollering.

"Get your transparent ass out here, Judd!"

Seamus settled down on the floor in the dining area, watching me as I wildly pulled food and drinks out of the fridge, my heart pounding.

"Whoa," Judd said from behind me. "Somebody having a party?"

I whipped around to look at him. He was wearing jeans and a black T-shirt, sitting casually on the counter, his arms resting on his knees. I pointed an accusatory finger at him.

"I should have known," I said. "I should have known that if you bought a house in the middle of nowhere, there'd be something more to it. But Jesus. You bought a house in a *magic* town? What the hell were you thinking?" I pulled out two Gladware containers and looked from side to side, stymied. "I don't have any garbage bags. Dammit." I set them on the counter next to Judd and wanted to smack him, but I knew my hand would just go through dead air. "What the actual *fuck*, Judd?"

"Calm down," Judd said, hopping off the counter. "Have some more lasagna. Pasta's good for the soul."

I gasped and put my hand over my mouth. "Oh! The lasagna!" I went into the fridge and pulled out the aluminum dish with the telltale serving missing from the corner. I dropped it on the counter like it was radioactive, and took a step back. Judd, being dead and stupid, leaned closer over it, trying to smell it.

"Was it good, Ellie? Tell me it was good. You don't appreciate food like that until you can't have it anymore." Judd eyed the pan with desire. "Eat some more, babe. Do it for me."

I swung my hand out to smack his shoulder, and was deeply unsatisfied when all I hit was air. "I'm not eating any more of that. That guy might be a *conjurer*. There could be potions in all of this stuff. Are you crazy?"

"No," he said simply. "Look at that lasagna. Why would anyone lace a lasagna like that? Lasagna's a sacred food, Ellie. A man goes to hell for something like that."

I put my hand to my forehead and tried to regulate my breathing. "It's been sixteen years. If he found me, he could have just called me, right? This is a lot of trouble to go to, just to get to me." I felt myself start to calm down a bit. "I'm being paranoid, right?"

Judd shrugged. "I don't know. He's your dad. You ran away and changed your identity to get away from him. Maybe he thought you'd send him straight to voice mail."

I paced a couple of times in the small kitchen space. "Okay. Okay. Okay." I turned to Judd. "Judd, I need you to focus, and tell me the truth. Why did you buy this house, in this town?"

His smile quirked up a bit at one side. Even as a ghost, he was working the charm hard. "Look, Ellie, you didn't tell me about the magic, and I didn't know about it. Like Dr. Fliegel said, I'm just a figment of your imagination. So my guess is as good as yours why I bought this house, but . . . I'm leaning toward coincidence."

"Oh, shut up. You're useless." I threw a hand towel through him and turned back to the refrigerator. All that food, and here I was unemployed and destitute and I couldn't eat any of it. But I couldn't throw it away, either, not until I had garbage bags. And a garbage can. And garbage service.

"Augh!" I said in a whiny, frustrated voice, and leaned my butt against the counter, facing Judd. "What the hell did you do to my life?"

Judd slid off the counter and moved closer. "I made it fun."

"Stop it," I said, my voice weakening.

"I love you, baby," he said, his voice soft. "I hate that you're so scared."

"Don't." I closed my eyes, and for a moment, in some parallel reality that had taken pity and revealed itself to me, he was there. I could smell his spicy Judd scent, and I could feel the backs of his strong fingers gently grazing my cheeks.

"Oh, babe, I miss you so hard it hurts," he whispered.

"Stop," I said, my voice cracking.

Then a British voice said, "Ms. Parker?" and it was

like a shock of cold water. I screamed, my heart pounding furiously as I gripped the counter behind me to keep from falling over. Judd was gone, but in my open front door stood the Brit from the bar, and my stupid, useless dog didn't so much as fart to give me a heads-up.

I swiped at my eyes and took out my aggravation on Desmond, who simply stood in my doorway, staring.

"What the hell is wrong with you? Don't you knock?"

"When a door is wide open? Not typically, no." He met my eyes and said, without a hint of shame, "I followed you home from the bar."

"Oh my God. *That's* not okay." I spoke as forcefully as I could, hoping he didn't catch the tremor in my voice. "You can't just follow women home from bars. Not unless you're a bad guy. Are you a bad guy, Desmond?"

"The answer to that question depends entirely upon whom you ask," he said, without a smile to indicate whether he was kidding or not. Jesus, he was the polar opposite of Judd. Judd never said anything without smiling. "I heard shouting. I was concerned."

"I was yelling at the ghost of my dead husband," I said, hoping the crazy would make him go away.

It didn't.

"Ah. I see." There was a long silence before he went on. "You seemed very upset, when you left the bar. I wanted to make sure you were all right."

"I'm fine. I just . . . I had a shock. A surprise . . ."

I stared at him, wondering what kind of magic he had. Conjurer? Conduit? Full magical? But really, it didn't matter. There was only one question I needed the answer to.

Just ask him, I thought. *Ask him and find out for sure.*

"This is a small town," I said. "You know everyone here?"

He shrugged. "Most of them. Is there someone you'd like me to call for you?"

"No," I said quickly. "Definitely not. But do you know . . . is there a man here by the name of . . . ?" I hadn't said his name in sixteen years. It felt weird coming out of my mouth. "Emerson Streat?"

Desmond's eyebrows knit together slightly, but I didn't see any name recognition on his face. "Why do you ask?"

I sighed, but my shoulder muscles didn't relax at all. "No reason. Nothing." I put my hand to my forehead. "My brain might be exploding."

"Are you all right? Can I fetch you anything?"

I pulled my hand away from my face, suddenly annoyed. "No. I'm a grown woman. If I need something I'll fetch it myself." There was no hint of either hurt or annoyance on his face, but I immediately felt guilty anyway. "I'm sorry. I didn't mean to be rude."

"It's all right," he said. "You're American. I've rather come to expect it."

"Hey!" I said in mock offense at what I presumed

to be a joke, even though he wasn't smiling. Maybe he wasn't joking. Who the hell knew? His face was impossible to read, and it was pissing me off. Judd's active, charming deceptions were preferable to Ol' Stone Face here. "Go away, please. I'm fine. It's just been a weird day, that's all."

"I apologize if I've upset you. I didn't mean to intrude. It's just . . ." He moved forward slowly, eyes on me as though I was some kind of wild animal that might strike at any moment, and placed the picture of Judd down on the counter in front of me. "You left this at the bar. I followed you home to return it, that's all. I thought it might be important to you."

I leaned forward, looking down at the picture of my stupid, grinning, lying jerk of a dead husband.

"Thank you," I said.

"Of course." He started toward the door, absently patting Seamus on the head as he went. He paused at the doorway and turned back. "Do you prefer the door open or closed?"

"Closed," I said. "Please. Thank you." *See? Americans are polite, you big jerk.*

Desmond nodded, and disappeared through the door, shutting it silently behind him. I stared at the doorway for a while, my vision going out of focus while my mental gears churned.

Judd hadn't known I was magic. I was sure of this because of one simple fact; if he had known, he would have built a con around it. He'd loved me, as much as

Judd had it within him to love anyone besides himself, but he was what he was. Tricking people out of their money was like breathing for him, and if he had any advantage, magical or otherwise, he would have used it. Used me. In a heartbeat.

But if Judd *didn't* know, did that mean it was just a coincidence that he secretly bought a house in a town with magical people in it? Maybe. Magicals were a very slim percentage of the population at large, and conjurers were even fewer in number, but they were out there, so in any given town, there could easily be one or two. And for all I knew, Desmond was the only one in town. The most comforting detail was that it was a small town; Desmond had been here for a year, and he hadn't recognized my father's name.

"C'mon, honey. Smile for me."

I looked up to see Judd grinning down at me. I couldn't help it; I smiled back.

"That's my girl," he said, his voice soft. "You know it's all gonna be great, right? New town, new life, new everything. Fresh start."

I gnawed at my lip and stared absently at my new front door. As annoying and dead as Judd was, his optimism was appealing. For sixteen years, I had been faithful to my mother's dying pleas. I'd drunk the potion she gave me to bind my magic. I'd used the identity documents she gave me and left my life as Josie Streat behind to start my life as Eliot Parker without question. I'd managed to stay away from both magic and my father, and as a result, he hadn't been able to use me in any more experiments, and no one else had died as a result, which was a very good thing.

But in that moment when I'd said my father's name again and Desmond hadn't recognized it, what I'd felt wasn't fear, or even relief.

It was disappointment.

"You've gotta get some sleep, babe," Judd said. "You look tired."

"Of course I'm tired," I said. "I haven't had a decent night's sleep in sixteen years."

He smiled at me, reaching his hand up to brush my hair away from my forehead, the way he used to. Of course, my hair didn't move, but it's the thought that counts. Judd wasn't any more use to me dead than he'd been when he was alive, but it was nice, in those brief moments, to feel loved again, even if it was by a figment of my imagination.

Chapter 3

The village of Nodaway Falls was cute, the kind of place you'd see on a 1950s postcard. Brick buildings all huddled up next to each other lined the street, with businesses on the ground floors and apartments up top. There was a drugstore, a waffle place, a little grocery store, and of course, Grace and Addie's antiques shop. I held Seamus's leash tight before opening the door and said, "If you break anything, I'll make you stand on the corner and dance for quarters to pay it off."

Then, we went inside.

I'm not sure what I was expecting. I think something like Mrs. Kim's shop from *Gilmore girls*. You know, every inch covered in something, chairs stacked three deep, breakable little trinkets covering every level surface. What I walked into looked less like an antiques shop than just someone's house. There was a glass hutch with knickknacks in it, but far fewer than my friend Del's grandmother had in her house when we were growing up. Rather than a dusty little room with no walking space where you'd find the odd treasure if you had the will to paw through all the junk first, this was a comfortable sitting area with mismatched furniture, from a Victorian couch that had been impeccably reupholstered in red stripes, to an overstuffed light blue chaise longue, to a mid-century oval coffee table that looked like it had come straight off the set of *Mad Men*. There was plenty of space in which to move and appreciate what was there, and lighting that made you feel like you'd just walked into a warm home on a blustery day.

"Hello?" I said, taking one step farther in. There was no answer, no sound. I looked down at Seamus.

"So what now?"

Seamus settled on the ground, putting his big head on his paws and being of absolutely no use to me. I gave him a warning look which he ignored, and moved a few more feet inside.

"Um . . . Addie?"

Again, nothing. I checked my watch; it was ten o'clock. Maybe she was running a little late. It seemed like someone should be in there to keep people from walking off with the merchandise, but then again, this was a small town and it seemed to be pretty tight-knit. Maybe it was one of those mythical places where you could leave your doors unlocked. I wouldn't be doing that, because in my experience it's the people you trust who are most likely to steal your television, but to each their own.

I ran my hand along the flawless wood frame on the couch as I passed, and that's when I looked at the shelf over the chaise longue and saw it.

"Oh my god, Seamus, the woman has an actual, honest-to-god record player!"

I walked over to it, my hands going out to touch the smoky-gray transparent plastic cover. I had grown up just as CDs were edging out records, but my father had been passionate about his vinyl. I ran my fingers along the spines of the albums that had been carefully placed there, with a very specific eye toward quirk and variety. The Beatles. The Supremes. Frank Sinatra.

"Seamus, this is amazing!" I clapped my hands together and plucked an album off the shelf. The blue and black cover was worn, and I ran my hand over it carefully, reverently. *"Rock 'N Soul!"*

I hesitated for the smallest of moments, then lifted the plastic cover off the record player and whipped the album out of its cover.

"My dad used to play this album all the time when I was a kid." I flipped the album cover over in my hands. "Solomon Burke. Everyone was so crazy about Sam Cooke and Ray Charles, but this guy was the real thing, you know?"

I carefully turned on the record player and lifted the head to place on the album, feeling almost giddy over the scratching sound the diamond-tip needle sent through the speakers as it made contact with the record. There was something about that sound that felt like home, like safety, like normalcy. I hadn't realized how much I had missed it. Like most everyone else, I loved the sturdiness of CDs, and later the convenience of MP3 players, and despite the fact that I'd often mocked music nerds for their obstinate insistence that vinyl produced better sound—*different,* yes; *better,* that's arguable—I couldn't resist the time-travel power the hiss and scratch of a real vinyl record had to transport me back. I set the record to play Solomon's plaintive "Can't Nobody Love You," then took the album cover and sat down on the blue chaise longue and promptly lost my mind.

"Oh my god," I said, sinking into its softness. "What do you think the chances are of Addie just letting us move in here?"

I was so absorbed in the music and the comfort of the chaise that I didn't even notice when Addie first walked in. If Seamus hadn't jumped up, tail wagging, to attack her with slobbering love, I might not have noticed her at all.

"Oh!" I hopped up off the chaise and turned off the record player. "I'm sorry. The door was open. Seemed okay at the time." I swallowed. "Now, I kinda feel like a criminal."

"Don't be silly," Addie said, her voice muffled by the kissy-faces she was making at Seamus. She was wearing a cotton dress with little blue flowers on it and a tightly tailored bodice that made her look like a well-aged Lucy Ricardo. "That's just silly, isn't it, Seamus? You were invited, weren't you?"

She laughed as Seamus hopped down and danced around her.

"He really loves you," I said. "You sure you don't want a dog? I'll trade him for that chaise."

"Are you kidding? Grace would kill me in my sleep if I came home with a dog." Addie laughed, straightening up after giving Seamus one last scratch behind his ears. "Besides, he's your dog."

He doesn't have to be, I thought, but instead of pushing the point I just said, "This place is amazing. It's like going back in time. I don't think I've heard Solomon Burke since my dad danced me around the kitchen to him, me standing on his toes." It was such a goofy memory, and I hadn't thought about that in years, but hearing that song again made it so fresh, it suddenly felt like yesterday.

"Aw, so sweet!" Addie said. "My father used to play tea with me with his grandmother's Revolutionary War china. Ooh, speaking of tea, I could really go for some. How about you?"

She walked past me, patting me on the shoulder as she did, and headed toward a door in the back. I followed her, keeping Seamus's leash held tight, into the next room, which turned out to be a full kitchen. It was a throwback to what I'd guess to be late fifties, early sixties. The cabinets were blue, the counters butcher block, the appliances classic stainless steel, and a wall covered in blue-painted pegboard sported an improbable array of copper cookware. Seamus sniffed a low-hanging saucepan and settled on the floor in front of the display.

"Wow," I breathed.

"Yes, it's wonderful, isn't it?" she said, grinning as she filled a copper-bottomed teakettle with water from the sink. "It's less a replica of Julia Child's kitchen—we have nothing like that kind of space—and more of an homage, but I love it." She cranked up the gas burner and put the kettle on.

"It's a working kitchen," I said. "Is it all for sale? There are no price tags on anything. Because not for nothing, I'd like to be buried in that chaise."

Addie smiled. "It is lovely, isn't it?"

"I'm serious," I said. "I know I can't afford it, but what is the price on that thing? A girl can dream."

"It's not for sale, yet," she said, motioning for me to take a seat at the long table, covered in a solid print burnt-orange cotton tablecloth. "I don't put tags on anything until I can bear to part with it."

"So . . . how is it a business, then?" I asked.

She shrugged. "My wife is independently wealthy. Her family is old Connecticut money, too busy exploiting the worker and raping the environment to reproduce. Both her father and her uncle left her everything, and while we don't have quite the moral fortitude to reject the cash altogether, we do give generously to the hippie liberals, which I'm sure made the greedy bastards whirl in their graves like rotisserie chickens." She giggled and sighed. "Twice a year we have a date night where we give a good chunk of their money to Planned Parenthood, drink one of their ridiculous bottles of old wine, and have sex on her uncle's bear rug, supposedly made from some poor animal Hemingway shot." She gave a good-natured eye roll. "Honestly, I prefer the wine that comes in the box, but it's really about the principle of the thing."

I smiled, liking her even more, but also pretty sure I didn't want to hear any more sex stories. Time to change the subject.

"So, I was wondering if you had leads on any jobs for me? I'm gonna need to buy some food soon." I dropped that last bit lightly, but it was sadly true. The first thing I'd done that morning was dig the trash bags out of my truck and throw in everything from the Welcome Wagon that hadn't been factory sealed. Then I drove to the IGA, threw the perfectly good food into the Dumpster in the back, and spent my last few bucks on a box of Cheerios and a half-gallon of milk. I had enough in my checking to pay the utilities, feed Seamus, and put gas in that stupid truck, but after that things were gonna get dire, fast.

"Oh, yes, of course, we'll get to that, but first . . . I need to talk to you about something." The teakettle started to whistle and she pushed up from the table to tend to it. "Herbal or classic?"

"Oh. Um. Classic. So, what's up?"

She dropped tea bags into a delicate floral teapot, and poured the boiling water, waiting until she was finished before looking at me with purpose. "Desmond Lamb."

I almost wanted to laugh at the seriousness on her face, but there was also a hint of genuine worry in her eyes, so I didn't. She set down a tray with a red polka dot teapot, two stoneware mugs, and a matching white porcelain creamer and sugar dish on the table. She poured a cup for me and a cup for herself, then motioned toward the cream and sugar. "Help yourself."

I pulled my mug toward me and said, "Thank you. Now, what is this about Desmond Lamb?"

She patted me on the arm. "It's okay, honey. There's no judgment here. We all make poor choices. I would tell you about some of the women I slept with in the eighties, but it might put hair on your chest."

"I'm sorry. Are you under the impression that I slept with Desmond Lamb?"

She gave me a disappointed look. "We're all women of the world. Let's not be coy. Larry told me that you two left his bar together yesterday."

"We didn't leave together, and . . . wait. Larry? *Happy* Larry, you mean?" I couldn't picture Happy Larry even noticing when I left, or with whom, much less caring.

"Yes," she said. "Speaking of which, you start working for him tomorrow afternoon, four sharp. But we'll get to that later."

"Wait. What? What do you mean, I start tomorrow? I haven't even applied yet."

"That's okay. You don't need to. I talked to Larry last night, and it's all set. He liked you."

Out of all the surprises in my life, that was probably the biggest one. Not necessarily that Larry had liked me, I'm delightful, but that he liked *anyone*. At all.

"I got you full minimum wage plus tips," Addie went on. "That's a hell of a deal for someone with your weird skill set, no offense."

"None taken," I said, "but—"

"Oh, and he said you could keep Seamus in a dog-house in the alley if you don't want to leave him home alone."

The surprises just kept on coming. "Wow. Really?"

She rolled her eyes, a gleeful smile on her lips, and I got the feeling that there was nothing that Addie loved more than managing other people's lives. "Larry puts on a show, but he's really just a big marshmallow. But don't distract me! We need to talk about Desmond Lamb first."

I picked up my mug and took a sip of tea. "I'm not sure we do."

She put her hand on my arm. "Now, I know he's all mysterious and British and good-looking in a beady-eyed kind of way," she said charitably, "but you have to trust me. Desmond Lamb is not a good man."

She said those words carefully, as though there was much more to the story, and it practically killed her not to tell me. But whatever had happened here with

Desmond, it was obviously more than just a story. It was personal, and she was genuinely worried about me.

"Yeah, there seems to be a misunderstanding here," I said. "I met Desmond Lamb yesterday, but there's nothing going on between us. Seriously. I'm freshly widowed, and dealing with that is enough for me right now."

"Good," Addie said, seeming to finally believe me. "You don't want a man like Desmond Lamb, especially not for your first after your husband died." Her eyebrows rose. "I'm sorry. I'm assuming he would be the first. How long ago did your husband pass away?"

"Eight months, and yes, Desmond would be my first."

Addie's eyebrows ticked up, and I realized what I'd just said.

"No, I didn't mean . . . he won't be. I'm not interested in Desmond Lamb. I mean, I find him . . . interesting. A little. Town like this, you meet a guy who's just sitting in a bar, reading Sartre . . ."

"Sip your tea, darling, you're getting a little red in the face," Addie said, a glint in her eye as she nudged the mug toward me.

"Stop that," I said, laughing. "Look, I'm interested, but I'm not *interested*. Curious, I guess, but not in a sexual way or anything. He's interesting. Just in the normal way that people interest other people." I took a breath to reset myself and met Addie's amused eye as I spoke the honest truth. "I'm not in a place where I'm ready to get into anything romantic."

Addie smiled and patted my hand. "That's fine, honey. If you say there's nothing between you and Desmond Lamb . . ."

"There isn't."

". . . then okay. I only wanted to warn you, just in case. Now, let's talk about the job."

"Okay," I said, and at that moment realized that I'd been so flustered at the idea of sleeping with Desmond that I almost passed up the opportunity to get more information about him from the town gossip. "What did he do?"

"Who? Larry? Well, before he inherited the bar he was going to college for—"

"No, Desmond. Why are you warning me about Desmond? He seemed perfectly nice to me yesterday. Is there . . . ?" I trailed off, trying to figure out the right word to hint at magic without actually saying it, just in case Addie was one of the vast majority who knew nothing and was better off for it. "Is there anything . . . different about him?"

I could see the struggle on her face, the struggle every gossip has when faced with the opportunity to share particular information she either doesn't want to, or can't, divulge. "He's just a bad man, that's all. Keep your distance."

I took that in, and my shoulder muscles tensed up. A possible-magical who was dangerous enough to frighten the town gossip . . . that wasn't a good sign. But I didn't have time to try and parse it all out now, so I shifted the conversation back to my gainful employment.

"So . . . this job at Happy Larry's. What will I be doing?"

"Bartending, some waitressing. You know, the usual."

"Waitressing I can handle," I said, "but I've never bartended in my life."

Addie shrugged it off. "Can you pour liquid into a glass?"

I nodded.

"That's about all anyone else has done in that job. You're a sharp girl. You'll pick it up."

I sighed. The good news was, I'd be making adequate money, and tips would give me cash before I starved. Plus, I wouldn't have to leave Seamus at home alone to chew up my shoes. But still . . . working for Happy Larry . . .

"There's really nothing else in town?" I asked.

Addie sighed. "Not really. There's a fair-to-middling chance that Amber Dorsey will get herself fired from her receptionist's job, but when I spoke to Emerson about it, he seemed like he was willing to give her another chance . . ."

My body processed what she'd said before my conscious mind could, and it was the cold prickle down my spine that made me realize what I'd heard.

"Did you say . . . Emerson? Like a . . . Mr. Emerson?" It wasn't an uncommon last name.

That's probably all it is . . . just someone with that last name.

But even as I was thinking that, I knew what was coming.

Addie shook her head. "No, she works for Emerson Streat, over at Community Cares. He has a little office just a few doors down . . ."

The shock of hearing his name rippled through me, and it took a moment for my brain to understand what was going on, so it helped that Addie just kept rattling on, making it unnecessary for me to respond.

". . . does such amazing work. He's been here less than a year, and already he's set up a farmer's market and a community garden . . ."

Emerson Streat, I thought. *He's here.* But it didn't feel real. It couldn't be real. Maybe it was just a coincidence. Maybe there were two Emerson Streats in the world . . .

"Sweet man, and he has the loveliest accent. I think he's from down south somewhere. Georgia maybe?"

South Carolina, I thought absently.

She sipped casually at her tea and kept on going. "I think he only puts up with Amber because he's just too much of a gentleman to fire her, but that girl is trouble. Last week, she went after her boyfriend, Frankie Biggs, with pinking shears and almost cut off his—"

I pushed up from the chair, almost knocking over my tea mug. "I have to go." I grabbed Seamus's leash and started for the doorway, and then turned around. "I'm sorry. Thank you. I mean—"

Addie stood up, concern on her face. "Eliot? Are you all right?"

"Fine. I'm fine." My voice was squeaky and unconvincing, even to my own ears. "I just . . . I remembered . . . there's a thing." I turned around and led Seamus through the kitchen toward the door. I just had to get through that door, to the air. I had to breathe.

"Eliot." Addie's voice came from behind me, following me. "Are you sure you're okay?"

"I'm fine. Thanks so much! I'll stop in again soon."

I hurried out, momentarily blinded by the sunlight. It felt like the world was spinning around me as I heard Addie's words repeating in my head.

. . . Emerson Streat. He has a little office just a few doors down. Sweet man . . .

I arbitrarily turned to the left, walking with Seamus tight on my heels, looking at the signs on the businesses that lined the village street. One was for lease, another was a real estate agent's office, then there was the waffle place, Crazy Cousin Betty's, on the corner. Across from that was the pharmacy . . .

I turned around and headed back the other way, quickly passing by Addie's shop and not looking in, hoping she wouldn't come out after me. She didn't. I passed by a pizza place, an independent bookstore, and then, on a freshly painted shingle hanging outside a modest storefront, there it was.

NODAWAY FALLS COMMUNITY CARES ORGANIZATION

And underneath that, a smaller rectangle hanging from delicate chains hooked into the bigger sign:

EMERSON STREAT, COORDINATOR

Chapter 4

I glanced through the storefront, keeping a tight hold on Seamus's leash so that I could feel him physically next to me, which gave me the strength I needed to not run away. The office looked much like every other non-descript office space my father had rented throughout the years. Beige carpeting, simple and forgettable décor, and a receptionist who drew attention and kept it off my father. In this case, it was a skinny redhead with wild, frizzy hair and eyes with so much crazy I could see it from the street. That must be the girl Addie had been talking about. *Amber.*

I took a deep breath. I could go in and see my father for the first time in sixteen years, or I could run.

I did neither. I froze, right where I was. I stepped back a bit, just out of sight so I could take a moment to think and make a decision about what I wanted to

do, but right as I was about to step back, the office door
behind the redhead's desk opened, and suddenly, with
no laser light show or evil musical motif, there he was.

My father.

Emerson Streat.

He was a bit more rotund than I remembered. His
red hair had lightened and thinned some at the top, but
even with those changes, he was shockingly the same.
He wore a modest brown suit and tie and his classic
horn-rimmed glasses, smiling like Santa Claus and
looking like everyone's favorite uncle. Even knowing
what I did, even having the history with him that I did,
my heart lurched with love at the very sight of him.

I put my hand over my chest and tried to breathe.
Now wasn't the time to get emotional, but I couldn't
help it. My father was a powerful, ruthless son of a
bitch, but he was also the guy who'd drawn my baths
for me and read *Goodnight, Moon* to me in silly voices
when I was a little kid. He'd insisted on teaching me
how to drive a stick shift because he wanted me to be
prepared for every possible situation. He held my hand
and made goofy faces at me as the doctor stitched up
the gash on my elbow after I fell off my bike when I
was seven, and when my power came in at thirteen,
he taught me how to use it, how to bend metal to my
will, how to hide it and control it so no one would see
it if I didn't want them to.

He loved me, and he'd been a good father to me. But
he'd also been single-minded to the point where I'd
watched my mother die because of his choices. My

best friend, her parents, and too many others. All dead, because of him. And those were just the ones I'd known about; in sixteen years, who knew how many more there might have been?

He's a killer, I thought, and then I touched my fingers gently to the glass and thought, *Daddy.*

"Ms. Parker?"

I swiped quickly at my face and turned on my heel to see . . . who else? . . . Desmond Lamb.

"You lying son of a bitch." My voice was low and dangerous as I moved toward him, angling us away from the storefront so my father wouldn't see us.

Desmond had the nerve to quirk his head at me in question, and that little move lit a fire of fury in my gut. I had enough presence of mind to know that Desmond Lamb wasn't the cause of all my anger, but not enough to stop myself from venting it all on him anyway.

"I asked you last night, *directly,* if you knew his name and you said no."

Desmond glanced up at the sign with my father's name on it, and his confused expression cleared a bit. "I didn't say no. I asked you why you asked."

"You did not—" I began, but replaying the conversation over in my head, I realized he was right, that was exactly what had happened, and the realization made me even angrier. "Of course. Of *course* that's what you did. That's what every man does to me. It's all charm and smiles and stupid sexy accents, but it's still lying, you asshole. What *are* you, anyway?"

Desmond stared at me, a blank expression on his face. "I'm sorry. What . . . *am* I?"

"You're not a full magical, I can tell that much. So what are you? A conjurer? Conduit? Are you one of those fetishists who only sleeps with magic women hoping some of the power will rub off?" A look of shock crossed his face and I stuck my index finger at him in accusation. "That's probably it. Pervert."

Desmond looked around, then back at me, his piercing eyes cutting into me as much as his dangerous tone. "I request that you lower your voice."

"Why?" I said. "Emerson Streat is here. The place is probably littered with you guys. Did he send you to spy on me? Did you already know who I was when we met yesterday?" I gasped with sudden realization. "Of *course* you did! The Sartre! Nobody reads Sartre in public unless they're trying to strike up conversation with an unemployed philosophy major. God, I'm so dumb!"

"Perhaps we should have this conversation somewhere more private." He touched my elbow, but I whipped it out of his grip.

"Don't touch me. I'm not having a conversation with you." I started down the street, away from Emerson's office and toward home, pulling Seamus along with me. But before I got far, another burst of rage ran through me and I turned back to Desmond to vent it at him. He obviously hadn't been expecting me to slow down, let alone stop, and he had to pull himself up short to stop from knocking me over.

"You probably work for him, don't you? You're not agency, I can tell that much, but neither is he anymore, and you're exactly the kind of slick-talking, Sartre-reading asshole he'd throw in my path to distract me. Son of a *bitch*."

"I'm not—" he began, but I said, "Shut up. Don't talk to me," and started down the road again. Desmond's long strides kept him easily at my side, even as I hurried to walk faster and get rid of him.

"Go away," I said. "I have to go home and fucking pack the fucking stuff I just fucking unpacked. *Fuck*."

We passed by Addie's antiques shop, and I couldn't believe that just a half hour before, I'd been happily sipping tea, planning my bartending career. It seemed like a lifetime ago now.

"I understand that you're upset," Desmond said, his voice quiet but firm, "but you're on the verge of making a public scene over something that the people in this town have worked very hard to keep secret, and I won't risk the danger you'd present in doing so. I'm walking you home."

I turned on him. "You're walking me *nowhere,* you limey bastard, and if I want to make a scene, I'll make a scene and you can't stop me!"

He grabbed both my elbows in his hands and pulled me closer to him, but nothing about the gesture was gentle. He glanced around to see if there was anyone close enough to hear us, and after deciding it was safe, he looked down at me, his eyes blazing.

"I *will* stop you from talking about magic in public," he said, his voice low and dangerous, "and I'll do it by whatever means necessary. Underestimating me will not serve you well, I can promise you that."

I met his eyes, saw danger there, and heard Addie's voice in my head.

Desmond Lamb is not a good man.

I let out a breath and opened my mouth to say something sharp and cutting, but I must have burned up all my anger, leaving me with nothing but grief left to express, and I started to cry, a hard, ugly, sobbing cry. Desmond released my arms immediately, looking almost as freaked out as I felt.

"Ms. Parker? Are you all right?"

"No," I sputtered, sobs breaking my words into pieces. "I'm not . . . all right, you idiot. I just saw . . . my father." I motioned back down the street, toward the office where my father was amiably going over bullshit office busywork with his crazy receptionist. "I haven't . . . seen him . . . for sixteen years." My voice cracked and my stupid eyes flooded with heat and tears and I began to whine like a radiator springing a leak, releasing pressure that would scald me if I got too close to it.

"Are you . . . um . . . would you perhaps . . . um . . . ?" he stammered. It was almost comical, considering how moments before he'd been idly threatening me, and now he was acting like Hugh Grant in his fumbling romantic-comedy phase.

Men. A few tears and they fall apart.

"I'm fine," I lied, swiping at my face. "I'm okay. Great, in fact. Never been greater."

"I have no doubt," he said. "I would still like to walk you home, if I may."

I sniffled and looked up at him. "Can I stop you?"

He had the decency to look a little ashamed even as he shook his head. *No.*

God, he was so . . . weird. He was wearing a crisp, white button-down shirt with brown pinstripes, and brown pants, and a brown tie. He looked so starkly different from the rest of the people in this town, and oddly, he made me feel . . . I don't know. Less alone, somehow. Plus, I'd been raised by one bastard and I'd married another; it maybe wasn't a sign of mental health that I felt comfortable around someone like Desmond, but it made a twisted sort of sense.

"Fine," I said, and pointed in the direction of home. "Let's go."

I swiped at my face as we walked. After a few moments of tense silence, he reached into his pocket and offered me a pristine white handkerchief, folded into a perfect square.

"I know they're horribly old-fashioned, but my mother never let me leave the house without a handkerchief," he said. "It's one of the enduring habits of my childhood."

I took it from him and swiped my face. I was beginning to feel calmer. The gentle rhythm of walking, with Seamus on one side of me and Desmond on the other, was helping me even out emotionally. Still, every few steps, I'd feel it rise up again . . . the panic, the sadness, the anger . . . and keeping it in check was exhausting me. I had to have a distraction.

"Talk to me," I said after a few moments, and he glanced around us again. There weren't many people on the street, but it was a summer day in a village, so there were enough, and he said, "I'd like to wait until we're in private."

"Not about . . . *that*," I said. "Tell me a story. Get my mind off things. Believe it or not, the thing with your mother and the handkerchiefs was kind of working."

"Oh. Right." He gently took my elbow and led me across the street, and we headed in the direction of my new home.

"I'm afraid there isn't much more to the story of my mother and handkerchiefs," he said after we'd crossed. "It really was just an absurd obsession of hers."

"So, tell me something else. Where are you from?"

"Southern Kentucky," he said, without missing a beat, and I laughed.

It wasn't quite a full smile, but there was a glint of humor in his eye as he looked down at me. "Is there something funny about that?"

"My apologies," I said. "So, what does your family do in Kentucky?"

"Bourbon, naturally."

"Oh, naturally," I repeated.

"And grudge feuds," he added.

"Professionally?"

"No, we were more grudge feud hobbyists. Cousin Hamish once—"

"Wait!" I said, holding up my hand. "Hamish? Seriously?"

Desmond blinked at me, all innocence. "Kentucky has a rich Scottish heritage."

"Maybe, but it breaks the fiction," I said. "Kentucky's more a Billy-Bob, Bobby-Jack, Jethro, Cletus kind of place."

"Is it your contention that there are *no* Hamishes in all of Kentucky?"

"I'm sure there are, but it's just not believable," I said. "It kicks me out of the story and then I have to come back to reality where my own crappy life awaits, like a pile of dog poop that's so big you can't help but step in it."

"That's quite the poetic imagery."

"I'm goddamn Yeats, Jethro."

The almost-smile played again in his eyes. "All right. May I continue with the story of my cousin Hamish . . ." He paused for a moment, then added, "Bobby-Jack?"

"Your cousin is named Hamish-Bobby-Jack?"

"My family's naming conventions are no concern of yours," he said, with an air of haughty dignity. "Cousin Hamish-Bobby-Jack . . . nickname, Cletus . . ."

"Thank you," I said.

"Cletus is a name of English origin, by the way."

"It is not!" I laughed.

He slid sideways eyes at me. "Who is telling this story?"

"I'm sorry," I said, leading us out of the village and onto the county road that led toward home. "Please continue."

"Well, Cousin Cletus was a drunkard of legend, which is a thing that happens from time to time in the bourbon-making families . . ."

"Occupational hazard," I added supportively.

"Yes, quite." He cleared his throat and went on. "As fate would have it, Cletus fell in love with a woman from a family of religious teetotaling Mennonites, a Miss . . ." His eyes narrowed and he looked at me as he decided on a name. "Miss . . . Hazel . . . Brown?"

I nodded. "Acceptable."

"You're very kind. Well, Miss Hazel would not accept Cletus's flurry of proposals until he gave up the drink, and Cletus, while being a burly man of great physical prowess, was sadly powerless over his addiction."

"Wow. Sad story."

"Yes, quite tragic." We crossed the street, making our way onto Wildwood Lane.

"One day," Desmond continued, "poor Cletus, wild with desire for both bourbon and Miss Hazel, was presented with a solution from our other cousin . . . Sir Harold—"

"Sir Harold? Please," I objected.

"Do shut up, Ms. Parker," he said, and while his face

was still deadpan, there was genuine amusement in his eyes. "Sir was his first name; Harold was his last. Kentuckians are as prone to whimsy as anyone else. Anyway, Sir Harold was a rapscallion and a rogue, but Cletus was desperate, so when Sir Harold suggested that Cletus allow himself to be locked in an empty whiskey barrel for four days as a cure for his condition, Cletus agreed."

We turned down my dusty driveway, and Desmond pushed the overgrowth at the mouth of the driveway up to gain free clearance for his height.

"Oh, this doesn't end well, does it?"

"I'm afraid not. Sir Harold, as it turns out, was also in love with Miss Hazel. She was quite the regional beauty, you see. In the four days during which Cletus was locked away in a barrel, engaging in his courageous battle against the demon alcohol, Sir Harold managed to convert to the Mennonite religion, woo Miss Hazel, and marry her. When he finally released Cletus from the barrel, the tragic wretch was too weak to kill Sir Harold with his bare hands, so he immediately went home to retrieve the weapon of choice of jilted lovers—"

"Oh!" I gasped. "Shotgun!"

Desmond let out an impatient sigh. "Dueling swords. Do I appear to hail from a family of savages, Ms. Parker?"

"No, you certainly don't," I conceded.

"Well, Sir Harold was no match for Cletus's brawn, even in his desiccated and sober state, but he had cleverness, an advantage which had always eluded poor Cletus, and he told Cletus that if he allowed Sir Harold to live happily ever after with Miss Hazel . . . now Mrs. Harold . . . he would sign over his entire share of the family bourbon fortune to Cletus."

"And Cletus gave up his one true love for *money*?" I said. "That's kind of a bummer ending."

"No, he gave up his one true love for more bourbon than a man could possibly drink in a dozen lifetimes."

"Still," I said. "Bummer ending."

"Perhaps, but only if you believe in one true love," Desmond said.

"You don't?"

He looked at me in silence for a long moment and said, "Possibly for those men who have the quality of character to truly earn it. Cletus was something of an arsehole."

I laughed, stepped up onto my porch, and turned to face him. Even with the porch step under me, he was still a little taller than I was.

"Thank you," I said. "I feel better."

"I'm glad." He met my eyes and held them, looking earnest. "I don't work for your father. We were professionally associated, some time ago, but not anymore, and I know he's a . . . complicated person. When you asked about him, I wasn't trying to dodge your question, I was just surprised that you'd mentioned him, and a little concerned."

Judd had taught me what to look for in people when

they lie. Either Desmond was telling the truth, or he was the most amazing liar I'd ever met.

"Okay," I said. "I believe you, and I'm sorry I yelled at you."

He nodded, then went on. "I am a conjurer, but I don't practice actively at the moment. I've never worked for either of the magical agencies. I didn't know who you were when you walked into the bar yesterday. I was reading Sartre for pleasure."

"Well, that's a lie," I said, snorting. "No one reads Sartre for pleasure."

He didn't exactly smile, but there was a light in his eye that seemed to be as close as he got.

"But I believe the rest of it, so . . . don't worry about it."

"All right," he said, and looked relieved.

I sighed and glanced at the house behind me. "I guess I'm going to pack up and leave now. Are you going to let me?"

"Is there anything I could do to stop you?"

"Do you want to stop me?" I asked, feeling a little strange at the phrasing of the question.

He nodded. "Yes."

"Why?"

He hesitated for a moment. "You're Josie Streat. The missing daughter who survived the disaster at Lott's Cove."

My heart flipped in my chest at the shock of talking to someone who actually knew my history. It was a strange sensation, having no secrets. "I'm not Josie Streat anymore. I haven't been for a long time."

He nodded, understanding on his face. "Fair enough. But your father is planning something, I'm fairly certain of it, and I think he needs you to finish. The only question is . . . are you here to help him, or to stop him?"

Having his suspicion land on me so suddenly threw me off a bit. "What? What the hell are you talking about? I'm here because my husband bought a house here without my knowledge, and you just saw me freak out at seeing my father again. Why would you think I was here to help him?"

"Why did you think I was sitting in wait hoping to trap you with Sartre?"

I sighed, understanding. "Because neither of us would put anything past Emerson Streat."

He nodded. "Your father went to a lot of trouble to get you here, obviously. Which only confirms my suspicion that he's up to something, and he must need you very desperately for whatever that is."

The confirmation of my own fears shot panic through me. "Why would he need me?"

He shook his head, his eyes locked on mine, actively recording any clue my expression might give him.

"I don't know," he said.

I watched him for a moment. Addie had warned me against him, and I'd seen what she was talking about on the street, when he'd grabbed my arms and threatened me. But for some reason I couldn't rationally

justify, I trusted him. I felt comfortable with him.
And if he was telling the truth, which I believed he
was, then we wanted the same thing . . . to stop my
father from hurting any more innocent people.

"I'm not staying," I said. "If he really needs me, then
the best thing I can do is leave before he gets what he
wants."

"I understand," Desmond said, "but if you could
answer some questions before you leave, it might help
me stop him if he decides to move ahead without you."

"Fine," I said finally, pulling Seamus with me as I
turned toward the door. "Come on in, Jethro."

I started with the kitchen, packing up what few utensils and kitchen stuff I'd brought to begin with. Packing wasn't going to be a big job, so I did it slowly and
deliberately, mostly so I'd have something to do while
we talked. Desmond sat on a three-legged stool I'd
brought with me, watching me from across the counter.

"Go ahead, Des," I said. "I don't have much to pack,
so if you've got questions, ask them now."

"Can you tell me what happened in Lott's Cove?"
he asked, his voice low.

I went quiet. It wasn't that I didn't want to tell him.
I did, if for nothing more than to reassure him that my
ass skipping over the town line was likely the solution
to his problem. I just didn't know how to start.

"I know it's probably not easy to talk about," he
said, reading my mind, "but if your information can
help . . ."

I took a deep breath, my stomach roiling. "So, you know my father was really high up in the agencies, then? Kind of like a magical J. Edgar Hoover, without all the cross-dressing?"

"I'm familiar with your father's history, yes."

"Okay . . . well. We moved around a lot. A *lot*. Being an agency kid was like being a military kid, always some new outpost you've got to go to. I didn't know much about what my father did for work, but after a while, even as a kid, I could put the pieces together. He was obsessed with giving power to nonmagicals. When he was a kid, his mother was killed for being a witch. It was in South Carolina, in the late fifties. She had elemental magic."

Desmond's eyes lit at this. "That's rare."

I nodded. "It is. Even in our family, she and I are the only elementals. She was water. I'm earth, metal mostly. Anyway, she and my father were walking home from the store one hot summer day, and she made it rain over his head to cool him down and someone saw. Two days later, someone lodged a firebomb through the bedroom window and my father was an orphan. And ever since . . ." I shrugged. "I guess his philosophy is, if you can't beat 'em, make 'em join you."

Desmond looked confused. I didn't blame him. "Why would he want to give power to his enemies?"

"Well, first, let's just say . . . most power is silliness anyway. Some magicals can't do any more than change the color of their eyes, which is fun, but not necessarily dangerous. People with real, applicable power are rare. I think mostly it was just that he wanted to be free of it all. Imagine . . . like, if a black person had the power to make everyone black. Then, suddenly, it's not a factor anymore. You can breathe, you can exist, without being afraid that some idiot is going to do something irreversible to you just because you're different. I mean, it's *wrong* with magic, it's dangerous and it gets people killed, but you can sympathize."

Desmond nodded, a little. He didn't entirely sympathize, but that was okay. He hadn't grown up a magical, and my father's obsessions were kind of screwing with his town. No one understood that better than me.

"So . . ." he pressed on, "that's what happened at Lott's Cove? He used you to make nonmagicals magical? How?"

I sighed. "I don't know."

Desmond gave me a look of frustration, and I said it again, to reassure him I wasn't playing games.

"I don't. I have no idea. I have elemental magic, and I work with earth. There are minerals and metal compounds in blood. That's how I can tell if someone has magic just by touching their skin; I can feel it humming in them. I'm connected, somehow, to other people's magic. My best guess is that it must have transferred that way . . . maybe?"

I could tell by his expression that he thought it was a weak hypothesis, but whatever. He wasn't there. I was.

"All I know is, one day, all I could do was make

friendship charms out of forks, and the next, I was magical Typhoid Mary."

I looked at my hands, which were mundane and sparkless, but in my mind, I could still see the electric-blue light dancing from my fingertips, hopping from one person to the next. Del, her mother, my teacher Mr. Gleason, the lady with the blue hair who played the organ, and, finally, my mother. My entire body was humming with emotion; for sixteen years, I'd shared this with exactly no one, and suddenly, I was dredging it all up for someone I didn't even know. My legs were shaking under me, and I was afraid I might wobble, so I leaned one hip against the counter and kept talking. Telling my story was upsetting, but it also felt kind of good. Freeing, I guess.

"I was seventeen, and there was a group of kids going on a trip to volunteer for Habitat for Humanity. Mom and I went down to the church with a bunch of other people to pack up toolboxes and supplies. I was the only active magical there, and—"

"Your mother wasn't magical?" Desmond asked, a curious lilt in his voice.

"It was daytime. She had night magic."

He nodded, understanding.

"Anyway," I went on, "we were in the basement and the lights went out, and there was a flash of blue light, but it wasn't regular light. It was like tiny, thin strings of lightning, dancing around the place. Like magical light." I held up my nonmagical hands. "*My* light."

"You felt it? Coming from you, I mean?"

I shook my head. "From me. Through me. Hell if I knew. I held up my hands. I saw it flash out in a circle from where I was standing, arcing from person to person. It was like static shock dialed to eleven. And then . . . that was it. The pastor found the fuse box and the lights came back on and we all finished packing the tools and went home."

I went quiet for a bit, gathering myself to tell the rest of the story. Desmond waited, perfectly still, until I was ready to talk again.

"We started hearing the stories of the magic within a few hours. Del called me on the phone that afternoon. Hers was the best. Perception magic; she made snow. But you could feel it, too, not just see it. It was such a cool, rare magic. We threw snowballs in her backyard, in July, and you'd look down at your hand, which felt cold and wet, but there was nothing there. It was pretty awesome . . . at first."

I could feel my heart pounding in my chest, and I willed it to slow down. Desmond waited, forever patient.

"Del got sick the fastest, probably because she used her power the most. I mean, *we* used it. Anyway, she just . . . collapsed, and they took her away."

"They?" Desmond asked, and I answered. "The agencies."

"And your father wasn't around?"

I shook my head. "Business trip, supposedly. I think he just skipped town for it. My guess is, he figured if it worked, it would give him plausible deniability with my mother, and if it didn't . . ."

There was a look of extreme sympathy on Desmond's face, and it made me uncomfortable, so I looked away.

"It had to be me, I think. Metal elemental. We're so rare, and he needed me to try this experiment, but . . ."

"He's a coward," Desmond filled in when I trailed off. "He couldn't face what he was doing, so he ran off."

My father was a lot of things, a coward just one of them, but I didn't want to talk about him. "Anyway, next was Del's dad, and her mom and then . . . my mom got sick."

"But she was already a magical," Desmond said. "Shouldn't she have been immune, like you?"

I shrugged. "Maybe. I don't know why I survived."

Desmond nodded. He wasn't taking physical notes, but I could see that he was putting all the details away in his brain, in case any might make sense later.

"Anyway," I went on, "that night, before they could take my mother away to wherever they'd taken Del and her family, she opened the safe and gave me my new documents. A fake birth certificate, a driver's license, a Social Security card, and the keys to her car. She . . . she told me . . ." I let out a breath. Sixteen years, I had never breathed a word about that day, to anyone, and the release of it was making me a little dizzy.

"Eliot?" Desmond said, his voice low and careful. "Are you all right?"

"Yeah," I said, more denial than outright lying. "She told me that it was me. She used the last of her magic to bind my powers so he couldn't ever use me that way again, and she told me to run and never see my father again. Then . . . she died."

The room was oppressively quiet. Even Seamus, asleep on the floor, wasn't snoring. A cool trickle of sweat beaded down my spine. I had stopped packing some time ago, and even though I knew my magic was bound, I felt hesitant about touching anything made of metal, so my utensils just sat on the counter like a pile of old scrap.

Desmond was the first to break the silence. "How long was the incubation period, between initial exposure and demise?"

"It depended on how much people used their new magic. Del went quick, a few hours. I was gone by the following night, but based on what I found out later, I think most people were dead within twenty-four hours."

"And what were the symptoms?" His expression was sharp, analytical. Like a doctor, looking for clues for his diagnosis.

"At first, the magic would happen accidentally. Magic is sparked by emotion, so someone would get mad or be surprised, their hands would tingle and their light would spark and *poof*, suddenly they'd change the color of pencil lead, or make a flower appear from thin air. A few hours of using the magic, and the power surges came. You know, where it just gets so strong, you can't control it anymore. After that, people just collapsed and then . . ."

"And no one in that basement was given anything to eat or drink?"

I shook my head. "I'm sure some people had coffee or a snack or something, but not all of us. He didn't use potions, if that's what you're getting at. It was some kind of electrical thing."

He nodded. "Your father wasn't in the room, correct? Do you think he might have given you a potion to spark the experiment?"

"Maybe, I guess," I snapped, sudden irritation surging through me. "I don't know. Do any of these details even matter?"

He gave me the patient gaze of the scientist. "Details always matter."

"Well, that's all I've got for you. Now, you can answer some questions for me."

He made a motion of permission with his hands. *Proceed.*

"So what makes you think that my father is going to try it again?"

"Emerson funded my research."

I closed my eyes. "Let me guess. Spreading magic to nonmagicals?"

Desmond lowered his eyes. "I was a doctor. And a conjurer. I thought I could figure it out, scientifically, using magic . . ." His expression was grim. "It was foolishness and hubris, and I'm afraid I'm the reason Emerson chose Nodaway Falls. I had some . . ." There was a brief pause, and Desmond's mouth twitched with distaste. ". . . *successes,* I guess you could call them, and he's been interested in this town ever since."

"Do you still work for him?"

He shook his head, and when he spoke, his voice was quiet. "Not anymore."

"But that's why you're still here?" I asked, putting my best guess on it. "To make it up to these people who hate you?"

Desmond seemed a little surprised by the comment, and I shrugged.

"Look, you were sitting by yourself in a bar reading Sartre; that's not a guy with a lot of friends. Plus, I saw the look Stacy gave you when she was in Happy Larry's yesterday. She does *not* like you. Even Liv seemed a little iffy about you. And today, Addie told me you were a bad guy and that I shouldn't trust you. Whatever you did to these people, they really hate you."

"Yes," he said simply. "They do."

"And you think you're going to make it up to them? Protect them from this danger, and make it all better?"

"No," he said carefully. "I threw a lit cigarette on the ground. It's irresponsible to walk away while the fire burns."

"Well, I'm leaving," I said. "If I'm gone, he can't do whatever he wants to do, and then you can move on. Sounds like a win-win to me."

He gave me a surprised look. "It's all hypotheses and conjecture," he said. "I have no idea what's really going on. Your father managed to create a lot of chaos without you last year—"

"You mean, with *you*?"

His eyes met mine and didn't flinch at all. "Yes. While your being here now can hardly be a coincidence, I take no comfort in your running off."

"Running off? Pardon my American rudeness, but fuck you, buddy." I picked up a pan and threw it in my box, anger coursing through my body. "Look, whatever's going on here can only get better if I leave. I'm sorry I can't give you a solid answer to everything you're looking for, but I didn't come looking for this. Now, just . . . tell me you didn't put an unbinding potion in the Welcome Wagon lasagna."

Desmond's eyebrows knit together. "What lasagna?"

I shook out my hands. "The one that came in the Welcome Wagon stuff. The one I ate yesterday."

He shook his head, concern on his face. "No. And I haven't made any potions that would unbind magic that anyone could have taken. Why?"

"Because," I said, panic running through me, "my hands are tingling."

Desmond hopped up from the stool he was sitting on and moved toward me, but I held my hand out to stop him.

"Your magic," he said quietly, not moving. "It's back?"

"There's only one way to find out," I said, and grabbed a knife.

Chapter 5

Desmond watched me carefully as I took the knife into my hand. Almost instantly, tiny blue strings of lightning danced around my fingers.

It was easy. Natural. What is it they say? Like riding a bike. I simply closed my fingers around the metal, and then, with hardly any effort or thought at all, it re-formed in my hand. When I opened my fist, a tiny stainless steel potion flask, wide at the bottom and thin at the mouth, sat in my palm. I handed it to Desmond who, to his credit, took it from me without fear.

"That's decorative," I said absently. "Steel corrupts potions."

"Yes," he said, staring down at the thing. "I know."

"Of course you do. Sorry." I let out a breath. "Well, fuck my fucking life, huh?" I put my hand to my forehead. I couldn't get in a full breath. "I think I might pass out."

Desmond touched my arm and guided me to the couch where he sat me down and leaned me over, putting my head between my knees. I heard him get up, and a moment later the faucet turned on. When he came back, I heard him set the glass gently on the coffee table. He put his hand at the base of my neck, and the strength of him was comforting, but I couldn't indulge that.

"You can't touch me," I said. "I'm not safe around nonmagicals. I think maybe I need to go off somewhere and be a hermit. It's okay. Age of Amazon, and everything, I can have supplies delivered to a cabin in the mountains by drones. I don't like people very much, anyway."

He didn't move his hand. "I'm not worried. You may have been a catalyst, but your father set off the original reaction, somehow. I'm sure of it. He may have unbound your magic, but I don't think you're a danger to anyone."

I pulled my head up and looked at him. "Hypothesis and conjecture. You don't know shit."

He gave a grim nod. "Fair enough. I would like to stay with you until sunset, though, just for observation. Will that be all right?"

I shrugged. "How long is that?"

"About six hours. We could run some tests, have you use your magic, test your control. But there's time for that. First, perhaps a nap would be in order."

I gave him a wry smile. "Is that your way of telling me I look exhausted?"

"Yes," he said.

I would have argued with him, but I was too tired. I stood up and walked over to Seamus, nudging his sleeping body gently with my foot. He opened one eye and looked up at me, then closed it again. I grabbed his collar and urged him to his feet. He may be a crappy watchdog, but no way was I sleeping alone right now.

"While you sleep, I'd like to make some phone calls, if you don't mind." He pulled his phone out of his pocket and swiped the screen, then looked up at me, waiting for permission.

"Fine." I shrugged, almost grateful that he was taking charge, because it was for sure I had no idea what to do. "Who are you calling?"

He didn't look up from his phone. "The cavalry."

Seven hours and one full chess set made from my flatware later, I was sitting in the eclectically decorated living room of Olivia Kiskey's Victorian house. Desmond had walked me to the house but stopped at the sidewalk, passing me and Seamus off to Liv like a prisoner exchange. Liv led me inside, settling me on a leather La-Z-Boy recliner while Stacy and Addie sat on a poofy floral love seat. Across the coffee table, Peach took up the center of the impossibly lime-green couch, flanked by Liv on one side of her and a woman in her seventies wearing a pair of blue sweats and a

Cookie Monster T-shirt—this was the eponymous Betty of Crazy Cousin Betty's waffle house, I was informed—on the other. Liv set a bowl of apple slices and peanut butter in the corner for Seamus, who went facedown in it.

Liv was wearing jeans and a brown T-shirt that read THE DUDE ABIDES. Peach was wearing a yellow sundress in which her round belly looked basically like the sun. On top of it she balanced a napkin with brownies on it, which she picked at lazily, as if nothing big was going on. Stacy sat with her arms crossed over her army-green tank top, her eyes narrowed and her stance ready for action. I didn't shrink from her stare, but I didn't engage with it, either.

At the moment, Stacy Easter was the least of my fucking problems.

"So . . . you really haven't had magic for sixteen years?" Addie asked, pouring a glass of lemonade for me.

"Nope."

"Wow," Peach said. "That must have been weird. How are you feeling?"

"A little wobbly," I said honestly, "but I'll be okay. So . . . you're all magical?"

"We'll ask the questions, thanks," Stacy said, eyeing me with suspicion.

Liv made a sound of disapproval in Stacy's direction, and Peach shifted a bit and pushed down on her stomach.

"Get your foot out of Mommy's ribs, sweetie," Peach

said, then smiled at me. "Liv's magical, and Betty. Stacy's a conjurer. I'm just a groupie."

"You're nonmagical?" We'd tested my powers after sunset, and they were fully gone, but the idea of being around any nonmagicals, especially a pregnant one, made me tense.

Peach picked at her brownie with one hand, and with the other, gave me a dismissive wave. "Ah, don't worry about it. I've been a conduit before, and it was cool. Besides, Desmond says he's pretty sure you're safe to be around. At night, anyway."

Stacy snorted. "Yeah, and apparently we're taking Desmond's word on things now."

Liv shot Stacy a sharp side-eye and then smiled at me. "Whatever's going on here, we'll figure it out. Don't worry. We've got loads of practice."

"Yeah," Stacy muttered, "because of *her* boyfriend."

"Barely know the guy," I said, but they all ignored me.

"Huh," Betty said. "I thought it was you who gave those potions to everyone last year, Stacy."

"Yeah, in flasks that Desmond laced." Stacy huffed and leaned forward. "And now we're hosting his little lady friend in your living room."

"Ignore her, Eliot," Peach said. "Stacy's just slow to warm up to people."

"I'm plenty fucking warm," Stacy said. "But you guys don't see a pattern here? Two years ago, magic came to town, and people got killed. Last summer,

Desmond tore my life apart. Now *this one*"—she made a face at me like I was a lab rat—"turns up and we just invite her in and give her lemonade and brownies? What the hell is wrong with you people?"

I shot a look at her, almost grateful for the confrontation that gave me something to put my back up against, and someone to vent my own anger at. "Yeah, well, all I know is, I came to this town after not having to deal with any magic for sixteen years. Then, I eat a little lasagna that you guys gave me and . . . thanks to a *conjurer*, by the way . . . I'm making rooks out of spoons. No one wants to know what's going on here more than me, trust me."

"That's just it," Stacy said, unruffled by my shooting back at her. "I *don't* trust you, I don't trust Desmond, and I don't want you anywhere near my friends or my town."

"Stacy, stop it." Liv's voice was quiet, but firm enough to silence everyone in the room. She picked up the brownie tray from the coffee table and held it out to Stacy.

"Two years ago, someone unbound my magic, and I was scared and freaked out, but at least I wasn't alone, and we're not leaving Eliot alone. She needs help and we're going to help her, so either get the hell out or take a brownie and shut up."

Stacy stared at Liv. For a moment, I thought she was going to leave, but then she took a brownie and sat back. Liv set the tray down on the coffee table and looked at me. "So. Desmond told us what happened with your father. I'm really sorry. That's got to be tough."

"I can't believe Emerson Streat is evil," Addie said, shaking her head. "You think you know someone . . ."

"He's not evil," I said, and then backed up. "Well, not exactly. He's single-minded, and he believes that the ends justify the means, so he does bad things. But . . ." I trailed off, feeling conflicted about defending the man who'd killed my best friend and my mother, and used me to do it. I didn't believe he knew they'd die for sure, but I did think he knew it was a possibility, and that was enough. And if he was going to try to do it again here . . .

"No," I said, finally. "Forget all that. He's evil."

"It's okay to have complicated feelings about it," Betty said. "I once dated a Fascist. Love is weird. The bottom line is, how can we help you?"

"I don't know." I picked up a brownie. I wasn't hungry, but picking at it gave me something to do, at least. "Maybe . . . tell me about your powers. What kind of magic do you guys have?"

"Nothing with teeth," Addie said casually. "The only one who could kill a person was Tobias, and he's gone."

A heavy blanket of silence fell over the room, and Addie's eyes went wide and she put her hand over her mouth.

"I'm sorry, honey," she said to Liv, the words muffled by her fingers.

"It's okay," Liv said, but I could see the pain on her

face. It almost made me want to not push, but I couldn't help it. I had to ask.

"So, Tobias . . . he was magical, too?"

Betty shot a wary look at Liv. "Yes. He's magical."

"Excuse me," Liv said, and hurried out of the room.

"Nice work," Stacy said, but when I looked up, she wasn't talking to Addie. She was looking at me. I didn't have time for her grudge, though, so I ignored her and turned to Betty.

"What happened with Tobias?"

Betty glanced in the direction Liv had gone, and then leaned forward, speaking in low tones. "He left her a note. Just a note. 'It's over. I'm sorry.' After two years of living together, practically married, he just—*poof*! Gone. All his stuff packed and moved out while she was at work. And you'd have never seen it coming. He adored her. You could tell by the way he looked at her, by the way he talked to her. He loved her. I think the agency he worked for called him away."

My entire body tensed, and my stomach went south. "Agency?"

"Yeah," Peach said. "He worked for Allied Strategical Forces. It's like a magical FBI or whatever, have you heard of them?"

I put on what I hoped was an impassive expression. "Yup."

Addie made a face. "Well, then you know that ASF isn't exactly the *good* guys, but they're not as bad as the other one. RIAS, whatever that stands for."

"Regional Initiative Action Services," I said automatically, and Stacy raised an eyebrow at me.

I swallowed. "My father ran RIAS when I was a kid. Before he caused the disaster in Lott's Cove and had to resign. I'd bet he's still got a lot of connections, though."

"Oh," Stacy said coldly. "Great."

"Regional Initiative Action Services," Betty huffed. "What does that even *mean*?"

"Nothing," I said absently, putting my picked-over brownie on the coffee table. "That's the point."

Addie touched my arm and lowered her voice, glancing in the direction Liv went. "*Whatever* about the agencies. Tobias loved Liv. And I don't mean he liked her a lot. He *loved* her."

"Loves," Stacy corrected gently, and she and Addie shared a dark, worried look. That's when I realized that they thought he might be dead.

Addie turned back to me. "I'm sure ASF called him away on some mission and made him write that note. He would never leave her on his own. He just wouldn't."

Maybe he wouldn't, I thought. *Maybe my father came to town and saw an agency guy, especially one from the opposing team, as a threat.* Guilt washed over me, not because it was my fault that my father had likely disappeared Liv's boyfriend, but that I was too much of a coward to voice my suspicions out loud.

At that moment, Liv walked back into the room, and we all shut up. She had something red and ceramic curled up in her arms like a pet, and at first I wondered how much of a toll Tobias's leaving had taken on her. She set the thing on the coffee table between us and I studied it. It was . . . weird. It had obviously been a red mug at one time, because the tail wasn't a fluffy bump at the back, but rather, formed from the ceramic handle. I was about to say something kind and nonjudgmental, but then the ceramic bunny wagged its tail and I jumped back.

"What is that?"

"That is Gibson," she said.

It waggled back and forth as the ceramic nose sniffed at the table, and the ceramic feet shuffled toward me.

"I made him when I first got my magic," Liv said. "Kind of accidentally. He's blind and deaf and a little clumsy, but . . . I don't know. I just love him, I guess."

"Oh my god," I breathed as I bent over lower to study the thing. "You have source magic? That's rare. I've never even seen it before."

"Source magic?" Peach said, looking up from the brownies balancing on her stomach. "What's source magic?"

Liv looked at her. "It's when you can give life to something independent of you." It appeared Tobias the Agency Guy had been schooling his girlfriend, which was good. At least there was one of them I wouldn't have to explain everything to. The rest of them, however, were watching me with interest, so I explained a little.

"There are different kinds of magic," I said, and

started rattling off my knowledge the way fourth graders rattle off state capitals. "Source magic, like Liv's, is when you can give life to inanimate objects. Elemental magic, people who work with earth, air, fire—"

"Fire," Addie said, perking up. "That's you, Stacy."

"You're a fire elemental?" I asked, feeling tense at the thought. You wanted your fire elementals to be the calm, rational sort, and Stacy Easter didn't seem that type to me.

"I'm a conjurer," she said, her voice even. "When I'm under the influence of someone else's magic, I start fires."

"Good to know." I squelched an instinct to apologize for being rude, but thought twice about it. I wasn't about to make myself submissive to Stacy Easter. If I'd offended her, she could just deal with it.

"Okay," I went on, "so, let me see . . . there's also kinetic magic, where you can affect speed and motion. Perception magic, where you can create visual impressions, but there isn't anything physically there. And there's creative magic, where you can make things appear from thin air—"

Peach snapped her fingers. "Like Betty! She can make baked goods just by snapping her fingers. Her baklava is amazing."

"Oh, it's nothing," Betty said humbly.

Gibson got to the end of the table, and I picked him up before he could fall off the edge. He already had a chip on his nose. I . . . well, for lack of a better word . . . *cuddled* him to my chest and looked at Liv. "Are you day or night magic?"

Liv's face tensed a bit. "Both. It's a long story, but . . . yeah. I can do it whenever."

It was clear that Liv understood exactly what she was, exactly how rare she was, and what that meant about her power, but her friends obviously didn't, because they didn't look worried at all, so I tried not to react too much. It was her place to tell them, not mine.

I handed Gibson back to Liv, and noticed that while Addie was petting Seamus and Peach was pushing the baby's foot out of her rib cage, Stacy was watching me carefully, and not missing a thing.

Liv leaned forward. "So, you think your father spiked your lasagna and unbound your magic? Why would he do that?"

"Because he needs me, I guess," I said. "It's really difficult to bind magic, practically impossible to bind a grown magical, but it's crazy easy to unbind it."

"Yeah," Peach said. "Liv got hit in the face with some herbs in a gym sock and that's all it took to unbind her magic. It was *crazy*."

I smiled. In a weird way it was kind of nice, being able to talk about this stuff again. "My father used to compare it to entropy. You know, chaos. Magic is a force that wants to be free, that kind of thing. So maybe my father dosed the Welcome Wagon lasagna—"

"Oh! Bastard!" Peach said, offended at the thought.

"But it's also possible my magic could have . . . I don't know . . . just come loose from being around"—I deliberately didn't look at Liv—"this much magical energy. Maybe. I don't know."

Stacy huffed, and Addie said, "What?"

"Seriously? You guys aren't seeing this?" Stacy looked at Liv. "*Desmond* walked her home from Happy Larry's last night." She said his name in the same tone people use for *politician* or *herpes*. "Desmond was with her today when her magic erupted. Maybe she's in on it, maybe she's just his victim, but I can't believe you guys don't see the common factor here."

Liv looked at me, torn. "I don't know. What do you think, Eliot?"

And all eyes were suddenly on me. I looked from one of them to the next and then said, "Hell if I know. You all know him better than I do."

"Well, let's start with the obvious. Did you drink anything in his presence?" Stacy asked. Her tone was less confrontational now than it had been before, but I guessed that was less about her coming to like me and more about the fact that she wanted information.

"He doesn't have to give her anything to drink," Betty said. "Remember what he did to Leo last year? With that hypodermic needle?"

A flash of pain crossed Stacy's face; apparently whatever Desmond had done to this Leo, it had been pretty bad.

"Who's Leo?" I asked. "What happened?"

"Leo's my boyfriend," Stacy said. "Desmond gave him a potion that wiped out his feelings for me."

"Oh, wow." For a moment, I felt some sympathy for Stacy Easter. Not enough to like her any better, but whatever.

"Desmond can't be trusted," Stacy said. "Don't think it's a coincidence that your magic unbinds the day after you meet him. I'll bet dollars to doughnuts, it's not."

"C'mon, guys," Peach said, making it obvious who the peacekeeper was in this group. "Desmond doesn't do that stuff anymore. He was under the influence of the potions at the time, too. Stacy cured him, and he's been . . . you know, okay. He's doing landscaping work for Nick this summer, and we haven't had any trouble with him all year. It might be time to give the guy a second chance."

Liv seemed to take this under consideration, and Addie gave a grudging shrug, but Stacy was having none of it.

"Do whatever you want," she said. "Just don't come crying to me when magic bites you in the ass. Again."

Liv gave Stacy a warning look. "I think Eliot would know if Desmond stuck her with a needle."

"He's smart," Stacy said. "And he's devious. He could drop something on her skin, she'd never know." Stacy looked at me. "Did he touch you?"

"I don't know. We shook hands, but . . . I don't think he administered anything to me. And the only other stuff I ate was that Welcome Wagon lasagna."

Addie's eyebrows rose a touch, and she gasped and put her hand over her mouth. "Gladys Night!"

I glanced around the group, thinking for a moment that perhaps Addie had just had one of those strokes that makes people say random words, but they all seemed to know what she was talking about.

"Oh, crap," Betty said.

"Wait," I said, leaning forward. "Are you guys talking about . . . Gladys *Knight,* Gladys Knight? What does any of this have to do with 'Midnight Train to Georgia'?"

"Nothing," Stacy said. "Gladys Night. No *K,* no Pips. She lives down the street from my mother. She's not magical. She's fifty-four years old and she believes that flowers bloom when angels fart. There's no way she'd put anything in that lasagna."

Stacy's mother's neighbor, I thought, and I looked at Stacy as I thought it. She looked back at me, reading my expression easily.

"Don't go pointing that fearsome intellect at me," she said. "I didn't lace your stupid lasagna."

Liv shook her head. "No. Stacy would never, ever, *ever* give anything to anyone against their will. Not after what Desmond did last summer. Just . . . *never.* Trust me."

"Never say never," Stacy said under her breath, eyeing me with mild threat in her eyes. She was like a cat, puffing up to look more dangerous than she really was, and despite the fact that she was pointing that puffed-up act at me, I could sympathize with where it was coming from. If I had friends and a town like this, I'd want to protect them, too.

"The *point* is," Betty said, getting us back on track,

"that Gladys Night spends every weekend doing volunteer work for Community Cares."

The room went silent. I sighed. "And my father runs Community Cares."

"Well . . ." Addie gave me sympathetic eyes. "Yeah."

"So we've got him on opportunity," I said.

"What's the motive, though?" Liv asked.

"The same as it's always been," I said, feeling suddenly exhausted. "To make all the nonmagicals magical."

Addie smiled and looked around. "Well . . . that doesn't sound too bad," she said. "Might even be fun."

"Yeah, it was sure a blast when Desmond did it to me and three other people last year," Stacy said. "It was a hoot until we all almost died."

"My mother *did* die," I said, and it was then that I saw the first spark of shame in Stacy's expression. "So did my best friend, and a bunch of other people from my town. I won't let that happen again."

If you can help it, a traitorous voice at the back of my head added.

"So," Betty said, ever pragmatic, "what do we do now?"

It was a good question, and none of us had the answer. Eventually, everyone shuffled out, and Addie gave me and Seamus a ride home. I slept, dreamt of a locked room filling with daisies, and when I woke up the next morning, pissed off and still tired despite a full night's sleep, I knew just what I needed to do.

Chapter 6

"Emerson Streat," I said breathlessly to the skinny red-head behind the desk. "I need to speak to him."

Amber Dorsey eyed me for a moment, sizing me up. She had hair like Little Orphan Annie, a wild fiery coif punctuated with little rhinestone dragonfly clips on either side. She wore low-rise jeans and a midriff top that exposed both her hip bones and lower ribs, which you could see clearly even when she was sitting down. Her eyes were dancing pinwheels of crazy, and she was exactly the kind of unexpected wild card Emerson would put on his front desk, the way someone else might install a fish tank of fascinating sea life for people to gawk at while they waited.

Some things never changed.

She cracked her gum and said, in a staccato and obviously put-on affectation of professionalism, "And what is your business with Mr. Streat?"

I could tell that, given a more natural environment, her response would have been, *Yeah, and what the fuck do you want?* My father always loved to play Henry Higgins to the town's most hard-edged Eliza Doolittle; it made him look like a hero to the people who liked her and a saint to the people who didn't. Plus, having crazy in the front office usually meant that people paid more attention to her and less to Emerson and whatever he was up to. This particular flower girl was fresh out of Covent Garden, as far as I could tell; the edges Emerson liked to smooth out on his front-desk women were still sharp and ragged.

"My business with Mr. Streat is personal. Where is he?" I pointed to the closed door behind her desk. "Is he in there? Is that where he is?"

Amber reached one hand, punctuated with bright red acrylics, toward the mouse. She cracked her gum again and clicked it without pulling her eyes away from mine.

"Let me *peruse* the calendar for Mr. Streat's next availability," she said coolly.

"Now," I growled at her. "He has an opening right the fuck *now.*"

She didn't move, just pulled her hand back from the mouse. Her body was still, but it was also lithe and dangerous, angry energy coiled and just waiting for an excuse to strike. He'd picked a live one this time.

"I will request that you maintain a professional tone in this—"

"Emerson Streat!" I shouted, giving up on getting anywhere with Amber Dorsey. "Get your ass out here, or I swear I'll—"

The office door opened and Amber shot up from her seat. "I told her she had to make an appointment, Mr. Streat. It's not my fault. She's obviously crazy. Do you want me to call the police?"

He smiled at me; it was obvious he'd been expecting me. At least he respected my intelligence enough not to feign surprise. He set the files in his hand on Amber's desk, and said, in a voice hued with a southern sunset and perfectly cracking with just the right hint of emotion, "It's okay, Amber. This is my daughter."

Amber's eyes widened, and she looked me up and down. "Are you sure? She doesn't look like you."

Emerson Streat chuckled and said, "No, she doesn't. She got her momma's genes. Proof of a benevolent god."

Amber blinked. She didn't appear to have any understanding of benevolence. Emerson pulled his eyes away from me and put a hand on her shoulder.

"Tell you what, Amber," he said, pulling some bills out of his pocket. "Why don't you take an early lunch? On me. I'll see you back here at two."

Amber, who obviously knew a good deal when she saw one, snatched the money out of his hand with her bright red talons and popped up on her toes to kiss him on the cheek.

"Thanks, Mr. S." She tagged me with one last look of caustic disapproval before shooting out the front door and leaving me alone with my father and my dog.

Emerson just stood there watching me for a while, a sad smile on his face. I tightened my grip on Seamus's leash, and I must have been putting out near-hysterical vibes, because the dog moved closer to me and rubbed his big rock of a head against my hip.

"You look beautiful, Josie," Emerson finally said. "The spittin' image of your momma."

"The name is Eliot now," I said. "But you know that."

He didn't even blink. "Yeah. I know that."

"You brought Judd out here," I said, sick with myself at how obvious it all was. How had I not seen it from the start? "How much did you pay him not to say anything to me about it?"

Emerson was quiet for a long time, and I relaxed a bit. He was quick with lies, a little slower when he was telling the truth. "There may have been a small monthly stipend."

My stomach turned. Judd had lied to me, all this time, for a small monthly stipend. Of course, that wasn't counting the lies he'd told me for free, but that was another issue altogether.

"And you gave him the money for the house." I stated it as fact, because there was no other way. Judd never had so much as two nickels to rub together. No way had he gotten his hands on one hundred thousand dollars cash, and if he had, he would have blown it in Atlantic City.

Emerson nodded. "Family is allowed to give a one-time gift for that sort of—"

"Did you tell him my real name? Did you tell him I was magic? Did—"

He held up his hands. "I told him I was your birth father, that we'd never met, that your mother had you without telling me. I told him that I just wanted to be sure you were taken care of. I flew him out here for four hours, to sign the paperwork, and that was all he knew. In case of death or divorce, you would get the house."

"And you expect me to believe that's all there was to it?" I held his eye, refusing to back down, even though my breath was ragged and my muscles were shaking.

Emerson undid his jacket button and sat one hip down on the edge of the reception desk, looking like every hometown politician ad ever made. *Just a good man doing a tough job*, his stance said.

Except I knew better.

"Whatever it is you want," I said, "you can forget it. I'm leaving town as soon as I can pack up my stuff. You can take that house back and sell it, burn it, give it to your little redheaded wildling, I don't care. But whatever you think is going to happen here, it's not happening."

He nodded, and hung his head a little bit in an affectation approaching shame. God, he was good.

He was so good, he almost had me fooled, and I knew him better than anyone else in this world.

"I don't blame you for being angry," he said. "All I was hoping for was a chance to see you again, maybe reconnect. Make up for the past. Start fresh."

"Yeah?" I could hear the squeak in my voice, but I pushed past it. "Then why didn't you just pick up a phone if you knew where I was? Why all the subterfuge, huh?"

He sighed. "Would you have taken a call from me? Would you have let me in if I showed up on your doorstep?"

"What do you think?"

"I think I did what I had to to see my daughter again. Maybe it wasn't the best way to handle it, maybe it was a little manipulative—"

I let out a huff at that. "A *little* manipulative? You bought a house for me without asking me. You paid my husband to *lie* to me."

"Josie—"

I held up my hand, but before I could correct him, he did it himself.

"*Eliot*," he said, tasting the name, and obviously not liking it. "That's the name your momma wanted to give you when you were born. I told her I wasn't giving my baby girl any man's name."

"George Eliot wasn't a man," I said. "She was a female writer who took on a man's name so she could write."

"Yeah, I know. And Parker for Dorothy Parker."

Emerson gave a little laugh, affection on his face. "She must have had those papers made up for you, just waiting in case I screwed up, and I had no idea. Your momma always was smarter'n me. It's what I loved most about her."

"She wasn't smart enough to survive being married to you." I felt a slight tinge of regret as soon as the words were out, because I could see that jab take a chunk out of him. For the all the weaknesses of character my father had, and he'd had a lot, I never doubted that he'd loved my mother, as much as he had the capacity to love anyone.

He gave me a small smile. "How 'bout I just call you 'punkin'? Like old times."

"Whatever," I said, waving a dismissive hand in the air. "What do you want?"

"Can't you believe that I just want a relationship with you? That this is all simply about an old man reconnecting with his only child?"

I took a moment, feeling slightly off balance. Could I believe that?

"Maybe," I said finally, "but you don't get to decide when or if that happens. *I* do."

He held up his hands. "Fair enough, fair enough." He smiled, that same old charming smile that had been the undoing of so many people. "But before you pack up and leave town, let me take you to lunch. There's a waffle house in town, makes the most amazing waffles you've ever had. If I can't convince you to stay, they might."

He pushed up off the desk and moved toward me. I stepped back, putting Seamus between us. "If you think I'm going to just go to lunch with you—"

"Now *that* is a majestic animal," Emerson said. He squatted down on his knees to commune with Seamus, and I willed Seamus to snarl, nip at him, or at least let out one of those huffing barks he made when he was hungry, but which sounded a little menacing if you didn't know what it meant. Weren't dogs supposed to have instincts about who was good and who was bad? Apparently Seamus had skipped that gene, because the traitorous little bastard sniffed Emerson Streat's hand and allowed himself to be petted.

"That's right. Good boy." Emerson pushed up to standing, grunting a little as he did and laughing a bit. "A man my age should know better than to overestimate what his knees'll do for him."

"You've been spying on me," I said, trying to get us back on track. This wasn't a friendly visit, and it was important that he understood that. He couldn't use my dog to get back into my heart. I wasn't that easily had.

"Yes," he said amiably. "Yes, I have."

"Did you know Judd was cheating on me? How much did you spy on us?"

He held up his hands. "I kept an eye on you, from afar. I wanted to be sure you were safe. I, uh, I found out about Judd and his lady friend. I gave him some time to realize his mistake and come clean to you, and when he didn't, I contacted him and bought the house. I wanted you to have something of your own if

the day came when you found out and left him. The
agreement was, if you left him, he was to tell you
about the house and sign over the deed to you."

"And three months later, he was dead." Much to my
shock and horror, my vision blurred. I sniffed and
blinked and the tears rolled down my face and dropped
onto my shirt. I could feel my chin quivering and my
lips quaking and I knew that the skin behind my eyebrows was turning bright red, the way it always did
when I cried hard.

Goddamn him, I thought. *Goddamn him.*

Emerson reached across Amber's desk, retrieved a
box of Kleenex, and handed it to me. He let me swipe
at my face for a moment, and just when I thought I had
gathered myself, Seamus moved closer to me, situat-
ing himself protectively between me and my father,
and that set me off again.

Dumb dog.

"Oh, punkin," Emerson said, his voice soft and full
of compassion. "I'm real sorry about that."

I swiped at my face and tried to keep my voice even.
"Did you kill him?"

He shook his head. "All I wanted was for you to
have a safe place to land if anything ever happened. I
never meant for it all to happen this way."

"That doesn't answer my question. Jesus. I shouldn't
have to parse every word to see if you're telling me
the whole truth. Do you realize how fucked up that is?"

"Watch your language," Emerson said. "I raised you
to talk like a lady."

"You didn't raise me at all," I shot back. "Mom did, and when she was gone, I finished the job on my own. You worked, and used us as lab rats."

Emerson sighed, and took a moment to compose himself before sidestepping that subject altogether. "I bought a house so you'd have a place to go when things fell apart. I wanted you to have a community, a safe place to land when Judd's cheating came out. I knew you wouldn't let me do that for you, so I used your husband."

I snorted. "A safe place full of *magicals*? You're gonna tell me that's just a coincidence?"

"It's who you are," he said.

"You don't know me," I shot back. "You don't know who I am. You had no right to dose that lasagna. I had Mom bind my powers for a reason, because that's what *I* wanted."

He looked at me, his expression sad. "You know as well as I do that your magic was always going to come back, someday. You can't bind magic forever. Magic always finds its way back, and I wanted to make sure you were in a safe place when it did. Did I go about that the wrong way? Well, maybe I did. And I'm sorry for it, but I'm just trying to protect you."

"What about these people?" I said. "What are you trying to do to them?"

He gave me a confused look. "What are you talking about?"

"Mom . . ." I said, barely able to choke out the word. "When she bound my magic. Before she died. She told

me that you'd try to use me to do it all again. She told
me I had to run . . ." I trailed off, staring at my father's
stunned expression.

"Punkin . . ." he said, and reached for me, but I
stepped back.

"Don't touch me," I said.

He watched me for a while, his expression per-
plexed, but I couldn't tell if it was genuine or not. I
was too upset. I took in a shaky breath and wiped
more tears from my face, willing myself to calm
down. I couldn't arm my bullshit detector if I was all
frazzled.

"I'm sorry your mother told you that," he said after
a long moment. "She was angry, and scared, and—"

"Because she was *dying*," I shot at him. "Because
of something *you* did."

His eyes flared, and his face reddened. "If I had
thought for one second that things would go as badly
as they did . . ."

"If you were so sure it was going to be okay, then
why weren't you in that basement with us?"

"Don't," he said, and in the force of that one word,
I felt like a little girl again, chastened and submissive
to the father she both feared and loved. "I lost everything that day," he said after a few moments. "I came
home to a town where I'd had friends to find them
dead. My wife, dead. My daughter, gone." He took a
deep breath, gained control, and met my eye. "I'm not
innocent. I was overseeing that experiment. I knew
what they were trying to do. I didn't know it would go

so wrong. You have to believe me, if I'd had any idea—"

"Stop." I shook my head and held up my hands, pushing the memories away. My mother's eyes going blank and turning toward the ceiling. Del's empty house, with lights on and the TV playing, as I drove my mother's car out of town to abandon it at a bus stop in Portland, Maine. "Twenty-eight people died, including Mom, and I had to watch it happen while you sipped chardonnay in Martha's Vineyard. So don't you *ever* talk to me about that day again."

"Okay," he said, nodding, his voice hoarse. "Okay."

We stood there, both of us breathing hard, and I tried to get a grip on myself. My hands were shaking, and I felt like the tiniest nudge could send me toppling over. I had taken the documents my mother had, in her prescience, prepared for me and run from it all. I had sealed off that part of my life, and thought about it as little as possible. That was how I'd gotten through it, and I had no desire to go back.

"I will say one thing," he said finally. "I don't know what your mother told you. She might have believed it, I don't . . . I don't know. She was angry with me, and she had good reason. I wasn't a very good husband. Wasn't a great father, either. But you are not a danger to the people here. You can stay, or you can go, but I need you to know that. I love this town. My work here is to make things better. There are magicals here, and I just wanted to give you a place where you didn't have to hide who you were. That's all I ever wanted for you."

"Stop," I said, and swiped at my face. I had no more will to fight him, and when he put his arms around me and held me to his chest, I broke. I leaned into him and God help me, even in the clutches of the dragon, I felt safe for the first time in a really, *really* long time.

"I am so sorry, punkin," he said, kissing the top of my head. There was emotion in his voice, and I believed it. I knew he loved me. I knew he missed me. I knew he was sorry, and that he wanted to know me. I just wasn't stupid enough to believe that was all there was to it, and that's what made it so hard. He was a wonderful, loving, funny, adorable man, but he was also one of the most ruthless bastards I'd ever known. Which Emerson Streat you got depended entirely on what he wanted at the moment, and I couldn't handle that. At least with Judd, I always knew he was working an angle. With my father, it was never clear, you never knew exactly where you stood, if it was in a safe haven or over a trapdoor that could drop you at any moment.

After a while, I pulled away from him. I ran through a handful of tissues getting all the tearful gunk off my face and pulled Seamus to my side as I headed toward the door.

"What can I do to make it up to you?" Emerson said. "Ask me for anything, it's done."

I stared up at him. I was exhausted. My mind was in a whirl. I had no idea what he wanted, and until I found out, there was no way I could leave. He'd just find another way to pull me back in again. Whatever dance we were doing, we were dancing it here, and we were dancing it now.

"There's a guy from town who kind of ran off a few months back," I said. "He was ASF."

Emerson's expression gave away nothing. Maybe he was the reason Tobias disappeared, maybe he wasn't. But either way, he had the power to help.

"He might have gone away because he wanted to, but if he didn't, if ASF called him away or if—god help you—you had something to do with it, I want you to get him back. Free and clear from either agency, if that's what he wants."

At least he didn't pretend that he didn't have the power to do exactly what I'd asked. "I'll do what I can."

"Good." I tightened my grip on Seamus's leash and resisted the urge, on the chance it might help Tobias, to tell him it wouldn't make a difference in our relationship no matter what he did. "I have to go."

"Wait." Emerson walked up to me, glancing quickly outside to see if there was anyone there who might see. There wasn't. He held out his hands, and golden light dashed around them. A moment later, he had the stem of a brilliant pink gerbera daisy in his hands, and held it out to me.

I stared at it, flooded with memories of a childhood filled with those daisies. Whenever he'd been gone too long on a business trip, whenever I skinned a knee, whenever I was sad or upset, he'd made me a magical daisy, and I'd loved every one. They'd fade away after a few hours, so you never had to watch them wither

and die. They were beautiful, and then they were—
poof!—gone.

And I'd been dreaming of them for years.

I looked up at his face in quiet wonder. Most of the
agency magicals were truly dangerous, with powers
that could kill. My father had creative magic, he made
imaginary *flowers,* for Christ's sake, and yet, there he'd
been, running the most dangerous magical agency
the world had ever known. I'd often wondered at the
more mundane skills he'd used to move to the top, to
inspire the loyalty and respect of magicals who could
kill him with just a thought. This man was capable of
things I couldn't begin to imagine, and yet, his essential nature was gentle.

And treacherous.

"No, thank you," I said finally. Then I pulled on
Seamus's leash and left.

Chapter 7

Once the decision was made to stay, there was really nothing left to do but go to work. My first shift at Happy Larry's was that afternoon, and I kind of liked it. I made a doggie lean-to out of pallets for Seamus, and set it up for him out in the back alley with food and water, shoveled up after him at the end of my shift, and it worked out pretty well. I'd tucked a pocket mixology book in the back of my jeans just in case, but mostly it was just pulling drafts and pouring the occasional whiskey neat. By the time I went home at 2:45 in the morning, I felt too tired to think about my father very much, and that was fine by me.

By my second shift the following day, I felt like I'd been working there forever. The crowd was mainly guys with names like Red and Skinner, sporting inadvisable facial hair and wearing torn jeans and old, faded flannel shirts, and who would say things like, "Fuckin' A!" and, "Wanna go and make out in my truck?"

"No," I told Frankie Biggs, and slid his beer across the bar to him. It was quarter after five in the afternoon, and I'd been on my shift for little better than an hour, but already I was in no mood for this bullshit.

"Why not?" he said. "I got air-conditioning."

"Well, in that case," I said, *"no."*

He grinned at me, and I still couldn't see his teeth for his big, thick moustache. "C'mon, Eliot. I never made out with a chick with a dude's name before. It's kind of hot."

"I've made out with chicks with dude's names." That wasn't really true, although I had kissed a boy named Kelly once. "Trust me, it's overrated."

Frankie hesitated for a moment, his head angling to the side a bit, like a dog who knows something interesting just happened, but isn't sure what it was.

"Did I just break you?" I asked after a protracted silence.

"No." He cleared his throat, put his hands on the bar, and went for it again. You had to hand it to Frankie; he wasn't smart, but he had determination.

"It's slow in here," Frankie said. "Come on outside with me. Life's short."

"Yours is gonna be real short if you don't stop bugging me."

"Give me one good reason why not, and I'll leave you alone."

"I'll give you two. One, I'm married." I held out my fist for him to check out the pathetic wedding set Judd had insulted me with; the only thing it was ever good for was keeping guys like Frankie off my back. "And two, you've got a crazy girlfriend."

I nodded toward the worn-out pool table in the corner over which Amber Dorsey gyrated to "Sweet Home, Alabama" while lining up her shot. She'd been there at five on my last shift, too; it was possible Emerson was sending her out to keep an eye on me, but it was more likely that she was just a hard-core barfly. Even if Frankie Biggs tempted me—and let's be absolutely clear, he didn't—I had no intention of getting between him and the wildcat.

"Aw, she's not my girlfriend," Frankie said.

"Either way, she's your problem, and I'm not making her mine." And with that, I made myself busy cutting lemons. I glanced around the room, and my eyes caught on Desmond, who was sitting in his booth in the corner, reading. I couldn't tell what he was reading this time, but it wasn't the Sartre, which was reassuring.

"Hey." Skinny fingers with long, red nails snapped in my face and I stepped back a bit to see Amber shoving her empty martini glass at me. "I want another Cosmo."

"You got it." I slid the lemons—and more importantly, the knife—way out of her reach, then grabbed her glass and smiled at her, remembering advice my mother had given me when I was very young; *don't poke the crazy bear*. If ever there was a woman that advice applied to, it was Amber Dorsey. I let her be as rude as she wanted, never complained that she didn't tip, and pretended I didn't hear her when she called me a bitch under her breath, which happened on occasion, usually after Frankie tried to get somewhere with me. I was grateful she didn't know that what I was serving her wasn't, strictly speaking, a Cosmo; it was Hawaiian punch decanted into a pitcher and pretending to be cranberry juice, mixed with a shot of the world's cheapest vodka and a dash of lime.

Larry might be happy, but that's only because he's a cheap goddamn bastard.

She watched me, her eyes narrowing. "Are you *really* Mr. Streat's daughter?"

I didn't answer, just pulled out the vodka and poured.

"He's a nice man," she said. "I don't think you're related."

I slid the drink across the bar to her, and she handed me a ten, keeping her slitted eyes on me. "I want my change. *All* my change."

I punched it into the register, and gave her three dollars. She took the bills, her eyes still locked on me, and tucked them all in the pocket of her painted-on jeans. I whipped my bar rag off my shoulder, pretended there was a spill at the other end of the bar, and went to attend to it.

"You don't think she's pretty, do you?" I heard Amber say to Frankie.

I closed my eyes. *Say no, dumbass.*

"Who, Eliot?" he said, which was a good start, but then he followed it up with, "Yeah. She's hot. What do you have to say about it?"

Oh, Frankie, you idiot. I filled a mug with draft beer, put it hurriedly on a round tray, and scooted over to the corner to check on Desmond, who was the only other patron there at the moment.

"Here you go, Des." I set the beer down in front of him, next to the one he'd ordered when he came in. It was still full, but had gone warm and flat, with a puddle of condensation at the base.

Desmond looked up from his book, setting it down beside him before I could read the title on the cover.

"I didn't order another beer," he said.

"Yes, but I need to avoid *that*." I jerked my thumb over my shoulder at Amber and Frankie.

"Asshole!" she yelled, and then he shrieked, "Stop throwing peanuts at me! Jeez!"

"You know what? I think it's my break." I sat down across from him. "So, how's it going?"

Desmond watched me for a moment. "It's going well, thank you. And you?"

I shrugged and jerked my chin toward the domestic disturbance at the bar. "I'll be better once they knock it off, or enough other people come in that I don't feel like I'm starring in an episode of the *Real Rednecks of Chautauqua County*."

More shrieking came from the bar. I slumped down in the booth a bit to avoid getting hit by any flying debris should Amber pick up a bar stool and whack it over Frankie's head, an event I was giving two-to-one odds on.

"Whatcha reading?" I grabbed a peanut from the bowl on the table and shelled it.

Desmond picked up the book and handed it to me. It was a spy novel.

"Wow," I said. "Wasn't expecting that."

"Yes, well, being well-read is as much about variety as it is about challenge." He landed his sharp brown eyes on mine. "Besides, I didn't want you to think I was trying to impress you."

I felt a *zing* up my spine as our eyes locked, and I couldn't help it; I smiled.

"Why are you worried about what I think, Jethro?"

He didn't answer right away, but instead just watched me for a long moment, a hint of puzzlement on his face.

"You're interesting," he said finally.

I snorted. "Me? Interesting? How so?"

"Don't ask a question unless you actually want the answer."

"I asked," I said, meeting his eye. "Now answer."

He hesitated for a moment. "You're an exceedingly contradictory person. You're intelligent, obviously highly educated, but your speech is almost willfully common."

"Unlike *some* people, I don't like to show off."

"Or, you want people to underestimate you."

I freed a peanut from the shell and popped it in my mouth. "Maybe I'm just quirky."

"Perhaps," he said. "You say you hate your dog, and yet you won't drop him at a shelter and be done with it."

"He's not my dog," I said, "and just because I don't want some shelter killing him doesn't mean I like him."

"You could find him a home yourself," he offered.

"Oh, yeah?" I said. "You want him?"

He shook his head. "No. Thank you."

"See? Finding a home for a shedding behemoth that poops in your shoes isn't as easy as it looks."

The edge of his lips quirked into something that was almost a smile. "I think that is perhaps the first time I've ever heard a person use both *behemoth* and *poop* in a single sentence."

"You have to get out more." I leaned forward, resting my chin on my hands. "Now tell me more about myself. I'm fascinated."

His eyes narrowed in a manner that was almost playful. "You have attractive features, but you put willful effort into hiding it behind a haphazard ponytail and Goodwill chic."

"Goodwill chic, my ass," I said, feigning offense. "These jeans were $12.99 on clearance at Target. That's some quality merchandise, at a hell of a bargain. And, for your information, I rock the ponytail."

He smiled—actually for-real smiled—and I was

surprised to see he had one crooked eyetooth. I hadn't noticed that before. I probably hadn't seen it before. I wasn't convinced that anyone ever had.

"Yes," he said. "You do."

Again, our eyes locked, and this time the *zing* went all the way to my cheeks, which warmed immediately, and that's when my breath caught.

What the hell am I doing?

You're flirting, Ellie, Judd's voice said in my head, and he didn't sound happy, which shouldn't have mattered, because he cheated on me and he was dead, anyway, and . . .

I lost my train of thought. My entire brain suddenly went blank, and my panic must have shown on my face, because Desmond's smile faded and his expression went from amused to concerned.

"Eliot?" he said, leaning forward a bit. "Are you all right?"

I picked up my little round tray and said, "Break's over," and got up to head back to the bar, but as soon as I turned away I saw a flat hand with red fingernails coming at my face. The slap was hard enough to knock my head back, and I fell, cracking my head on the edge of the booth table on my way down, and the last thing I heard before I blacked out was, "Stay away from my man, *bitch!*"

I wasn't out for long, because everyone was still scuffling when I came to. Amber's legs were spiraling in the air as she struggled against the restraining hold

Frankie had her in from behind, and she was screaming something. I couldn't quite process what it was exactly, but I could tell it was directed at me, and it wasn't flattering. Desmond stood protectively between us, his back to me. I tried to push up on my elbows, but the room spun, and I closed my eyes and lay back down, listening to the hubbub around me.

"Amber!" Frankie said. "Calm the fuck down!"

"*She* better calm the fuck down!" Amber shouted, which of course didn't make any sense at all since I was presumably passed out at the time, but then again, Amber wasn't exactly the Rhodes scholar of Nodaway Falls.

"What the hell's going on out here?" Apparently, Larry finally decided to come out of his office.

"Amber assaulted Eliot." *Desmond.* Even if I didn't know his voice, he's the only person within twenty miles of Nodaway Falls who would use the word *assaulted* in casual speech. I felt the heat of someone's body kneeling down beside me. A moment later, a warm hand touched my face, and I knew it was him. Rather than look at him and face the embarrassment from my flirting—or from booting the burger I'd had for lunch all over his shoes which, at this point, was also a distinct possibility—I kept my eyes shut and pretended I was still out cold.

"I'll slap her again!" Amber shouted. "That slut was hitting on my man!"

"That is a creative distortion of the facts," Desmond said, and I could feel his arms slide under my shoulders

and legs. *Oh, God, he's carrying me.* I kept my eyes
shut, trying to avoid the complete humiliation of it all.
If I stayed out long enough, maybe they'd call an am-
bulance and admit me to the hospital, and they wouldn't
let Desmond in because he's not family, and then I
could run away when no one was looking. It wasn't a
great plan, but it was the best I had at the moment.

"There's a couch in my office," Larry said gruffly.
"Put her in there."

Desmond moved easily through the bar, hardly jos-
tling me at all as he did. Unfortunately, I was supposed
to be blacked out, so I couldn't protest about being carried to Larry's couch, which was an old orange thing
of questionable origin. This was getting worse and
worse. Why couldn't he have just left me on the floor?
I would have gotten up on my own eventually.

Frankie's and Amber's voices faded as I heard a
door shut, and the next thing I knew I was laid out on
Larry's couch. I lay there, trying not to move, or
breathe much, hoping Desmond would leave.

No such luck.

"You can open your eyes now."

Busted.

I opened one eye and looked at him. "You knew I
was conscious?"

He crossed his arms over his chest. "Yes."

I groaned and sat up, putting my face in my hands.
"It's okay. I'm fine. You can go now. Leave me here to
die of embarrassment, please."

"Why are you embarrassed?" he asked, and I heard

a note of anger in his voice. "You were attacked. That's not your fault."

I straightened. Right. *I was attacked.* Maybe I could ride that horse out of this barn.

"Amber Dorsey is eighty-five pounds dripping wet," I said, trying to sound as though I were upset about being slapped, instead of embarrassed by flirting with Desmond. "How would you feel if she knocked you out?"

He shrugged. "Actually, she only surprised you. It was the booth table that knocked you out. Speaking of which . . ."

With a concerned look, he moved to sit next to me on Larry's couch. I flinched as he reached toward my head, and he froze with his hands in the air.

"May I?" he asked, his eyes darting back and forth, looking into both of mine, and for a moment I thought he was asking to kiss me. My stomach lurched and I was so flummoxed by all of it, but especially by the tenderness in his voice, that I just swallowed and nodded.

He shifted my hair aside carefully, drew in a breath, and said, "You're not bleeding, but it's going to bruise a bit, I think." He lowered his hands and looked at me. "You weren't out long, but you were out. I think you should let me drive you to hospital."

"No," I said, resting my aching head against the back of the couch. "This is hardly my first bar fight. I'll be okay." I released a breath, trying to keep my mounting tension out of my voice, and succeeding only a little. Why did he have to sit so close to me, anyway? And why did I have to like it?

"I don't have health insurance," I said, not looking at him. "I can't afford an emergency room visit."

"That's not a problem. I'll pay for it."

I shifted away from him, putting some distance between us, although I couldn't put much, because my butt was already half on the arm of the couch. "What? That's crazy. It's not a steak. You can't just pay for it."

"It's not an inconvenience. I don't mind." He touched my shoulder, and I felt that stupid *zing* run through me, and it was too damn much. I hopped up off the couch like it was on fire. It was one thing to have Addie wiggle her eyebrows at me over Desmond; that was idle gossip, and it meant nothing. But I had flirted with him, and I'd liked it, and that was too much.

"I'm not . . . look, I know I told you a lot about me and maybe I gave the impression that I liked you, but . . ." I put my hand to my forehead and closed my eyes. "I'm not ready."

There was a long silence, so long that when I opened my eyes, I half expected Desmond to be gone. But he wasn't. He just sat there on Larry's ugly orange couch staring up at me, looking at me like I was crazy.

"If I've given you the impression that I have romantic intentions toward you . . ." he began, but I waved my hand at him, unable to stand it.

"You didn't. It's me. My husband died eight months ago, and I've just met my father again for the first time. I'm confused and emotionally unstable. I might talk a good game, but I can't back it up. Nothing can happen here."

"Of course," Desmond said kindly. "I'm so sorry if I made you feel—"

"You didn't do anything wrong. I flirted with you, and now I'm freaking out, and I kind of wish Amber had hit me hard enough to knock me out for a day or two."

"I sympathize." There was a long moment of awkward silence, and then Desmond stood up. "If you're quite well and don't need me, perhaps it would be best if I left. You might be more comfortable . . . perhaps?"

I nodded. He stood up, then turned to look at me.

"I hope you won't take this in any unintended way . . ." he began, and I waved a dismissive hand at him.

"I flirted with you," I said. "I know, it's all me."

He paused, seeming to choose his words very carefully. "I'm glad you decided to stay."

With that, he left. As soon as the door shut, I leaned forward and put my head in my hands.

"You always did have rotten taste in men. You know that, Ellie?"

I looked up and there he was, ghostly arms and legs spread out over Larry's couch, taking up all the space in the room the way he always did.

"Oh, great," I said. "It's you."

Judd's eyes twinkled as he looked at me. "I was worried about you. You took quite a hit to the ol' noggin out there."

"Don't give me a hard time about Desmond," I said. "I'm not in the mood."

"I wasn't gonna give you a hard time," Judd said. "What makes you think I was gonna give you a hard time?"

I gave him my best dead-eyed stare. Judd gave up the pretense and leaned forward.

"I don't like that guy, Ellie. I get a bad feeling. You shouldn't be making friends with him."

"Gee," I said. "You want me away from the handsome British guy. What a surprise."

Judd got up and moved toward me, his ghostly form crowding me on the desk. "Look, you want to move on, move on. You have my blessing. Just don't do it with him."

"I'm not doing it with *anyone*," I said. "Didn't you hear me? I'm crazy. You made me crazy. You broke me and you left me here, all broken, and now I'm not getting involved with anyone else because between you and my father, I may never trust a man again. So congratulations, Judd. You got what you wanted, and I got the mess you left behind."

Judd stared down at me, his eyes soft, the way he used to back when I thought he hung the moon. "You're still my girl, Ellie."

I was about to argue with him, tell him that I wasn't his *anything* anymore, but then the door opened and Judd disappeared into a single point of light, like an old TV snapping off. I straightened my posture, my heart speeding up, and it wasn't until Larry closed the door behind him that I realized, one, that I'd been expecting Desmond, and two, that I was disappointed when it wasn't him.

Oh, that's not good.

Larry trudged over to the desk. "You okay?"

I nodded. My head hurt a bit as I did, but it wasn't too bad. "Yeah." Something about Larry's presence, cranky and mundane, was comforting. I motioned toward the bar. "Everything okay out there?"

"Frankie and Amber left, so, yeah. You need to go to the hospital or something?"

"No," I said. "I'm okay."

Larry eyed me suspiciously. "You're not gonna go after Amber now, are you? Because I can't have that personal vendetta shit going on at my bar."

"No," I said, and hopped off his desk. "I think I can let it go."

He grunted approval. "You gonna sue me?"

I smiled. "Not unless you grab my ass, Larry."

He nodded, and his shoulders seemed to relax a bit. "Can you finish your shift, or do you need me to cover for you?"

I clasped my hands over my heart. "Aw, Larry. You would do that for me?"

His eyes narrowed and he tried to look gruff, but I had seen it, and he couldn't make me unsee it; Larry cared about me. Or at least he cared about the possibility that I could sue him, since I was attacked on his property. Either way, I was kinda touched.

"It's okay," I said. "It's only five-thirty. I don't want to leave you stranded for the night."

"Good," he said, walking over behind his desk. "There are thirsty people at the bar, and I've got work to do. Shut the door on your way out."

I smiled, even though he wasn't looking at me, and put my hand on the doorknob . . . except, I didn't. I didn't actually touch it, but I could feel it, the workings of the metal as the inner shaft twirled and the door opened, as if on its own power.

Except it wasn't on its own power. When I looked down, I could see disappearing trails of electric blue light as my hand clasped around the doorknob, just a second after it opened for me.

I hadn't even been trying.

I turned around and looked at Larry in a panic. He was less than ten feet away. There were no tendrils of blue light, nothing dancing around the room, but still.

"You feeling okay, Larry?" I asked. "Any . . . um . . . tingling in your hands or anything?"

Larry looked up from his computer. "What the hell are you talking about?"

"Nothing." I looked at my watch; it was barely six o'clock, and the sun wouldn't be down for another three hours. I could go home, but I needed the tips.

"Bar's on the other side of the door," Larry grumbled, and I went out and finished my shift.

Chapter 8

Three days later, there was a knock on my door.

At first, I was annoyed. It had been my first day off since starting at Happy Larry's, and my intention was to spend it in solitude. Bartending was keeping me in lights and kibble, but being surrounded by people every day was making my essential misanthropy worse. Although Amber Dorsey had had the good sense to stay away after the attack, between Frankie Biggs and the rest of the idiots who hung out at Happy Larry's, I was beginning to think that Sartre was onto something with his whole "hell is other people" shtick. So when the knock came, I was inclined to ignore it, except that the windows were open, and whoever it was could probably hear my laptop playing the DVD I'd gotten at the library.

I hit the pause button and looked down at Seamus,

who sat next to me on the couch, not moving as usual. I pushed his shoulder off my hip and went over to the front door, hoping I had the energy to politely turn away whoever was fool enough to knock on it.

The man just stood there, unstable on his feet, his eyes glassy and unfocused. He had a full dark beard shot with a few touches of silver, which seemed premature, since he looked to be mid-thirties at the most. His clothes were new; as a matter of fact, the size sticker on his cheap jeans was still stuck to his thigh; he wore a 34 x 32. His shoulders were broad, but slumped, and he squinted as though he'd just stepped into the sun from a dark place.

"Who are you?" I said, but the second I said it, I knew. My heart started pounding in my chest, and I stepped out onto the porch to look around, to see if there was a trace of whoever had dumped him on my porch.

"Oh, Jesus," I said, and put my arm around Tobias's waist as I led him into my house. "It's okay. Everything's okay. Can I get you some water?"

I led him to the couch, sitting him where I had been a few moments before. Seamus moved out of the way just in time, and then sniffed at Tobias's leg as I sat on the coffee table in front of him.

"Tobias? I need you to look at me, okay?"

I pulled my phone out of my pocket, hit the flashlight button that turned on the flash by the camera lens, and pointed it at his eyes. He shrank away from

me, but I put my hand gently on his face to keep him
from turning away.

"I just need to see," I said, but he couldn't stand the
brightness enough to keep from squinting his eyes. I
turned off the flash and hit Desmond's number, trying
not to think about what it meant that Tobias had been
so unceremoniously deposited on my doorstep.

"Eliot?" Desmond's voice came crisply through the
phone. Wherever he was, it was too quiet to be Happy
Larry's.

"Desmond, I need you to come over, right now.
Bring your magical emergency kit."

"What's happened?"

I hung up on him and dialed Stacy Easter's number, grateful that Addie had come into Happy Larry's
during the week and programmed the essential Nodaway Falls magical phone book into my phone. While
it rang, Seamus put his head on Tobias's lap and set it
there, and Tobias just stared at me. Well, less *at* me
than at a spot somewhere over and past my left shoulder. I reached out and touched his hand. "It's going to
be okay."

"Hello?" A man's voice answered Stacy's phone;
I assumed it was the much-talked-about boyfriend,
Leo.

"Is Stacy there?"

"She's out back. Who's this?"

"I'm Eliot. I'm new in town."

"Eliot? I've heard about you." There was a pause,

indicating that what he'd heard probably hadn't been great.

"Leo, I need you to get Stacy, and the two of you need to bring Liv to my house, right now, okay? Don't let her come alone."

There was a moment of taut silence, and Leo said, "Is everything okay?"

I hope so, I thought, but all I said was, *"Now,"* and hung up, and then, because there was nothing left for me to do, I waited, with my thoughts circling around me like debris in a cyclone. Tobias had been returned, which was good news, but I didn't know what it meant. My father had gotten Tobias freed from wherever he was, which was what I'd asked him to do. He'd kept his word, so there was that. It had happened pretty quickly, though, which confirmed my suspicions that Emerson had had something to do with Tobias's disappearance in the first place, and judging by Tobias's appearance, wherever he'd been hadn't been the Ritz. If Tobias had simply been pulled out of Nodaway Falls by ASF and been assigned somewhere else, I doubted they'd just send him back immediately; it would be weeks to extract him from his assignment and replace him, not days. Then again, in the magical world, when Emerson Streat made a phone call . . .

"Oh, god." I put my hand to my forehead, as if that would stop my thoughts from spinning out of control. The fact was, there were no sure conclusions to draw from any of it, not until Tobias could tell us where he'd been and what had happened. I took Tobias's hand in mine.

"It's going to be okay," I said, although I wasn't sure who I was trying to convince, him or me. Didn't much matter; either way, I was being disingenuously optimistic, and he didn't seem to be listening, anyway.

There was a quick knock at the door, but before I could get up to answer it, Desmond was already inside.

"Eliot?" he said, his voice taut. He rushed over to me, and froze once he came around the couch and saw who was sitting there. The stark worry on his face subsided, and with work to be done, he was all business. He snapped a finger in front of Seamus's nose, and Seamus jumped down off the couch. Desmond sat where Seamus had been and put his hand on Tobias's shoulder. "What happened?"

"He just knocked on the door, and he was like this."

Desmond set his briefcase down next to Tobias and flicked it open. "When?"

"I called you the second I got him to the couch. He's disoriented, sensitive to light, I was worried that maybe he'd been given . . ." I stopped. This was no time to be coy. "There's a memory potion the agencies used to use a lot. I can't remember everything that's in it, but I think it had something called . . ." I closed my eyes and tried to remember. "I want to say beets . . . stock? Something like that?"

"*Bayatsah tsvyetok?*" he said quickly, and looked at me for my response.

I shrugged, frustrated. "Gesundheit. I don't know what you just said."

"Bayatsah tsvyetok," he said again, a little slower. "It's Russian. Is that what he used?"

"Yeah . . . maybe. I don't know. It was a long time ago. What is it? Is it yellow, ugly, kinda weedy-looking?"

Desmond sighed. "Yes. So are about twelve other things. I can't counteract anything if I don't know for certain what he's been given. You suspect your father had something to do with this?"

Guilt stabbed through me, even though I knew none of this was my doing or my fault. "He wanted to know what he could do to prove himself to me. I told him to send Tobias back to Liv. It was all I could think of."

Desmond watched me for a moment, and I could see gears churning madly behind his eyes, but I had no idea what they were coming up with. Before I could ask, there was another knock on the door. Desmond stood up, on alert, and I put my hand on his shoulder.

"I called Stacy and told her to bring Liv," I said.

He looked at Tobias, and then at me. "Bugger."

"I *had* to call her."

He nodded, his expression contrite. "Of course you did," he said, and nodded toward the door.

I walked over and turned the knob. Liv's hair was wet; she must have been in the shower when Stacy came to get her. Behind Liv, Stacy stood with her arms crossed over her stomach, and a tall man with messy brown hair, a crooked nose, and wide, kind eyes stood with his arm around Stacy's waist. I took him to be Leo.

"Hi," I said.

"Are you okay?" Liv reached out and touched my arm. "Stacy said you needed to see me?"

I stepped back to let her in. She moved inside, looking confused. She said, "Hello, Desmond," with a question in her voice, and then she froze. A sound caught in her throat and she looked at me, and I said, "He just showed up on my doorstep." Liv's eyes filled with tears and I added, "He's a little disoriented," which was the understatement of the year, but when she moved closer and said, "Tobias?" he turned his head toward her, just a little. I looked at Stacy and Leo, both of them staring at me, a thousand questions in their eyes, but all I could say was, "I don't know."

Seamus had relocated to the love seat in the corner, and I shoved him over and sat down next to him, trying to disappear into the scenery as Liv sat down next to Tobias. I felt voyeuristic, but I couldn't look away, either. She didn't touch him immediately, just stared at him wide-eyed, tears absently dropping from her lashes. She looked as if she was afraid that it was all an illusion, and that if she touched him, he'd disappear.

"Tobias?" she said again, her voice cracking in a million places, and he turned to look at her. His eyes seemed unable to focus, but he was trying.

She was bringing him back.

She reached out and touched his face, laughing a sad laugh through her tears. "You have a beard."

She sniffed, and ran her hand through his hair. "I've never seen you with a beard."

His eyes squinted a bit as he looked at her, the way they'd squinted in the sun earlier.

"Liv?" he said, his voice barely more than a whisper.

Liv nodded and burst into violent, shaking tears. Tobias reached out for her as best he could and she fell into his arms. Desmond, who had been standing quietly by the wall, stepped forward.

"Liv, I think maybe Tobias should lie down."

Desmond glanced at me for permission. I nodded, and he led both Tobias and Liv down the hallway to my room. I grabbed Seamus's collar and walked him over to where Stacy and Leo were standing. Stacy's eyes were red-rimmed; Leo's were dry but harried-looking, and his grip around Stacy's waist was visibly tight.

"Um," I said in low tones, uncomfortable with speaking at full volume. "You're a conjurer, too, right?"

Stacy said, "Yes," and at the same time Leo said, warily, "In training."

I got right down to it. "Between you and Desmond, you should be able to help him. I don't know what he was given, but he probably shouldn't go anywhere today, and he definitely shouldn't go to a hospital. We're not sure what he's got in his system, and hospitals can make this sort of thing worse. He needs rest. He and Liv can have my bed. You guys can have the couch and love seat, if you want. I'll sleep . . ." I motioned vaguely in the direction of my truck parked outside. "Somewhere."

I started toward the door, but Stacy's hand came down in a firm clamp on my arm.

"Wait a minute," she said. "You're not going anywhere, Eliot."

"Stace," Leo said, but she didn't take her eyes off me.

"You come to town, tell us you're the magical daughter of an evil agency dude, and suddenly Tobias shows up on your doorstep? Is that all supposed to be coincidence?"

I pulled my arm out of her grip and stepped a little closer to her, letting her know that she wasn't going to intimidate me.

"You think *I* did this?"

"I think you know something about it, yeah," Stacy said. "And if you think I'm letting you out of my sight, you've got another think coming."

A strong, British voice came from the hallway. "Leave her alone, Stacy."

Stacy looked over at Desmond, but I kept my eyes on her. After being clocked by Amber Dorsey the other day, no way was I turning my back on another unpredictable chick from Nodaway Falls.

"Oh, so, what? I'm supposed to trust *you* now, Des?"

Leo visibly tensed as Desmond walked over to us, the muscles in his arm going taut as he pressed his hand protectively against Stacy's hip. It looked like it was all he could do to not hit Desmond, and when

Desmond moved closer, Leo twitched for a moment, as if holding back a swing.

"I'm pretty sure it's *bayatsah tsvyetok*," Desmond told them coolly, seemingly undisturbed by their palpable hatred of him. "Some of his memory will just be gone, there's nothing we can do about that. He'll be sensitive to light for a while. But if we can get the counterpotion fast enough, he shouldn't lose much more than a few months. Maybe a year."

The color drained from Stacy's face. "A year? Of his *memory*?"

"A few months, if we act quickly," Desmond said. "And you can thank Eliot. She suggested it, and I have reason to believe she's right."

Stacy glanced at me, looking like she had absolutely no intention of thanking me for anything.

Desmond went on. "Would you like the recipe, or shall I make the counterpotion?"

Stacy's eyes narrowed, and she said, "Give me the recipe."

"You make it," Leo said over her, and he met Desmond's eyes. He didn't like Desmond, that much was obvious, but he seemed to respect him.

"Leo," Stacy said, and Leo looked down at her, his expression instantly softening.

"You told me emotions mess with the process," he said, "and you're full up on emotion right now. Desmond . . ." He looked up at Desmond, obviously not liking what he saw. "Desmond doesn't have that problem, do you, Des?"

The icy expression Stacy held when Desmond had been talking warmed instantly as she looked at Leo. "Look, they *say* emotions mess with the process, but—"

"They say it because it's true," Desmond said, his voice calm and direct. "Now we can argue or we can help Tobias, but we don't have time for both. I agree with Leo, it should be me, but if you don't trust what I'll bring back to you, then you do it. Either way, someone needs to take action. Now."

"Go," Leo said, and before Stacy could argue, Desmond had his hand on the small of my back, leading me and Seamus out the door.

"You'll come with me," he said, not asking. He opened the back door of his silver sedan and snapped his fingers in front of Seamus's face. Seamus instantly hopped inside.

"How the hell do you do that?" I asked, staring in amazement as Desmond got in the driver's side, but he didn't answer, so I got in and rode with him in silence to his place.

Desmond lived a little farther outside of town than I did, still within walking distance of the village, but it was far enough to be full-on rural. The roads out this way were as much dirt as pavement, and the only neighbor I could see was a red farmhouse so far in the distance that I couldn't even tell if anyone actually lived there. We turned onto his driveway, which was newly paved and led through a copse of trees to a small clearing where his house, a small, contemporary structure, sat.

"You know, living out here probably doesn't do much to combat the impression that you're a bad guy," I said as I got out of the car. "I can think of a few Bond villains who might go for this place."

Desmond was halfway into the house by the time I shut the passenger-side door; I was pretty sure he hadn't even heard me. Which was just as well. I opened the back door for Seamus and he ambled out, then followed me down the step-stone path that led to the front door, which Desmond had left wide open.

The house was fairly new, and extremely well kept. It was a simple, open layout, with wood walls and exposed beams and huge windows that showed off the heavily treed property. I shut the door behind Seamus and took off my shoes; this was the kind of pristinely kept space that made you super conscious of any dirt you might track in. I padded past the kitchen area—stainless steel appliances, quartz countertops, everything in gleaming neutral tones—to the living room, where a cream-colored rug covered the walnut-colored floor between a living room set of an overstuffed, latte-colored couch and matching love seat that stared each other down over a simple, dark wood coffee table. It looked like no one had ever actually sat on the couch, which I could believe. The riverstone fireplace had three fresh logs sitting in it, and it didn't look as though a fire had ever been lit in it. Next to the fireplace was an open wood-slatted staircase that led up to what appeared to be a loft bedroom. Apparently, Desmond's magical lab was downstairs, because I could hear occasional sounds coming from the open door at the other side of the kitchen, but I didn't go over there. Desmond had important work to do, and I wasn't going to distract him. Seamus sniffed around for a while and then jumped up onto the love seat, ignoring me when I said, "Seamus, no!" but then, I thought, *What the hell?* It was a nice love seat. Someone should sit in it.

I couldn't sit. I felt nervous, twitchy, worried. Desmond's house felt like a safe haven, but I knew I wouldn't be there for long, that eventually I'd have to face the reality that was waiting for me. I snooped through his refrigerator and pantry, finding nothing but healthy snacks and a single container of yogurt past the expiration date. No wonder he was so thin. I wandered around the living room a bit, and saw a hardcover book sitting on the bottom shelf of an end table. I sat down on the couch and pulled it out. It was an old hardcover book, and I smiled as I read the title: *Witness to My Life: The Letters of Jean-Paul Sartre to Simone de Beauvoir, 1926–1939*. Tucked inside the cover was a library receipt from the Henrietta Comstock Community Library, dated the day after we'd first met at Happy Larry's.

I sat with the book in my hands for a while, staring down at it. It was the same version I'd read years earlier. Possibly, it was the only printing they'd ever done of it. It felt odd and intimate, holding that book.

I wondered what he thought of it, and how he'd feel if he knew I'd seen it, an obvious indicator that he'd been thinking about me in the time since we first spoke. In the end, I decided to put it back exactly where I'd found it and went upstairs to check out his loft bedroom.

Hey, if he didn't want people to snoop, he should have gotten a television.

The bedroom, at least, looked like it had been used. The sleek platform bed was covered by a fluffy white duvet and sat under a slanted roof, more window than anything else, and while the bed was neatly made, the pillows at least had dents in them. There was an en suite bathroom that was cleaner than my kitchen, with the exception of a tiny clump of blue toothpaste in the sink basin, which I was inexplicably gratified to see. Proof the man was human, I guess.

I walked back out into the bedroom and stood there for a while, staring at the bed. It looked so soft, and it had been a hell of a day. A gentle rain had started up, pattering on the windows over the bed, and I took that as a sign that the gods obviously wanted me to rest, so I flipped back the duvet to reveal sleek silver-blue sheets and crawled inside. The bed smelled like Desmond, a combination of Ivory soap and man, and as my body sank into the mattress, I had only time to moan, "Ohhhhh, Tempurpedic," before falling into a soft comfort coma.

Chapter 9

It was dark when I woke up, and it took me a moment to remember where I was. When I did, I shot up, horrified to realize that I had drooled a bit on my hand . . . and on Desmond's pillow. *Oh, god.* I hopped out of the bed and quickly flipped the pillow over and pulled the covers back up before I padded down the steps. When I got to the living room, I saw that Seamus was still sleeping on the love seat but the door that led to the secret lab downstairs was closed. I was trying to decide if Desmond had known I'd fallen asleep in his bed when the front door opened and he stepped in, mildly damp from the rain outside.

"I didn't fall asleep in your bed and drool on your pillow," I said as he shut the door behind him. He was carrying what looked like a bag of takeout in one hand, and my small purple suitcase in the other.

"What a suspiciously specific denial," he said. "I hope you rested well."

"I did. Thanks."

He set my suitcase on the floor by the door. "I took the liberty of fetching some of your things while I was at your house. By the way, Liv wanted me to extend her thanks to you for giving them your house for the night. We should be able to move Tobias home tomorrow, but it's a good idea to jostle him as little as possible tonight."

"Aw, it's nothing," I said, waving a dismissive hand in the air.

Desmond was quiet for a moment. "I hope you weren't alarmed when you woke up alone in the house. I didn't want to wake you when I had to leave."

"You mean you tried, but I was snoring so loud I didn't hear you?"

He smiled. "You are uncommonly self-aware."

"Yeah, I get that a lot." I sat on one of the bar stools at the kitchen island. Despite being sleek and industrial-looking, the stool was fairly comfortable. "You got grub?"

Desmond put the bag of takeout on the island. "Yes. Burgers and fries. I hope that's all right with you."

"Are you kidding? If they're bacon burgers, I might have your children." I reached in and pulled out the Styrofoam containers while Desmond sat down next to me. I opened mine, lifted up the bun, and said, "You know I was just kidding, right?"

"I think we should name the first girl Eloise," he said casually.

I felt a small flush in my cheeks, and my mind raced against the clock, trying to think of a wiseass answer before things got weird. I'm not good under pressure, though, so all I said was, "I like Sam for a boy."

Desmond considered it. "Sam's a good name."

We tucked into the food for a while. I was quiet until I got my equilibrium back, and then I said, "So, why all the guilt and brooding? And don't try to deny it. You're one long black trench coat away from being freakin' Rochester on the moors. What's up with that?"

Desmond stopped chewing and stared at me for a moment, then swallowed before speaking.

"I apologize," he said. "For reasons that surpass understanding, your bluntness continues to surprise me."

"I know some of it," I said. "You were researching potions to give powers to nonmagical people. Stacy said you almost killed her and a couple of other people, and you dosed Leo with a potion that made him forget he loved Stacy. That it?"

Desmond lowered his head. "Hardly."

I popped a fry in my mouth and chewed while I thought. "Look, it sounds bad. I'll give you that. But you obviously feel bad about it, and from what I can tell, no one died. All's well that ends well, right? If they hate you, they hate you. You've gotta get over it."

Desmond was quiet for a while, and when he finally

spoke, he kept his eyes low, deliberately not meeting mine.

"I wanted a nonmagical subject who had gained powers to work with me as proof of my success," he said, his voice matter-of-fact. "I was ruthless in my attempts to obtain that subject."

I took another bite of my burger. "Ruthless . . . how?"

He had stopped eating, apparently having lost his appetite. "I withheld the potions that could mediate the effects. I withheld the potion that could reverse them. I risked the lives of many people here."

"Okay," I said, not sure what else to say. I'd gathered that much from the clues I'd been given.

He looked straight ahead, staring into the middle distance, not meeting my eye. "By way of explanation . . . not excuse, simply explanation . . . I had been self-administering a potion that dampened my own emotions, my sense of right and wrong, and my empathy, and I was . . . ." He swiped crumbs off the table, his long fingers delicate and steady. "I'm not a good man, Eliot."

"So I hear." I processed all this for a moment, and was surprised by how little his confession truly bothered me. "I don't know. You've been pretty good to me."

He finally looked at me, with anger in his expression. "You're a fool if you think you know me."

"You're a fool if you think anybody knows anybody, and—"

"People have *died* because of me." He said it quietly, but with a force behind the words that made me pause before pushing it further. But of course, eventually I did push it, because I'm me.

"Who?" I asked. "Someone from this town?"

He didn't answer. It was almost as if he hadn't heard me ask the question. If his jaw muscles weren't working so furiously in his cheek, I would think he hadn't.

"I had a fiancée, once. Alysia. She took her own life, because of the experiments I did. I couldn't have been more responsible if I'd killed her myself."

"And that's when you started self-administering the no-emotion potion?" I asked, taking a bite of my burger.

"Are you making light of this?" His eyes were fiery as they landed on me.

I swallowed my bite before speaking. "I'm sorry. No."

He relaxed a bit. "Alysia wasn't the last to come to harm because of my ambitions. I came here, and the experiment saw some success, but at a cost. I put people in grave danger, all in pursuit of my ambition, and I . . ." His eyes went dark with self-loathing. "I assaulted her."

"Who?"

"Stacy."

I put my burger down. I couldn't picture it. I couldn't see Desmond hitting anyone, least of all a girl, and I certainly couldn't see anyone raising a hand to Stacy Easter and living to tell the tale.

"On two occasions," Desmond continued off my silence. "I meant to kill her the second time, and the only reason I didn't was because she managed to stop me."

He didn't look at me as he spoke, and he held perfectly still as though waiting for me to . . . I don't know. Step back in horror. Run away, I guess.

I didn't move.

"Okay," I said.

He turned on me, his eyes lit with surprise and a hint of anger. "*Okay?* You think it's okay that I hit a woman?"

"No," I said. "Obviously, it's not *okay*—"

"I took my fist and bashed her in the face, splitting her lip in the process. On yet another occasion, I smashed her into a wall, and she fell to the floor in a slump, unconscious. I wanted to kill her. I intended to kill her. I imagined doing it, with my bare hands, and I took joy in the thought of it." He looked sick as he spoke, every muscle in his body visibly taut, and I could see within him the violence he was describing. I waited to speak until his breathing evened out again.

"You're not that guy anymore."

"You can't excuse that sort of behavior," he said, looking down at his hands as though they were traitors. "It's unforgivable."

"Bullshit."

His head popped up in shock, and his eyes narrowed as he looked at me as though I were insane. "What?"

"I call bullshit." I got up and started clearing away the food, partially because I could tell the discussion of his past was turning Desmond's stomach, but mostly because it gave me something to do. "You were under the influence. People do terrible things when they're on drugs, and whether it was magic or not, you were on a drug. You're not now. You're different now. You're not that guy. I'd venture to say you never *were* that guy. Something took over your body for a while, but it's gone now. Or it would be, if you would let it go."

I could see the mental process on his face as he first considered and then rejected my premise. "A person either is or is not capable of things," he said, his words clipped.

"Not true." I pulled two bottled waters out of the fridge and tossed him one, standing across the breakfast bar from him. "Everyone is capable of everything."

He remained silent, sulkily staring at the water bottle in his hand, unwilling to give me an inch.

"Tell me this," I said. "Since you stopped 'self-administering,' or whatever, have you hit any women? Done anything to hurt anybody?"

Something between a smile and a grimace graced his lips. "I fail to see how that's relevant."

"So, that's a no," I said. "And before . . . were you all soul-shriveled and evil before the potion? Did you do anything deliberately, knowing it would hurt someone?"

Desmond said nothing.

"Another no," I said. "You did bad things under the influence of a powerful potion you shouldn't have been messing with in the first place. I'll admit, you were stupid as all get out, but I don't think that makes you evil."

"It makes me weak," he said, his voice thick with self-disgust. "That can be worse."

"Whatever. Look, I may not know much about this town, but I know bad people, and they don't feel bad about it. They don't worry that they're evil, and they don't hang out in a town where everyone hates them trying to make things right. Either way, now you're off the sauce and on the leash and everything's okay. It's time to take off the damn hair shirt."

There was a long silence. I could tell that nothing I'd said made him feel any better about himself, but to be honest, nothing he'd said made me feel any worse about him. My father had been at least indirectly responsible for the deaths of twenty-eight innocent people in Lott's Cove, and I loved him fiercely despite all that. Judd was little more than a thief who entertained you while he fleeced you clean, and he had been my world. I knew that goodness wasn't an absolute in anyone's soul, no matter how much they played the angel, and I also knew that devils could be the most honorable people in the world if the circumstances were right. Black and white were concepts, not realities, and there was nothing in Desmond's confession that had convinced me otherwise.

"Have you ever heard of wild magic?" Desmond asked after a long silence.

"Wild *hmm*?" I said.

He angled his body toward me, watching my face. "Wild magic. It's magic that you can run through another person, without the aid of potions. It's rare. There are no well-documented cases of it, but there have been a lot of stories about it over the years. It's typically linked to people with elemental magic. Earth elementals, actually."

I stared at him for a minute, understanding descending upon me. "Wait. You think *I* have wild magic?"

He shrugged. "You say your magic ran through you to the others in Lott's Cove, correct?"

"But . . ." I shook my head. "But you said wild magic would be my magic, running through someone else. Their magic was different from mine. It was—"

"I would guess that your father did something to amplify your magic, use it to jump-start what latent abilities the others had." He watched me carefully, not taking his eyes off my face. "It also would explain why you survived, and your mother didn't. Have you ever had an incident where you touched someone, ran your magic through them?"

I shook my head. "I don't . . . think so. I mean, I think I would remember something like that."

He nodded and spoke the next bit very carefully. "You know, there is a way to find out."

I stared at him for a moment, then picked up the

remains of our fast food and started to clear it, mostly for an excuse to move away from him.

"No. Absolutely not."

Desmond dashed around the counter, opening up the cabinet under the sink to expose the garbage can. "It's just a theory. You might not even have wild magic."

I stuffed the garbage in the can and turned to look at him. "And what if I do? What if it was wild magic, my wild magic, that killed those people?" My heart started pounding and I was beginning to regret eating that burger.

"Try not to panic," Desmond said, moving closer. "When nonmagicals use magic, it exhausts the chemicals in their brain. I have spent years studying exactly this; trust me, I know how it all works. I have potions that can allay and even reverse the effects."

I crossed my arms over my stomach and backed away from him. The sun was down, but still. He was freaking me out.

"Yeah, and what do you know about the effects of this . . . wild magic? *Nothing.* You said yourself, all your information is anecdotal. What if I manage somehow to do this, to . . . whatever, run my magic through you, and your potions don't work?"

He shrugged, as though it was no big deal. "Then we have more information."

"Then you *die.*" I walked away from him, and stopped short as my eyes caught on Seamus, asleep on the couch. "Oh, hell. I can't accidentally . . . ?"

Desmond shook his head. "Magic doesn't transfer to animals."

I barely had time to sigh in relief before he started in again.

"But you could transfer it to me. We could get answers—"

"You could get dead."

"It's a minimal risk, and one I'm willing to take."

"Yeah, well, I'm not." I walked across the room, putting the kitchen island between us. "Is it so important to you to make it up to these people—these people who hate you, by the way—that your first thought is to risk your own life?"

"Can you think of anyone else we can test it on?"

"No, that's the point," I said, feeling breathless and panicked. "Look, I know you're used to using human trials in your research and everything, but that's a *bad thing*. Normal people don't do that."

He shut down almost immediately. His face, which had been animated in his enthusiasm while trying to convince me, turned to stone. He straightened and nodded.

"Yes," he said. "I know."

"Oh, man," I whined, feeling terrible. "I'm sorry. I didn't mean—"

"You did mean it," he said, "and you should." He raised his eyes to look at mine. "I don't think this will kill me, but if it does, what has the world lost, really?"

"Desmond, stop," I said. "Don't go all broody on

me. I know they love it in the romance novels, but it gets old. Trust me. You can't live your life feeling guilty all the time. It'll kill you."

"It's not guilt," he said quietly.

"What?"

"It's not guilt," he said, louder. "It's shame."

"What's the difference?"

He spoke carefully, enunciating each syllable. "Guilt is when you feel bad about what you've done." He met my eyes; his own were cold. "Shame is when you feel bad about what you are."

"Yeah, and what are you, Desmond? Are you some kind of monster? Is that what you really think?"

He didn't answer. Instead, he stepped past me, heading toward the door that led to the downstairs lab. "There are fresh towels in the bathroom, if you wish to take a shower. I asked Liv to pack some things for you, so please don't fret that I've pawed through your delicates."

"I don't care about that," I said.

He didn't turn to face me, just angled his head over his shoulder as he rested one hand on the doorway. "I do."

"All right," I said, my voice feeling hoarse. "Thank you."

"Of course." He stood where he was, in the doorway, not leaving, but not looking at me, either. "If you'd like Seamus to sleep in the bed with you, I have no objection."

"I can take the couch," I said. "You don't have to give up your bed."

Desmond cleared his throat. "It's okay. I won't be sleeping much tonight. Tobias will need more of that potion to get him through the next few days."

"I'm sorry," I said. "I didn't mean to make you feel bad."

Desmond finally met my eye again, and his expression softened a bit. "You didn't. Good night, Eliot."

"Good night, Desmond."

He disappeared downstairs, and I watched the empty space where he'd been standing for a while before picking up my purple suitcase, walking over to Seamus, and dragging him upstairs to the loft.

When consciousness began to dawn the next morning and I realized I was lying in bed next to a warm body, I snuggled closer, my hazy brain thinking for some reason that it was Desmond. But then Seamus huffed at me and licked my arm, and I said, "Eww! Gross!" and wiped it on his fur.

"Ugh." I rolled over and got out of bed. I washed my hands and finger-brushed my teeth in Desmond's bathroom, got changed into fresh clothes from my suitcase, and when Seamus and I finally toddled down the steps from the loft, Desmond was fixing coffee in the kitchen.

"I'd offer to wash your bedding, but I don't have any laundry at my house, and it's kind of an awkward thing to do anyway, so let's just pretend a big dog didn't spend the night drooling all over everything." I picked up the cup of coffee Desmond set in front of me and took a sip. "Mmmmmm."

"That's quite all right," Desmond said. "We can also pretend that all the drooling came from the dog if you'd like."

"Oh, I'd like that very much."

"Yes," he said dryly. "I thought you would."

Desmond grabbed a bowl from the cabinet and put it on the floor, then filled it from a red bag of Iam's dog food I'd gotten a few days earlier. He must have brought it over from my house the night before.

"I don't get it," I said as Desmond walked over to where Seamus was staring out the window. "He doesn't respond to anything, even the sound of the kibble hitting the bowl. I mean, what kind of weird-ass dog doesn't come running for food?"

"A deaf one," Desmond said simply. He put one hand lightly on Seamus's shoulder and Seamus looked up, seeming surprised by Desmond's sudden appearance. Desmond held his hand in Seamus's line of sight and pointed to the bowl of kibble. Seamus ran right to it while I watched.

"Oh my god," I said, stunned.

"You didn't know he was deaf?" Desmond asked.

"No." My mind whirled, putting the pieces together. "All those times he'd ignored me, I thought he just hated me. He loves Addie, though. I couldn't figure it out."

"Addie talks with her hands," Desmond said simply, imitating the kinds of movements Addie makes with her hands when she talks. "She's physically demonstrative. She hugs, she moves."

"I never touch him," I said as I watched Seamus wolf down the kibble. "I only yell at him and tell him he's a jerk."

"Well, if it's any comfort, he can't hear you. He's pretty old for a dog. I'd guess he's at least eleven, maybe thirteen. What did your vet say?"

"I haven't taken him to the vet." I gasped in sudden panic. "Am I supposed to take him to the vet? Nothing's wrong with him, right? I mean . . . aside from the deaf thing, he seems okay. He's okay, right? I've never owned a dog before."

Desmond smiled. "It's all right."

"No it's not!" I put my hand to my forehead. "I'm such an idiot. It's not his fault his owner was a two-bit whore who slept with my husband, but I've been punishing him for it this whole time. Oh my god, I'm a monster."

Desmond walked over to me, put his hands on my shoulders and turned me to look at him. I focused on his deep brown eyes, and my breathing stabilized.

"You'll take him to the vet," he said. "It's okay. He's fine."

I looked past Desmond to see Seamus finishing the last of his kibble. I walked over to him and sat on the floor in front of him.

"Hey, buddy," I said, and reached out to pet his big

rock of a head. I smiled at him, and felt tears welling in my eyes. "I'm sorry."

I put my arms around his neck and hugged him. He was warm, and soft, and he let me hug him until I pulled away, at which point he licked my face with his gross, slobbery tongue. I laughed and wiped at my face with my sleeve.

"I had a deaf dog when I was growing up," Desmond said. "Just put your hand in his line of sight, and he'll respond to you. You can even train him to learn certain hand movements as commands."

Desmond reached his hand down to me and pulled me up off the floor, and without thinking, I put my arms around him and pressed my face against his chest. There was a moment of hesitation, but then he settled his arms around me and hugged me back.

"Thank you," I said. "This has been a weird couple of days, and I'm a little emotionally unstable." I hesitated for a moment, wanting to pull back, but not sure how to do it gracefully. "And now I'm making it weirder by hugging you."

I could hear the rumble of Desmond's laughter in his chest, and what was weird was that it *wasn't* weird. Having his arms around me felt comforting, and I didn't want to pull away because I was afraid that *then* it would be weird. I wanted to stay there, my face pressed against his chest, forever.

But I didn't, because I couldn't. I stepped back, and put my hand to his chest, where my face had been, right over his heart.

"I may have gotten dog slobber on your shirt," I said, swiping at the wetness that remained on my chin. "He's kind of disgusting."

"It's not a problem."

I looked up at him and he was smiling down at me with so much warmth that I couldn't imagine this guy ever doing anything to hurt anyone.

"Whoever you were when you did that stuff to Stacy," I said, "you're not that guy anymore. I think you should know that."

He pulled back from me, and his face went stiff. "Yes. Well."

We both went back to the counter and drank our coffee in silence for a while until the awkwardness abated, and then I said, "Can you drop me off in town? I can walk home from there."

"Of course. Any place in particular?"

"My father's office."

Desmond was quiet for a moment. "Are you sure that's a good idea?"

"He brought Tobias back. Ball's in my court. If we're going to figure out what he's up to, I'm going to have to get close enough to him to find out."

"Yes, but that doesn't mean you have to see him right now. You can give yourself some time, you know."

I waved a dismissive hand in the air. "The more I think about it, the more I'm gonna psych myself out, so best to do it before I lose my nerve and just go out for ice cream."

Desmond looked at his watch and said, "At nine in the morning?"

"Are you suggesting there's a bad time for ice cream?" I asked, and he smiled.

"Silly mistake on my part. Carry on." He put his mug in the sink. "Would you like me to go with you to see Emerson?"

I thought about it, then shook my head. "No, thanks. I need you in my back pocket. If I go parading you into his office, he'll know we're friends and I'll lose my secret weapon."

"I'm your secret weapon, am I?"

"You bet. You're tall, you're smart, you're British, and you're evil. If anyone is going to give my father a run for his money, it's you."

Desmond looked at me, the hint of a smile lighting in the corners of his eyes. "I don't know. I rather think it's you he should be watching out for."

Chapter 10

Desmond dropped me off at my father's office, then drove off with my suitcase and Seamus, heading back to my place to check up on Tobias. I felt weird without Seamus by my side; unprotected. Even though there wasn't much that a big, dumb, deaf dog was going to do for me, there was something about being able to clutch his leash that made me feel anchored. Possibly it was just because he outweighed me by a good twenty pounds.

I pushed into the reception area to find my father standing by Amber's desk, leaning over and squinting at her computer over the reading glasses perched on his nose. It took them both a moment to notice me; when they did, Emerson straightened up and smiled. Amber straightened up and didn't.

"Punkin." Emerson walked over to me and pulled

me into a hug. He gave my hair a sniff and pulled back. "That's an interesting perfume."

"Thanks. It's called Big Dumb Dog." I went silent, and looked meaningfully at Amber. "Maybe we can talk in your private office?"

Amber shot up out of her seat. "No, that's okay. I need to run these things to the post office." She picked up an armful of document-sized envelopes and started toward the door. She'd almost made it when my father cleared his throat.

"Amber?" he said, and her shoulders visibly stiffened. She paused for a moment, her back to me, and then turned. She pulled on a crackling rictus of a smile, and looked straight at me, as though she had been practicing.

"I'm sorry I attacked you," she said through her teeth. "It was a momentary lapse into old behaviors which I realize now are beneath me."

I looked at Emerson, who was watching her with a smile on his lips, but something colder in his eyes, and a chill went down my spine. I looked back at Amber and said, "Yeah, don't worry about it."

Something passed between Amber and Emerson, and then she quietly turned and left. I waited until the door had shut behind her before saying, "She's afraid of you."

"She should be," Emerson said. "When I heard what happened, I read her the riot act for two days straight. That's no way for a person in my employ to behave in public no matter what, but attacking *you* . . ." His eyes blazed with protectiveness, but then he sighed and shook his head. "I damn near fired her, sent her back to work in the dirty roadside mechanic shop where I found her." He looked at me, his expression softening. "You all right?"

"I'm fine," I said, wishing that I had Seamus's leash to hang onto, to keep me anchored and stop me from falling into this display of fatherly protection. "Really. No big deal. She didn't even hit me that hard. It was the booth table that knocked me out."

"It is a big deal," Emerson said, his voice booming. "When she's out there, she represents me and this office, and it is not okay for her to behave like a goddamn wildcat." He let out a breath and smiled at me. "I'm glad you're okay."

"I'm fine." We both went silent as the Tobias-shaped elephant in the room stood in the space between us. I waited for him to bring it up, and he was obviously waiting for me, only I wasn't sure what to say, so I said, "I'm going to need you to tell me the truth. The absolute truth. No evasions, no loopholes, no technically-the-truths. Okay?"

He leaned against Amber's desk, his hands amiably tucked in his pockets. "Okay."

"Did you make Tobias disappear?"

He looked me dead in the eye. "No."

"Did you hurt him, drug him?" I paused, and Emerson opened his mouth to speak, and then I added, "If you had him hurt or had him drugged, that counts."

"No," Emerson said. "I had nothing to do with it."

"Do you know what happened to him?"

Emerson nodded.

"Will you tell me what happened to him?"

He shook his head. "Can't do that, punkin. You know that. I may be retired, but agency business is agency business. If I tell you what I know, that puts you in danger, and I can't have that."

I stared him down in silence, and he sighed.

"I can tell you it was just agency business. They needed him for something, and they pulled him out of Nodaway Falls. I called in a favor, and got him back for you. That's all there was to it."

"Then why did they have to wipe out his memory?"

Emerson shrugged. "You'd have to take that up with the boys in ASF, and they won't tell you, so it's best to let it lie. You got your man back, and that's all you're like to get."

I watched him, wanting to ask a million questions. *What do you want? Why are we here? What is your plan? How do I fit into it?*

Or was the real trick that there was no plan, that he just wanted me in his life again, in a town where I wouldn't be the only magical? A town I could call home? If I was a parent, that's what I'd want for my kid.

"What are you doing Saturday night?"

I blinked, shaken out of whatever fugue state I'd gotten into. "Saturday? I don't know. Working, probably."

He smiled, sadness in his eyes. "It's your birthday."

"No, it's . . ." I started automatically, but realized . . . actually, he was right. Since I'd transitioned from Josie Streat to Eliot Parker at the age of seventeen, my birthday had been in the fall. But originally, I was a June baby.

"The town is having a celebration out at the park," he said. "It's the Nodaway Falls bicentennial. Gonna be fireworks, big barbecue, some bands playing. One of 'em's even good, so I hear. Bunch of Irish fellas."

"That's nice," I said warily, watching him.

"Take the night off," he said, his voice soft. "Be my date, Josie. Come see the fireworks with me. Remember how you loved fireworks when you were little?"

"My name is Eliot," I said quietly. The door behind me opened and Amber returned. Emerson and I watched each other as she quietly made her way to her desk and sat. I tore my eyes from him and really paid attention to Amber for the first time since I'd walked in. Her hair had been tamed into ringlets that framed her face prettily, rather than the wild fuzz that exploded into the space around her head. Her dress was clingy and short, but modest by Amber's standards; I had a clear view of neither her midriff nor her cleavage, such as it was. Her nails were short, clear, and natural, buffed to a shine. She wasn't chewing gum, and her makeup was still heavy, but the colors were a little more subdued.

"Hey, Amber," I said in a friendly tone. Her eyes were blazing, on instant defense when she looked up at me, but she turned her focus to Emerson and he smiled kindly at her. Her entire being seemed to relax a little bit, and while she was still swimming in crazy, I could see her anchor herself to him. He kept her calm, instilled self-regard in her, gave her balance, and in that moment, I was proud of him.

"Hello, Eliot," she said after a bit. "Is there anything I can do for you?"

She watched me, her eyebrows raised, her body language open. She was genuinely asking me if she could do anything for me. She was trying to be a reasonable person, and I could see the strain it took on her, but also, I could see that she was doing it for him. In a weird way, kind of like a daughter, she loved him, and she wanted him to be proud of her. His influence on her was good.

Wow.

"I was just wondering . . ." I trailed off and stole a glance at Emerson, who was watching Amber with no small amount of pride in his expression, and then I looked back at Amber. "Um, I was wondering if you're going to the bicentennial fireworks on Saturday?"

This took her off guard, but after a moment of tension, she smiled—an actual real smile.

"I think so," she said. "It should be fun. Are you going?"

"I'm not really sure yet." I reached absently for the leash that wasn't there. My anchor was gone, and I felt oddly off balance without that huge, stupid dog by my side, like one leg was shorter than the other or something. I looked up at Emerson, feeling more conflicted than ever. It would have been so much simpler if he was all good, or all bad. This in-the-middle stuff was unsettling. "I have to go now."

I started toward the door, and as my fingers touched the door handle, Emerson said, "Good to see you, punkin," and I turned around and smiled at him.

"Yeah, you, too." And I meant it.

Seamus was in the yard when I got back to my place, chewing lazily on a tennis ball which he must have found on the ground somewhere. I ran to him, patting my legs.

"Hey, buddy!" I waved my hands at him, and he got up, wagging his tail, and walked over to me. He seemed happy to see me. I laughed and waved my hand at him again, and he made a feint, like a playful puppy. I walked over to the tennis ball and threw it, and he ran after it.

"I'll be damned," I muttered, and went inside to find Desmond in my kitchen, doing the dishes.

"Wow," I said. "Talk about a full-service conjurer. You do windows, too?"

"Liv and Tobias have gone," Desmond said. "I offered to clean up after them."

"How's Tobias?" I rolled up my sleeves and walked over to the sink. I nudged him out of the way to wash my hands and face, covered as they were with dog.

"He's well," Desmond said. "He's still a bit confused, and he can't remember anything after about two weeks before he left. Honestly, that's quite a bit less memory than I thought he'd lose. Your quickness saved the day." He put a clean coffee mug in the rack, and I picked up the towel and dried it.

"How's Liv handling everything?"

Desmond's expression darkened. "She seems to be having a tougher time. She still doesn't know if he willingly left her or not, and neither does he, so I imagine it's not easy for them."

"They told you all that?"

He gave a small shrug. "I surmised."

Desmond put a saucer in the rack, and I took it to dry. "You didn't have to clean up, you know."

"I don't mind. How did it go with your father?"

I walked over to the cabinet to put the saucer away, grateful for the opportunity to hide my face. "I don't know. He told me he didn't have anything to do with Tobias's disappearance. But considering that Tobias was the only agency presence in town, I could see why Emerson would want him out of the way." I turned to face him, playing with the towel in my hand. "Any chance Tobias will get his memory back?"

Desmond put the last coffee mug in the rack and shut off the water, angling his body to face me. "It's possible. Unlikely, but possible."

"Poop," I said absently as I grabbed a mug to dry. If Tobias didn't get his memory back, then I'd never know whether my father had been behind his disappearance or not. Which meant that I either needed to take my father's word, a dangerous proposition, or never trust anything he ever said again, which was a heartbreaking one.

"Eliot?"

"Huh?" I turned my attention back to Desmond. "What?"

"Is everything all right?"

I took a moment to figure out how to answer that question.

"When I took on my new identity, my birth date changed to September. I never really thought about it. I changed my name, my Social Security number . . . everything changed. My birthday was really the least of it. I never celebrated it, anyway."

Desmond waited in silence, not pushing, just listening. I liked that, the way he just knew there was more, and was willing to wait until I was ready to tell him.

"My real birthday is Saturday. My father wants to take me to the bicentennial fireworks to celebrate."

"Did you accept the invitation?"

"No."

"Do you want to?"

"I don't know. I love him. He's funny and smart and sweet and if it weren't for the occasional bouts of evil-doing, he'd be the perfect father. I miss him. It's been a long time since I've had . . . you know . . . family." I continued to dry the mug in my hand, even though it was already dry. I just wanted the busywork.

There was a pause in the conversation in which Desmond took the dry mug from my hand and set it on the mug tree by the coffee maker. "There's nothing wrong with it, you know."

"Wrong with what?"

"Loving him," he said simply. "He is your father."

"I'm not worried about it being wrong. I'm worried about it being stupid." I looked out the front window to see Seamus's tail wagging as he plodded by. "It looks like Seamus found a tennis ball."

"Oh, yes. I had one in the back of my car."

I pulled my attention away from the window and looked at Desmond. "You gave him that ball?"

He pulled his car keys out of his pocket. "It's been ages since I've played tennis, so I threw it out for Seamus. He seemed to enjoy it. Well, if you don't need me for anything else here, I think I might . . ." He trailed off, catching my expression. "You look strange. Are you well?"

Without thinking much about it, I pushed up on my tiptoes and kissed him. I didn't realize what I was doing until it was done, and his shoulders went stiff under my hands and we just . . . froze. It wasn't so much a kiss as two sets of lips touching, with no apparent idea why. Just when I was about to pull back and run out the front door, something changed. Desmond's lips softened, moving against mine, and I moved my hands up his shoulders to clasp at the back of his neck. His hands slid around my waist, pulling me closer, and our lips opened to each other and it felt like . . . I don't know. Music. Communion. A slow, slow dance to which there were no steps, only the crashing waves of . . . hell, I didn't even know what. I couldn't mix another metaphor, I just knew that suddenly, out of nowhere, I wanted this man more than anything I had ever wanted in my life.

The moment, like all of them, finally ended, and we regained consciousness of ourselves. I pulled back and looked up at him, and he stared down at me, his arms still wrapped around my waist, my fingers still woven into his hair. We were both breathing hard, and I felt like if he let me go, I'd fall for hours.

"Little more," I breathed, and he bent his head down and kissed me again, and while the first time had seemed more me than him, his enthusiasm was apparent now. It was like falling into him, through him, only to be restored to myself again. I felt happiness in my toes. I didn't even know that was possible.

After a few minutes, I pulled back again, pressed the flats of my hands against his chest, and rested my forehead between them. Unable to look him in the eye, I stared at his chest and smoothed his shirt under my hands.

"I mean . . . thank you," I said lamely. "F-for the tennis ball."

We sort of froze there for a while, his arms around my waist, my palms resting against his chest, the *thump-thump-thump* of his heart growing faster under my fingers. It was like being on the edge of a precipice, and knowing that a single move will send you toppling one way or the other, but the edge is so nice, you kind of want to stay there a while and enjoy it.

His finger tucked under my chin, urging me to look up at him. When I did, he smiled down at me, his deep brown eyes so soft and so full of . . . well, whatever this was that was happening between us. He touched my face, his fingers moving hair away from my forehead in this gentle movement, so deliberate, so careful. He didn't want to topple away from this, either.

Slowly, he lowered his head and put his lips to mine, softly moving them against my mouth with agonizing deliberateness. I put my hands to his face, pulling him closer in, and at first, I thought the power that surged through us was just sexual excitement gone haywire, but then my eyes opened and I saw the blue light dancing around my hands . . . dancing around him . . .

Dancing *through* him.

"Oh my god!" I yelled, and jumped back from him, but it was too late. The light traveled down his shoulders, to his hands, and then he hollered and threw the keys that had been in his hand to the floor, and they skittered across the floor into the dining room.

"No," I said, feeling like I was going to throw up. The room spun around me, but I focused on finding those keys. I had to find those keys, and they had to still be keys, because if they weren't still keys . . .

"Oh, god. No, no, *nonononono* . . ."

"Eliot." I heard Desmond's voice behind me, but it might as well have been echoing on the end of a tinny phone line for all I noticed he was there. I was focused on the keys. I found them under the table, picked them up, and held them in my hands.

There had been three of them, attached to the keyless car fob. A house key, I guessed. Something that looked like a post office box key. Something else. It didn't matter, because they weren't keys anymore. They had molded into the shape of a potion flask, with the word *Kwikset* still engraved on one side.

"No!" I said. "No! Goddammit!"

"Eliot." Desmond's hands were on my shoulders and he pulled me up from under the table, sitting me down in the chair. He left and I could hear the refrigerator door open, but I couldn't see anything but that stupid metal potion flask in my palm. The stupid metal potion flask he had made, because of me. Because I couldn't have had the common fucking sense to realize that if there was a chance I might have wild magic, and my magic was so strong that I could turn a doorknob without even trying, *maybe* I shouldn't go around kissing people.

"Hey." Desmond appeared in my line of sight, kneeling before me, holding a glass of water. "Drink this, okay?"

"No," I said, still staring down at the potion flask. My vision blurred, and tears dripped down my face, but all I could see and feel was that flask, cold and real in my hands.

Desmond put the glass on the table and touched my face, forcing me to look at him.

"I'm so sorry," I said. "It wasn't on purpose. I didn't send that magic through you on purpose. I would never, ever—"

"Trust me, I know that," he said, his voice completely calm. Considering that he'd just had wild magic surging through him, you would have expected him to be a little more ruffled, but he was completely cool. Cucumber cool. He took the potion flask from my hand, set it on the table, and then took both of my hands in his, holding them even as I weakly tried to pull them away.

"It's all right," he said. "I feel fine."

"So did Del, at first." I pushed up from the seat, away from him, and started for the living room, pacing back and forth as I talked. "Okay. Okay. You have potions, right? You said you have potions. We can go back to your place and you can take them and then we'll go to my father. Maybe over the years he's figured it out, and he has a cure or something. Maybe . . ." I trailed off, knowing that if my father knew how to give power to nonmagicals without dire consequences, this whole town would be lit up with magic by now.

Desmond put his hands on my shoulders and forced me to stand still. "We don't know what we're dealing with just yet. I'm not going to take potions I don't need. It could do more harm than good. Right now, I'm more worried about you. You need to calm down, Eliot. Please. Look at me."

I met his eyes and wanted to burst into tears again. But he was holding me, he was anchoring me, and if he wanted me calm, then I was going to be calm.

"It's twenty-four hours, right?" He held my hands in his, comforting me. "Twenty-four hours from initial exposure to . . . ?" He had the courtesy to not finish the sentence with the word I couldn't hear: *death*.

"Yes." My voice sounded like someone else's, like a calm person speaking. Inside, I was trying like hell, but I was anything but calm. "About twenty-four hours. First you'll get powers of your own, and then . . ." I trailed off, unable to think past that point.

"All right." He put one hand on my shoulder and pressed firmly, sending some of his calm shooting into me. "We have twenty-four hours to monitor the situation, and I am not afraid. I think I'm going to be fine, but even if . . . even if the worst happens, it'll be okay."

"I won't be okay," I said. "If the worst happens, I will never be okay again. You know that, right?"

He put his hands on my face, his eyes so confident and determined that I felt my heart rate slow down just from looking into them. "Then we won't let that happen."

I held his gaze a while longer, taking strength from him until the vise of cold fear that clutched at my heart released its grip a little bit. "Promise me."

He kissed me instead, and while I knew he was doing it to avoid making me a promise he couldn't keep, I took it as a promise anyway. It was the only way I was going to hold it together and be any help at all for the next twenty-four hours.

Chapter 11

Desmond drove us to his house in silence, the only sound coming from the backseat where Seamus panted and gnawed on his increasingly gross tennis ball. Once we got to Desmond's, he tossed my overnight bag and Seamus's food by the door, and walked me over to the couch, where he sat me down and took my hands in his.

"We need to talk about some things," he said. "Do you need anything? Water? Tea?"

"No," I said. "I'm okay."

"When magic manifests," he said, "it's usually centered in the limbic system . . . the emotional centers of the brain. Often a shock, a sudden burst of fear or happiness . . . those are the things that tend to bring on the first incident. So the first thing we need to look for is my developing any power independent of yours. So far, we just have the potion flask which was made on the burst of your magic. I haven't felt any other effects."

"Really?" I asked. "You're not just saying that to make me feel better?"

He shook his head. "No tingling sensation in my arms or hands, and no evident light phenomena." He held out his hands and looked at them as if they were some rare artifact he'd never seen before. "Of course, temporal constraints aren't necessarily transferable."

I blinked. "Sorry. What?"

He seemed distracted by his own thoughts, but then looked up and gave me a comforting smile. "You have day magic, but the magic that each person manifests is contingent upon their individual potential. Some people are day magic, some are night. We won't know for sure what I am, if indeed I am anything, until evening falls. Which is . . ." He looked at his watch. "We're in midsummer, so it will be another seven hours at least."

"And you have to have an intense emotional experience in order to spark it?" I asked. "To jump-start the limbic system?"

He gave a half nod, half shrug. "It's mostly conjecture at this point, but based on available data, that would be my expectation."

"So, how do we create an intense emotional reaction in you? Should we . . . I don't know . . . talk about your childhood? Maybe . . . did you have to put down that deaf dog of yours or something?"

Desmond met my eye. "I believe we've already tested thoroughly for day magic."

It took me a moment to understand, and when I did, my breath caught. "Oh. You mean . . . when we kissed? The, uh . . . the second time?"

"Yes. Also . . ." He looked at his hands as he spoke. "I want desperately to . . . for you to not worry or upset yourself on my account. I find it very . . . extremely, um, well . . . *vexing,* for lack of a better word . . . to be unable to relieve your distress."

"Vexing?" I let loose with a light, mildly hysterical laugh. "So, when you get stressed out, you get, like, more British? Is that how it works? If I started pelting you with a BB gun, would your monocle just suddenly pop off?"

He met my eyes and smiled. "Had I a monocle, yes. That's exactly how it works."

I held his gaze. Desmond's smile faded, and his eyes lowered quickly.

"Although I think for the moment, considering how much time we have between now and nightfall, we should both be thinking in terms of stress *relief* rather than . . ." He choked a bit on the words and his face reddened a little bit. "What I mean to say is . . . I'm not suggesting . . ."

The silence fell over us, and I let it sit there. There were maybe two feet between us, and suddenly all I could think about was closing that distance and touching him, everywhere, but it was exactly that instinct that had created this whole disaster in the first place.

Until night fell and my magic wasn't active anymore, I didn't want to risk touching him again, so finishing his obvious thought and bringing up the topic of sex would not help at all.

"Badminton?" I offered finally.

"Pardon?"

"For stress relief," I said. "You're not suggesting . . . badminton, right?"

"Yes," he said, meeting my eyes. "I think . . . *badminton* . . . would complicate an already complicated situation."

I smiled, amazed at how safe he was making me feel, even given the day I . . . well, *we* . . . were having. "Good, because that may be too British, even for you."

He laughed lightly, and my heart sang at the thought that I had made him happy. I didn't know what his emotions were doing right now, but mine were in overdrive, and it was best to calm everything down for a while. I took in a deep breath and let it out slowly. "Okay, so we've got seven hours to kill, we need stress relief, badminton's off the table . . ."

"I have a bottle of Glenfiddich," he offered. "And a pack of cards."

"Sounds perfect," I said.

"Well, we've learned one thing," I said a few hours later, gathering up the cards from the coffee table. "You are the worst spit player in probably the history of the world."

"I consider that a positive quality. Spit is a terrible game."

"Spit is the best game ever," I said. "Del and I played it all the time when we had sleepovers."

"And thank you for making my point for me," he said dryly.

I shifted on the floor, where I sat next to a sleeping Seamus while Desmond stayed on the couch. We'd been slow with the whisky, stretching a few small glasses over a late lunch of brie, baguette, and grapes, and what seemed like endless games of cards. So far, Desmond appeared to be having no response to the wild magic, but then, the sun hadn't set yet. I glanced out the window, the way I had been every twenty minutes for the last six and a half hours. The sky was pink now, not the bright blue of earlier, but still. Night was coming, and I wasn't sure I was ready for whatever came next.

"So, you pick the game, then," I said, shuffling the cards. "Something British and sophisticated. Perhaps a round of whist?"

Desmond sighed, and I looked up to see him giving me a plaintive look.

"Stop thinking what you're thinking," I said. "I'm not leaving."

"I promise to call you immediately if anything happens," he said. "Which it won't."

I tapped the deck on the table, twice, punctuating my determination to stay. "Fine. If you won't make a suggestion, let's do blackjack again."

I started to deal the cards, but Desmond reached for my hand, and I pulled away on instinct.

"Eliot, stop. You're like a skittish cat. You're not going to hurt me."

"Right." I put the cards down. "Because I've already hurt you."

"No," he said, his voice firm. "You didn't. If anything happens to me, which it won't, it will have been an accident. Please. Let me drive you home."

He got up from the couch, walked over to the breakfast bar, and whipped the useless potion flask keys attached to his car fob off the counter. The car fob still worked, and he obviously meant to take me home.

I stood up, crossing my arms over my chest. "I'm not going anywhere."

"I'm asking you to go," he said. "If I ask you to leave, and you refuse, you do understand that's trespassing, don't you?"

I stood my ground. "So, what? You're going to call the police and have me forcibly removed? Because that's what you'll have to do."

"Fine." He pulled his phone out of his pocket. I didn't move.

He tapped his security code in. I didn't move.

He opened his phone app and dialed.

"Oh, if Roni Kittering answers, tell her that she left her earrings at Happy Larry's. They're in the lost and found."

"Dammit." He shut the phone down and looked at

me, eyes blazing. "You are the most bullheaded woman I have ever known."

"We haven't even scratched the surface yet, buddy."

"I don't want you here," he said. "I'm asking you to leave. I don't understand why you won't respect that."

"Why do you want me to leave? Because you don't want me to worry? Like I won't be out of my mind if I'm not with you. Why in the world would you think that would be any easier on me?"

"Nothing's going to happen to me, but if it does—"

"Then it won't matter if I'm here!"

He raised his voice, speaking over me. "*But if it does,* I don't want you here to see it! Dammit. Why are you being willfully obtuse?"

"Because you're being willfully a dumbass!" I said, walking over to him. "I'm here to help. Who's gonna get the potions down your stupid gullet if you collapse?"

Desmond motioned toward the kitchen counter, where a line of small, glass potion flasks stoppered with corks sat in a neat row. "They're right there. If something should happen, which it won't, I will be perfectly capable of administering the correct dosage, and if I'm not, then you wouldn't be able to help me, anyway."

I must have looked as horrified as I felt at that, because his face softened and I could see guilt in his eyes.

"You're upset," he said. "This is exactly what I wanted to avoid."

"Then stop asking me to leave."

It took a little while, but eventually, he nodded. I glanced outside; there was still a trace of pink light in the sky.

"So, you've been reading the letters," I said suddenly, motioning toward the end stand in the living room. "I noticed the book earlier." He looked at me blankly, so I added, "Sartre and Simone?"

"Oh. Um. Yes." There was still tension in his voice, but it was softening a bit. "They're quite engaging. I think you got it exactly right with those two. A crazy lid for every nutty pot, was that what you said?"

I smiled. "Something like that, yeah. I think if anyone else in the world called her 'my dear little girl' she would have castrated the guy. But when he said it . . ."

I trailed off, and we stared at each other for a long while, a new tension building between us.

"My dear little girl," he said quietly, and I swear to god, it almost killed me trying to hide how it made my insides go to jelly.

"So, um . . . how are you feeling? Emotionally, I mean?" I motioned to the window. It was almost full dark. "Should we start?"

"Start . . . what?"

"I don't know. Emotions. Stirring things up. Talking about that dog that died, or . . ."

I hadn't realized that we'd been closing the space between us, but now, we were close enough that I could feel his breath swirling in the air between us. It smelled of whisky, and it was intoxicating.

"Or?" he said.

"Or . . ." I swallowed. "Or we could play . . . badminton." I let out an involuntary giggle, feeling stupid and reckless and drunk on something more powerful than the hooch. "Unless, I mean . . . I'm assuming you feel emotion when you play . . . badminton. Some people don't, and that's okay."

"I think . . ." He cleared his throat. "We're trying to test a hypothesis. Perhaps it's time to be direct with each other."

"Should we have another glass of whisky first?"

"Yes, excellent idea." He poured the whisky while I sat down. He handed me my glass and settled across from me on the couch, his body turned toward mine. I knew my face was flushed, and I drank a big gulp so I could blame it on the Glenfiddich.

"Just being around you is enough to spark an emotional reaction within me," he said, his words coming careful and even. "I don't need to touch you or have sex with you for you to . . . affect me."

I nodded and laughed, unable to bear the tension anymore. "I actually tend to spark reactions in a lot of people. Every time Happy Larry sees me, steam comes right off the top of his head."

"What I'm feeling isn't anger." His voice was calm and even. He took a sip of his whisky, keeping eye contact with me as he drank, making me feel dizzy.

"What . . ." My voice cracked, so I swallowed and took another run at it. "What are you feeling?"

He took a breath, seeming to think about it for a moment. "There's an odd . . . I don't know how to describe it. A lightness of being, I guess."

I wanted to make a joke out of the way he was speaking, anything to take down the electricity between us, but I was too caught up. I could barely speak, let alone joke. "You mean . . . I make you happy?"

He let out a light laugh and lowered his eyes. "Yes. But more than that. You make me forget, however temporarily, that I've ever been unhappy."

"Oh." I wasn't sure how to respond to that, so I took another drink.

"When you speak, I'm fascinated." He kept his head low, staring into his glass, which he swirled absently in his hand. "Your intelligence, and your willful attempts to veil it . . . I find myself ensorcelled. I don't hear anything else, just your voice, even when there's all manner of commotion around us. Everything else just fades away. Watching you move toward me makes me light-headed, and when you walk away, I can't pull my eyes from you until you disappear from view, and even then, I stare like a fool at the space you vacated. When you smile at me, I want so badly to be the man you see in me. And when I make you laugh—" He raised his head, his expression embarrassed, but then he saw me swiping at my face and his eyes widened. "Oh, bollocks."

I waved my hands in front of my face as he shifted toward me on the couch.

"I'm sorry, I'm sorry," I said, taking the handkerchief he held out to me and dabbing at my eyes. "It's just . . . no one has ever said anything like that to me." I lowered my eyes, too embarrassed to look directly at him. "I mean, even Judd. When he proposed, all he said was, 'I'd rather have you on my side than the other guy's.' No one says stuff like this." I hit him playfully on the shoulder and sniffled. "I mean, who says stuff like this?"

"Someone should say this to you every day," he said, so softly that I almost didn't hear him. I looked up, and his face was just inches from mine. I reached out and put my index finger on his lips, and he gently kissed it. I glanced outside.

The sky was black.

"Are you feeling . . . a lot of emotion right now?" I asked.

He swallowed, and nodded. I reached down and took his hand in mine.

"No evident light phenomena," I said.

He smiled and shook his head. "No. No, there is not."

"H-how are feeling? Are you feeling light-headed?"

"Yes," he said, his voice quiet and intent. "But I don't think it's magic."

We sat there, frozen in that space, for what felt like a really long time, then I got up and took his hand in mine. Silently, I led him past Seamus's sleeping body and up the steps to his loft bedroom. I turned to him and started to unbutton his shirt. At first he tensed up, but I pressed my lips to his chest and he sighed and I knew he wasn't going to resist. Whatever powers we may have had, none of them were more powerful than this.

We moved slowly, together, as though time wasn't a consideration. It wasn't that we took off each other's clothes; it was as though they just fell away. He lowered me onto the bed and kissed my belly, and I pulled him back up to kiss my lips, hungry for his mouth in a way that almost made me dizzy. I had been ready for him for what felt like hours, and now that we weren't holding back any more, every moment without him was an eternity. We fished through his bedside drawer together, giggling, and when I took him in my hand and sheathed him, his sharp intake of breath at my touch intoxicated me. I moved over him, tasting his mouth as I slid myself down over him, and held myself motionless, looking into his eyes as we melded together. He sifted his fingers into my hair and pulled me down to him and it felt like falling into safety, into comfort, even as the waves we rode slammed us together, the power of each crash increasing until I reached down and touched myself between us, unable to wait any longer. I cried out, bucking against him, and he held me tight to him until the spasms subsided. A few quiet moments, and slowly he moved within me, and I kept his pace until he shouted out, then went still and fell down beside me. I curled myself up next to him, my head resting over his pounding heart, and closed my eyes.

I don't know how long my eyes were closed. I might have fallen asleep for a bit. I was drowsy, drunk, and postcoital, so I wasn't paying careful attention. It wasn't until I felt Desmond's arm move that I opened my eyes to see Desmond holding his hand up in the shaft of moonlight coming through the window.

"No evident light phenomena," I murmured drowsily, and Desmond kissed the top of my head.

"I have felt as much emotion this evening as I have in a lifetime before." His voice was soft, calm, and lulling. "If I had any magic in me, it would be bouncing all over this room."

I was quiet for a bit, and then I said, "So . . . do you think it's possible that everything's okay? That nothing bad is going to happen? My father just wants a relationship with me, and that's it?"

"It's possible," he said, his voice sleepy and soft.

"Hmmm. This is weird."

"What?"

"Living in a world where I feel safe." I snuggled into his chest and he wrapped his arms around me. He smoothed my hair with his hand, and it felt so good that I let out a little sigh of contentment.

"Are you comfortable?" he asked. "We don't have to cuddle if it prevents you from sleeping."

"I can sleep anytime, anywhere, in any position. It's one of my many charms." I created a little swirl in his chest hair with my index finger. "Feel free to shove me over in the night. I won't notice."

"I'm content as we are, for the moment," he said,

shifting down a bit into the pillows, but still keeping his arms around me.

"Yeah, it's kind of weird how well we fit together," I said on a yawn, and closed my eyes.

"It is at that." He kissed the top of my head, and we fell asleep.

The next morning, things were strangely comfortable. We woke up at dawn, still entwined, and moved into quiet, dreamy morning sex without any awkwardness. We talked and laughed over a small breakfast of coffee and English muffins, and Desmond seemed fine. When the twenty-four-hour mark of the moment I'd shot magic through him came and went without event, we figured it was time to get back to life as usual. He drove me home and we kissed in the front seat of his car for a good ten minutes before Seamus's whines from the backseat killed the moment. Before leaving, he asked if he could take me out to a birthday dinner before the bicentennial on Saturday, and that was it.

I, Eliot Parker, cheated widow and magical freak show, was apparently in some kind of . . . relationship.

Happy Larry was not happy.

"What's the matter with you?" he asked, giving me a strange sideways look as he wiped down the bar during my shift that night. "You're all . . . smiley."

"I am not," I said, and put my hands to my cheeks. I had been smiling so much, my face hurt. But I couldn't stop. Every time I tried to channel my typically cranky self, I'd think about Desmond and my face would break into this stupid, gummy smile and I'd feel like an idiot, but I couldn't help it.

Larry picked up a bottle of gin and inspected it, shooting me a look. "You skimming off the top?"

"No," I said. "When I drink, I actually get more cranky."

He handed me the bottle. "Then take a shot on the house. You're weirding me out."

I laughed and put the bottle back. "Get used to it."

He seemed mildly ameliorated by my insolence, but not enough to look entirely comfortable. Instead, he muttered something I couldn't hear over the jukebox and disappeared into his office, which was just as well.

About an hour later, Peach Easter waddled in behind a huge belly full of baby, looking like a fifties pinup girl who had swallowed a beach ball. She was wearing a bright orange dress that splayed out to her knees, with her hair pulled up into a matching bandanna. Her makeup was expertly applied, and even her manicure was flawless. She somehow managed to settle herself on a stool, even if she had to sit sideways to the bar in order to do it.

This woman was my goddamn hero.

"You still haven't had that kid yet?" I said, placing a coaster in front of her.

"If the little monster doesn't come out on her own by Monday, I'm sending a team in to get her," she said, one hand resting on her taut belly. "Walking is supposed to induce labor. I've been walking all over this damn town for two days. *Nothing*. Having sex is supposed to induce labor. Nick's at the point where he's making excuses. *Nothing*. I've been an obstetrics nurse for ten years, and I always thought those women who shot evening primrose oil up their hoohas to get the baby out were crazy, but I'm telling you now . . . I get it."

"Are you hoping that gin induces labor?" I said, grinning. "Because I'm not sure I can serve a pregnant lady." I thought about it and shrugged. "I could possibly look the other way while you snag a bottle from behind the bar, though."

Peach laughed and patted her stomach. "No. I haven't had a drop since the stick turned pink. No booze, no caffeine, not for nine months." She slapped her hand down on the bar. "No! Ten! Nine months is a myth. Forty weeks, four weeks per month, that's *ten* months. Plus the extra week she's been in there cooking, just taking her damn time." She looked down at her belly and raised her voice. "What do you need, kid? An engraved freakin' invitation?"

"How about a seltzer with lemon?" I said. "On the house."

Peach looked back at me and nodded gratefully. "That would be great."

I went about making the drink and Peach leaned sideways to get a little closer to me.

"Hey, what are you doing Saturday night, before the bicentennial?"

I put the drink down in front of her. "Oh. Well.

I have a . . . thing." It felt weird to say it was a date. Desmond and I were undefined at the moment, and that was good by me.

"A thing? What thing? Like a date?"

I shrugged, feeling uncomfortable. "It's not a date. It's just dinner." *With a guy I had crazy sex with all night.*

She clapped her hands. "Perfect! Bring him along!"

"Um . . ." I paused for a moment, trying to figure out if I'd missed something in the conversation. "Bring him where?"

"We're having a dinner party, at Liv's," Peach said. "Stacy and Leo, Liv and Tobias, me and Nick, *unless the baby decides to break out.*" She directed that last bit pointedly at her stomach, then picked up her drink and sipped through the tiny red straw and winked at me. "Power of suggestion. Worth a shot. Anyway, we thought it would be nice if you could come. Liv's really grateful for how you helped with Tobias and everything. And we like you."

I couldn't help but smile at her diplomacy. "You don't *all* like me."

Peach rolled her eyes. "What, Stacy? You can't take her seriously. She talks to all of us like that. Her mother is a harridan, and she treated Stacy like crap her whole life, and so Stace doesn't know how to behave around people. She likes you just fine. Seven o'clock okay? That'll give us enough time to get to the bicentennial for the fireworks."

"Oh, um, I don't know . . ." I hesitated, not sure

if I was ready to talk about what was happening with Desmond, but there wasn't really any way to avoid it. "Desmond is the guy I was going to dinner with."

"What a surprise," she said flatly, her eyes glittering with amusement as she sipped innocently on that tiny straw. She put the drink down and grinned at me. "Don't look so shocked. You live in a very, very small town. Clementine Klosterman saw him driving you home this morning, and she called Liv. She was worried that maybe he'd kidnapped you or something." Peach shrugged. "She's still a little skittish around him. A lot of people are."

"You're not," I said.

She shook her head. "When Nick says he has a good feeling about someone, I've just learned to trust him. He works landscaping. Nobody tries to impress Nick. He sees them exactly as they are, and he's the best judge of character I've ever known."

I pulled out some lemons to cut while we talked so that if Larry came out from his office he'd think I was working. "But . . . Stacy's his sister. Didn't he want to kill Desmond after all that stuff happened last summer?"

Peach nodded. "Yeah. He did. He was so mad. Desmond did a number on my mother-in-law, too." Peach rolled her eyes. "Desmond gave Lillith magic, and a little bit of power in a bitch like that is a really bad thing. Nick wanted to kill Desmond for a long time. Then, he tried."

I stopped cutting and looked up. "He tried to kill him?"

Peach waved a hand in the air. "The way men are always trying to kill each other. Nick went for a walk around town one night, saw Desmond, and just laid into him. I wasn't there, but I heard the story from, like, twelve people. Nick hit Desmond, and Desmond just took it. He didn't argue, he didn't say anything to defend himself, didn't raise a hand to deflect the blows. Just stood there and took it. Nick hit him hard, knocked him down, and when he shouted at Desmond to fight back, Desmond didn't say anything. He just got up and stood there. He was gonna take his punishment until Nick got tired or killed him, whichever came first. Nick swore at him and took him to the hospital to get his eyebrow stitched up and his ribs wrapped. The whole time, he told me, he was waiting for Desmond to press charges, and he was thinking about how much I was going to kill him when I had to bail him out of jail. But Desmond told the doctors that he fell down the stairs, and that was that. Desmond came to work for Nick the next week, and it was all fine." She rolled her eyes again. "Men."

I went back to cutting the lemons, not wanting Peach to see how affected I was by the story. I knew that Desmond had done bad things, but the idea of anyone hurting him, even if he deserved it, made me a little shaky. We were quiet for a while. Peach reached out and touched my hand. I looked up to find her giving me a sympathetic smile.

She watched me for a moment, then leaned into the bar. "Still, I was completely against it when Nick hired Desmond to do landscaping work for him. I mean, between dosing Leo and hitting Stacy . . ." She raised her eyes to watch me, her expression wary. "Did you know about that?"

I nodded. "Yeah. He told me."

Peach eyed me for a moment. "Good." She took another sip of her seltzer, then set it down and sighed. "Anyway, Nick said he was hiring Desmond, and I said, 'Nick, you're crazy,' and Nick just said, 'He's a good guy.'" She smiled and let out a small laugh. "And then, two weeks later, Nick went down to Pittsburgh to check out a new paving stone supplier, and he had Desmond redoing the walkway at our house. It was April or so, I was still cute-pregnant, not mammoth-pregnant like I am now. My ankles were still normal-sized and I was wearing these really cute strappy sandals, and this adorable little pink baby doll outfit." She gave a wistful sigh. "Anyway, I tripped over my own feet and Desmond was there before I even realized what was happening. He caught me and carried me into the house and set me down and wouldn't leave until he was sure the baby and I were both fine. Luckily the kid was turning cartwheels that day, or I think he would have carried me all the way to the hospital if he had to. Did you know he used to be a doctor?"

I shook my head. "No."

Peach nodded. "You think that's weird? That he tells you he hit a woman, but not that he used to be a doctor? Of course, he lost his license for doing magical tests on cadaver brains or something, so maybe that's why." She shrugged. "Men, who can figure 'em, right?"

"Right," I said, and fiddled with my bar towel.

"So, Saturday? Seven o'clock?"

I smiled. "I'll talk to Desmond."

Peach patted the bar twice, then used it as leverage to push herself up. "Hopefully, I'll be in the hospital *with a baby in my arms*." She aimed that at her stomach, then looked at me and smiled. "But if not, it would be great to have a doctor at dinner, just in case the little monster decides to crash the party." She winked at me and waddled toward the exit. I watched her go, feeling a strange happiness run through me at the thought of a real, adult dinner party. With real, adult friends.

"Hey!"

I looked up from the bar to see Larry frowning at me from his office door.

"Quit smiling and go get that table's order!" he said, pointing to a table in the corner where a couple just sat down. I grabbed a pen from the cup below the bar and grinned at him.

"You bet, sunshine!" I blew him a kiss as I hurried past him. He grunted something unintelligible and slammed the office door.

It was turning out to be a pretty good day.

Chapter 12

I woke up in the dead of night to the sound of crashing dishes. Seamus, sleeping on the rug by my bed, of course heard nothing. I nudged him with my toes as I got out of bed, he jolted up and walked beside me as I moved down the hallway into my kitchen. I flipped on the light and saw a dinner plate go flying from the kitchen over the dining room table, and into the front window, where it exploded into a thousand ghostly pieces that dissolved into nothing as they hit the floor. Seamus panted at my side, but when I let go of his collar, he just ambled over to his water dish and took a drink.

After all, there was nothing for him to see.

Judd sat on the kitchen counter. The cabinet holding my small collection of sad, mismatched dishes was open, but I'd probably left it open. Between Judd's legs there was a ghostly bottle of Jim Beam which had maybe a third left, and Judd took a gulp when he saw me. He reached into the cabinet, grabbed a ghostly dish, and threw it at the window again. Once again, it shattered and dissolved into nothing. All my plates were undisturbed, in the cabinet.

"It's all imaginary," he said, staring at the window. "The dishes, the booze. I can make them appear, but they don't have weight. They don't have *heft*. They don't have shit." Still, he took another drink, because he was Judd, and he'd never met a self-destructive behavior he didn't take to like a fish to water.

"Just go toward the light, Judd, okay?" I said, rubbing my eyes. "Maybe they'll have real booze over there."

"You won't let me!" He hopped off the kitchen counter and came toward me. "You're holding on to me, and until you let go, I'm stuck here!" He stopped just short of walking through me, and when I looked up at him, all I could see were wild eyes staring down at me.

"But . . . no." I rubbed my arms, trying to come awake. Was this a dream? "You're just a reflection of my inner whatever. You're not you. You're just . . . me. I can't hurt you, because you're not you. What the hell time is it?"

I glanced at the clock on the wall, but my eyes wouldn't focus, so I walked through Judd to get a closer look.

"Oh, god, it's four o'clock in the morning. I've had two hours of sleep."

"You think you can't hurt me? How do you think I felt, watching my wife have sex with that fucking limey asshole?"

I turned to face Judd. He really did look distraught. I couldn't even begin to figure out what kind of psychological break I must be having. It was just too early in the morning. So instead of trying to figure it out, I decided to treat this mirage like it *was* Judd. Really, actually Judd. Not some extension of my subconscious, not some imaginary security blanket. And the second I made that decision to see this whatever as *really* Judd, I was pissed.

"Are you seriously kidding me?" I said, moving toward him. "What about you and Christy McNagle? What about those poor cops who had to come and tell a woman that not only was her husband dead, but he was sleeping with someone else, too? What about all that debt that ate up everything we had? You gave me nothing when we were together, and you left me with less than nothing when you died. I'm not going to apologize for not living like a nun, Judd."

"I had *sex* with someone else, yeah," Judd said, jabbing a finger to his chest as though he was making some kind of self-righteous point. "That doesn't matter. That's body parts. That's nothing."

I laughed a furious laugh. "Even dead, you're delusional. A person would think you'd get some kind of clarity in the great beyond, Judd, but you're just as much of an idiot as you were when you died."

"Don't change the subject," Judd said. "The point is, I didn't fall *in love* with anyone else, Ellie. I loved you. Only *you*."

"Yeah, you loved me so much you cheated on me and lied to me about meeting with my father. My *father,* Judd. How could you not tell me about that?"

He put his hands on his hips, his lips thinned with anger. "You love him?"

I threw my hands up in the air. "What? Yeah. I don't know. Maybe." I shrugged and sighed. "I don't know. He's my father. It's complicated. He's . . . complicated. I'm still figuring all that out. And what the hell is it to you, anyway?"

"No," Judd said, his voice forceful and cold. "Do you love . . . *him*?"

I froze, my thoughts in a jumble. "What? Who? Desmond?"

Judd held his hands out in a gesture of frustration, and if he'd had a neck, I would have throttled it.

"That's none of your damn business," I said. "We're not married anymore, and *you* cheated on *me*. I am the one here who's done *nothing* wrong. Let's keep that straight."

Judd took a hard swig from his ghostly bottle and made a face. "I see how you are with him. The way you laugh, the way you touch your face when he looks at you . . ."

"I don't touch my . . . *agh!* I'm not having this conversation." I closed my eyes and scrunched up my fists. "Go away, Judd. Just go toward the light. If you're a real ghost, then I release you, and if you're not, then I want to trade you in for something else. Maybe a psychosomatic facial tic with no goddamn opinions. Just *go!*"

I kept my eyes closed for a while, and everything was quiet. I could hear Seamus's feet shuffling across the floor and the gentle thud of his body hitting the living room rug, stretching out to go to sleep. I listened carefully for any other sound, real or imagined, but there was nothing, so I opened my eyes.

Judd was standing right in front of me.

"Oh, man," I whined. "Why are you still here?"

"You tell me." His voice wasn't angry anymore, and there was a smile in his eyes as he looked down at me. "Why am I still here?"

I shrugged and moved into the kitchen to get away from him. I grabbed a glass and filled it with water.

"I don't know."

"You need to figure it out," Judd said. "Neither one of us is going to move on until you do."

I drank the water, thinking. "I don't know. I miss you, maybe?"

"Why?" Judd said. "I was never home. I cheated on you. I left you in debt. I lied about your dad."

"Trust me, I haven't forgotten." I ran my hands through my hair, suddenly feeling bone-tired. "I don't know why I keep you around. I really don't."

"Wanna hear a theory?"

"No."

"Because I loved you."

I couldn't help it. I laughed. "Oh, yeah. You made that patently obvious, what with the sleeping with other women and leaving me alone with less than nothing."

He moved closer, close enough to kiss me, if he'd been corporeal. "I loved you. And when you were with me, you knew I loved you. And you're afraid I'm the only one who ever will love you. If you let me go, that's it. You're alone."

I felt a stab in my gut at his words, which meant they were probably true, and that seriously pissed me off. "Oh, please. Spare me your armchair psychology. If the way you loved me was the best I could ever do . . ." I trailed off, not sure how to finish the sentence, and looked up at him. Judd. My dumb, beautiful, fucked-up Judd.

"Oh, Ellie," he said softly. "If I had anything, I would give it all to be able to hold you right now," he said. At that moment, I felt a hard nudge at my knee, and there was Seamus, rubbing his head against my leg affectionately.

"Oh, sweetie," I said, and dropped down to hug him. I had no idea how he knew I was upset; he couldn't hear a damn thing. But as I hugged him and snuggled into his massive furriness, he wagged his tail and nuzzled me, and I felt better.

Some time later, I don't know how long, I looked up and Judd was gone. I pushed up to stand, walked over to the cabinet and shut it, then led Seamus back to my bedroom, where we both passed out cold.

The next evening, I clutched the neck of the wine bottle in my hand and looked up at Desmond as we walked down the street toward Liv's house. Things between us were sexually charged, but relaxed about it. No casual kisses at the door, no hand-holding, no talk of being boyfriend and girlfriend or anything goofy like that. At the same time, I had every expectation that we'd be having more great sex at the first opportunity. It was pretty much the perfect friendship.

Or it would have been, if Desmond didn't look so miserable.

"Are you sure you're okay?" I asked.

Physically, he looked great. He was in his usual getup of a shirt and tie and trousers, and I was wearing a little swirly dress in a deep blue that matched his tie, a little coincidence that I found really sweet. But as fine a figure as he cut in his clothes, his face was understandably tense.

He forced a small smile. "I'm fine. This will be . . . fun."

I stopped and turned to face him. We were about two houses down from Liv's, and this was our last chance to run.

"We don't have to go," I said. "I'm perfectly happy to run off to the park and drink this on the swings, just the two of us." I held up the wine, enticing him. "Come on. I saw on YouTube how you can open a bottle of wine with just a shoe and a hard surface."

"No," he said quickly, and followed it up with a smile. "No. For better or worse, this is the magical community here, and it's time to face the music. This was bound to all come to a head sooner or later. At least this way there will be alcohol."

I reached up and touched the hairline scar on his eyebrow, the one visible scar that had to be the tip of an iceberg full of invisible ones. "I never noticed that before."

He touched his eyebrow self-consciously and said, "Oh, yes. I did that to myself."

I pulled my hand down, but didn't push him on it. "Yeah. I've got a few of those, too."

He took the wine from my hand. "Ready?"

"Yeah." We walked the rest of the way down the street, and before we could hit the doorbell, Peach threw the door open, her arms splayed out in enthusiastic greeting.

"Eliot!" she said, and pulled me into a fierce hug. I hugged her back, matching her enthusiasm. She released me and smiled up at Desmond.

"Hey, there, you," she said. She was gentler reaching out to him, but there was genuine affection in her eyes as she put her arm around his neck and pulled him down to kiss her cheek. Behind her, a bald guy who was only an inch or so taller than Peach approached us.

"Oh, Eliot! This is my Nicky!" Peach reached out

to a swarthy bald dude with smiling eyes and pulled him toward our group. I was kind of amazed, looking at him. It wasn't that he wasn't attractive; he was obviously well toned and there was a sharpness in his eyes that belied an above average intelligence, but he was also on the shorter side and, overall, kind of average looking. It was hard to see how he could be related to someone as stunning as Stacy Easter, never mind winning the love of a bombshell like Peach. But then, not everything is about raw physical attraction, and good people got more attractive as you got to know them, the same way that bad people got less attractive. Nick smiled a warm, crooked-toothed smile, and in an instant, I saw the appeal. I held out my hand to him.

"Hi, Nick. It's so great to meet you. Peach has told me so much about you."

"Yeah, I'm sure all good, right?" He winked at Peach, then pulled me in to kiss me on the cheek. He stepped back, looked up at Desmond, and while his smile waned a bit . . . this was, after all, the same man who had viciously attacked his sister . . . he was all cordiality. Peach had worked on him, it was pretty obvious, but if Nick had any remaining hard feelings for Desmond, he didn't let them show.

"Glad you could make it, man," he said, and shook Desmond's hand.

Desmond's smile was tight, and I felt his discomfort, but he didn't shrink away. "Thank you for the invitation."

"Okay, enough pussyfooting around," Peach said.

She took the wine from Desmond, handed it to Nick, then stepped between me and Desmond and tucked her arms in our elbows. "Let's go face the firing squad."

With that, she led us down the foyer and through the archway into the living room. Stacy and Leo sat in a corner of the couch, and Tobias—clean shaven, and looking healthy if still a little thin—smiled and waved as we walked in.

"Eliot, Desmond," he said. "Thanks for coming."

"Hi, Tobias," I said, and Desmond nodded austerely in Tobias's direction.

Peach cleared her throat. "Okay, this is gonna be painful, so I say we just strip naked, paint ourselves blue, and run at it screaming, what do you say?"

She angled me and Desmond toward Stacy and Leo, and I said, "I'm not sure what that means, but it sounds kind of alarming."

"It's how the Scottish used to go into battle," Desmond said. "To terrify the enemy."

"It's not working," Stacy muttered.

"Stacy has some unresolved feelings about Desmond," Peach said, "and I think we should just resolve them, don't you guys agree?"

"Oh, no," Liv said. I looked up to see her standing in the archway that led to what appeared to be a formal dining room, a platter of appetizers in her hand. She waved at me and Desmond, her smile worried. "Hey, guys. Welcome to my home. Peach, what the hell are you doing?"

"Don't worry, sweetie," Peach said. "We're finishing this up here and now, for good, so we can have a nice dinner."

Tobias and Liv exchanged a look, and Tobias said, "I'm gonna go get a corkscrew."

"Yeah, I'll help you with that," Liv said, escaping behind him out into the dining room.

Peach moved from between me and Desmond and waddled to the big easy chair. "Would you guys like to sit down?"

Desmond and I demurred as she plunked down into her seat. "Okay, who's gonna get us started?"

There was a long silence, and then Desmond cleared his throat. "Perhaps . . ." He visibly swallowed. "Perhaps . . . I . . . sh-should . . ."

Another long silence. Nick leaned one hip against the side of Peach's chair and muttered in singsong, "Told you this was a bad idea."

"Nope," Peach said. "I'm a thousand months pregnant and I have no patience for this crap anymore. Stacy, Leo . . . you guys gotta get over this. Eliot's good people and Desmond is really sorry for what he did. I think you need to give him a second chance, and I think it should start now."

"That's great, Peach," Stacy said coolly. "Want me to tell you what I think?"

"No," Peach said, giving Stacy a loving but firm look, and I could see the mom in her already. "Look, if we were all just people here, then I'd say, 'Whatever,' and let it go. But you guys are all magical. You're going to need each other. When Tobias came back, it was Eliot and Desmond who saved him. Would you have jumped in like that, no questions asked, if the roles were reversed, Stacy?"

Stacy shrugged, but didn't argue.

"Now Eliot's here, and no one knows what the hell is going on with her, but when that shit hits the fan . . ." Peach made a gesture of apology toward me. "Sorry, honey, but we've got some experience here and the shit always hits the fan eventually."

"No, that's fair," I said.

Peach smiled and looked back at Stacy. "When the shit hits the fan, if Desmond is the one who comes to you in need, and you hesitate even for a second, people could get hurt. I won't have it. No." She shook her head and crossed her arms, resting them on top of her massive belly. "It all gets cleared up now. To-night."

Leo had one arm protectively around Stacy's shoulders, but the other hand made a fist in his lap, and I could see his jaw muscles working under his cheek. Desmond looked as horribly uncomfortable as I'd ever seen him, and Stacy was staring blue murder at Peach.

I was on Nick's side; this did not seem like a good idea.

"Maybe we should just go," I said, and touched Desmond's elbow as I moved toward the door. He stayed where he was.

"Perhaps we should, but first . . ." He stepped away from me, toward Stacy and Leo. "I'm not asking your forgiveness. I cannot see how an apology could be adequate for what I've done. I don't blame you in the least for—"

"I don't care whether you blame us or not," Stacy interrupted, her eyes blazing. "Why the hell are you even still here? That's what I don't understand. Why didn't you just leave town, like any *decent human being* would have done?" Her eyes narrowed as she stared him down. "Oh, well, I guess I just answered my own question."

I waited for Desmond to defend himself, to explain that he was here protecting them, but he didn't say anything, just kept his eyes low and stood with his feet braced, like a man on the bow of a ship facing down a hurricane.

"Look, Desmond," Leo said finally, his voice soft and calm, in stark contrast to his girlfriend. "I can forgive what you did to me—"

"I can't," Stacy said through clenched teeth, but Leo squeezed her hand, and she seemed to calm down a bit.

"But I can't forgive what you did to her." Leo's jaw muscles worked, and I could see the toll that staying calm and reasonable was taking on him. "I've tried, but every time I see you, man . . . I just want to kill you. I mean it, I want to smash your head into a wall. It's not who I am. It's not the man I want to be, but . . ." He shook his head, and looked at Peach. "I'm sorry, Peach. I really am."

Again, Desmond said nothing. He just stood there, still as stone, and took it. Much the way he'd taken the punches from Nick in that story Peach told me. He wasn't going to walk away. He wasn't going to deny them their justice. If Leo got up at that moment and tried to kill him, Desmond would let him do it.

Well, I wouldn't.

"You know why he's still here?" I said, stepping forward. "To protect *you*."

"Eliot," Desmond said, but I ignored him.

"Desmond knew that Emerson Streat was probably up to no good, and he stayed here to watch over you, over all of you, and no matter what you do to him, he's going to stay until he knows you're all safe. No matter how much you hate him." I looked at Nick. "Or how badly you beat him."

Nick dropped his eyes to the floor, and I felt a twinge of guilt for making him feel bad, but I had to make my point.

"I wasn't here last year," I said. "I know it was bad, but I didn't see it, so maybe it's easier for me to see him for what he really is. Desmond told me what he did to you, and I know he feels terrible—"

"Eliot," Desmond said again, his voice a little firmer now, but I was already worked up, and not ready to stop.

"He was under the influence of a powerful potion," I said. "He wasn't himself. He's different now. He's kind, and smart and generous. He didn't hesitate to help Tobias when you needed him. Just a few days ago, he asked me to risk his life to protect *you,* and—"

"Eliot!"

The force in his voice was enough to get my attention, and when I looked back at Desmond, his face was red and his eyes were blazing. Not at them.

At me.

"That's enough, Eliot." His voice was even and firm, but he was visibly upset. As our eyes met, the turmoil in his calmed a bit. "Please. Enough."

I looked back at Leo and Stacy, then at Peach and Nick. I couldn't say anything else in Desmond's defense. All I could do was stand beside him.

So that's what I did.

He didn't move. He didn't turn to go toward the door. He didn't speak. He just stood there, ready to take his punishment. I stood steady at his side, ready to take whatever was coming with him.

The silence was long, and excruciating. Peach watched all of us, expectant, and when Nick opened his mouth to say something and break the incredible tension, she put her hand lightly on his knee, and he shut up.

Finally, Leo spoke.

"When you took away my emotions . . . my feelings for Stacy . . ." Leo cleared his throat, and when he spoke again, his voice was gentle. "She was heartbroken. I watched her fall apart, right in front of me, but I couldn't feel anything about it. I left, because I felt it was best for her, but . . . even loving her as much as I did, even knowing how much it would devastate her for me to abandon her . . . I just felt cold about it. It was easy to leave." He raised his head and met Desmond's eyes. "Is that how it was for you?"

Desmond took a while to answer. "I knew what I was doing was wrong."

"But you couldn't feel it," Leo said. "You couldn't *feel* that it was wrong."

Desmond didn't say anything. I moved closer, silent at his side.

"That was *one dose* of that stuff, Leo," Peach said after a while. "Desmond had been taking it, over and over, for years."

Desmond's head moved slightly to the side as if he was dodging something, as though hearing the slightest word in his defense made him physically uncomfortable.

"And you know how guilty you felt when you came back, Leo?" Peach continued, her eyes locked on Leo. "I remember that night you came over and got drunk with Nick. I remember how terrible you felt about leaving Stacy. Desmond got hit with so much more than that, all at once, when Stacy shot him with that reversal potion. Just imagine what that must have been like for him. He could have run off, but he didn't. He stayed. He faced all of us, over and over again, every day."

I was close enough to Desmond that I could feel the tension in his body. His face was stone, his head raised, his body taut, ready to take whatever came at him.

There was another long silence, but then Leo stood up, walked over to Desmond, and held out his hand.

"All right," Leo said. "If you're good, I'm good."

It took Desmond a moment, but he took Leo's hand and they shook. Peach made a sound, and when I looked, I saw tears in her eyes, which made me want to tear up, but I couldn't. I was going to match Desmond's strength, face it all with him, and that meant withstanding whatever the storm threw at us.

Leo stepped back, and all eyes were on Stacy, who stood up as well and walked over to Desmond. She looked him in the eye, crossing her arms over her stomach.

"I felt sorry for you," she said. "That day, when I hit you with that dose, and brought you back. You were so destroyed. Five minutes before, you were going to kill me, and then you were just lying there, a pathetic, weeping huddle on the ground. Peach didn't see it. Neither did Nick, or Leo. I did and it was . . ." She shuddered, remembering. "It was devastating."

She took a deep breath, released it, and went on. "I was ready to forgive you right then, as long as you left. But you stayed, and every time I saw you on the street, or even thought I saw you out of the corner of my eye, it all came back, and it made me afraid. I don't like being afraid. That pissed me off."

Desmond nodded. "I understand."

She glanced at Leo, and her stance softened a bit as she looked back at Desmond. "But I can kinda see now . . . that the guy I'm afraid of *did* leave. He's not here anymore. And I can't forgive you, because you're not him. So . . ."

It was the most awkward hug I've ever seen. Stacy

lifted her arms a little, started to put them back down, and finally placed them stiffly around Desmond's neck. Just as stiffly, Desmond patted her on the back with one hand, and after a moment, they both seemed to relax into it. He held her tighter, with both hands, and in what I imagined to be a rare moment of sweetness from Stacy Easter, she kissed him on the cheek.

"Oh!" Peach stood up as they released each other, and hugged Stacy, then Leo, her eyes brimming with tears. She laughed and looked at Nick. "Bad idea, my *ass*!"

That broke the tension, and everyone laughed, and then Peach looked at me and said, "Don't worry about those two. It was *forever* ago that they slept together, and it didn't mean anything at the time, anyway."

Four sets of wary eyes landed on me, and Nick said, "Jesus, Peach."

"Oh, crap!" Peach put her hand to her mouth and turned wide eyes to me. "Did you not know about that?"

"Oh, that's okay. It doesn't matter. We're not . . ." I motioned awkwardly between me and Desmond. "I mean, we're just . . ."

"Friends," Desmond said, smiling down at me. "Good friends."

My heart did a little jig in response to the warmth on his face. "Yeah. Good friends."

"Oh, *please*," Peach said, and everyone laughed, even Stacy and Leo, and suddenly, it was all okay.

Peach, in direct defiance of all reason, had actually been right about how to fix the situation, and I made a mental note not to underestimate her so easily again.

Liv poked her head in from the dining room at the sound of our laughter and smiled. "Oh, good. Everyone's still alive. You guys hungry?"

"Oh, hell yes," Peach said, and led the charge toward the dining room. Desmond and I were at the back of the pack, and he took my hand and held it, stopping me from moving forward with the crowd. The living room cleared out, and we were alone. I turned to face him.

"You okay?" I asked.

He released a deep breath, and I could see the stress on his face that he refused to show during the confrontation. He took a moment, gathered himself, and gave my hand a squeeze, releasing it quickly.

"Yes," he said finally, and led me into the dining room.

Chapter 13

Peach was tired after dinner, so she and Nick went back to her house next door, and the rest of us walked into town. The sun was lowering, providing a soft pink glow, and as I walked next to Desmond, with the air sweet and warm on my skin, I felt happy and peaceful.

"Did you enjoy dinner?" Desmond asked me when we found ourselves lagging at the back of the pack.

"Yeah," I said. "You?"

"Not at first." He let out a light laugh, less of humor and more of relief. "But . . . yes, I did enjoy it." He stopped and turned to face me. "Thank you for . . . well, just thank you."

"For what?" I snorted. "I didn't do anything. That was all you."

He smiled down at me. "Has anyone ever explained

to you that the proper thing to do when someone thanks you is to graciously say, 'You're welcome'?"

"You Brits," I said, and started walking again. "So mannered. Chill, will you?"

We laughed and walked the rest of the way in comfortable silence, weaving through the crowds and the food carts and the platform where the band played. We found a picnic table on the edge of the celebration, and we listened to the band and waited for the fireworks, making casual chitchat. I don't remember what we said, exactly, because my focus was on searching the crowd for Emerson.

"Would you like to go find him?" Desmond asked me after a while.

"What?" I met his eye and smiled. "I'm sorry. I just . . . I haven't spoken to him since . . . you know . . ."

Desmond jerked his head toward the crowd. "Go on."

"Are you sure?" I glanced at Stacy and Liv, who were laughing about something.

"I think I can take them if they attack. Go. I'll be right here until you get back."

"Okay." I got up and the other four looked up at me. "I'm gonna go . . . try to find my father."

Stacy smiled at me. "Good luck. I've got booze in my car if you need it when you get back."

"Thanks," I said, smiling back at her. "I just might."

The sunlight was starting to dim, and I wandered through the crowd, looking for the familiar, slightly balding red head of Emerson Streat. After a few minutes, I heard his voice say, "Who are you looking for there, punkin?" and I twirled around to see him behind me.

"Oh, hi!" I looked around, thought about making an excuse and escaping, but I just smiled up at him. "I was looking for you, actually. I was wondering if you still wanted to watch the fireworks with me?"

He smiled so wide it took over his whole face, and as he held out his elbow for me to take, I felt strangely awash with happiness, like I had when I was a little girl and he would take me out for ice cream, just the two of us. We walked a little farther out, where the band music wouldn't keep us from being able to hear each other.

"I wanted to tell you something," I said, feeling a little awkward. How do you tell your father that you maybe don't think he's a liar and a cold-blooded, ruthless monster anymore? It's a tough conversation to start.

I never even got the chance to start it, because Emerson held up his hand to silence me, and motioned toward the band, who had started playing Solomon Burke's "Can't Nobody Love You."

Emerson held his hand out to me. "I was going to request that they play 'Happy Birthday,' but I thought this might be better."

Hesitantly, I took his hand. Emerson pulled me into his arms, and we danced. For the first time in memory, I rested my cheek on my father's shoulder and relaxed.

"Do you remember how we used to dance to this when you were a girl?" he said, his voice thick. "You used to stand on my toes and I would twirl you around?"

"Yeah," I said, my own voice quavering. "I remember."

"I wish I could have danced with you like this at your wedding," he said.

I laughed. "No one danced at my wedding. It was at a county courthouse, and then we went out for pizza."

"You should have a big wedding," he said, pulling back to look at me. His eyes were a little misty, which was as close as I'd ever seen my father come to crying.

"Yeah, that won't be happening for a while," I said. "But if it does, maybe we'll dance again then."

"You've grown into such an amazing woman," he said. "I'm really proud of you. I want you to know that."

I took a deep breath. "It's okay. We don't have to do all of this right now. There's time."

He stopped dancing and stepped back from me, holding my hands.

"Well, punkin, things are gonna be different here after tonight," he said. "I wanted to be sure we had this moment first."

"Um, okay," I said, and my heart started pounding, an automatic response to my instinct knowing something my conscious mind was still resisting.

He took my hand in his and walked, leading me

toward where they were setting up the fireworks display. I followed, trying to listen carefully despite the commotion around us.

"You know the story of what happened to your grandmother. My mother." I couldn't see much of his face in the fading light, but I could hear the seriousness in his voice.

"Yes," I said warily, and the muscles in my shoulders tightened.

He gave me a brief smile and looked away. "They talk about the Salem witch trials like that kind of thing is in the past, but it's not. Magicals die every day at the hands of people who don't understand what we are. And no one knows why it's happening, because we hide. We don't talk about who we are. We live on the edge of every society, and if you let it slip for one minute . . ." He took in a deep breath. "If you stop on a road walking for miles with your son on a hot day, a moment where you think you're alone, and have the audacity to make a little water fall from the sky to cool your boy, all it takes is one drunken asshole to see it, and you pay with your life."

I felt the shock at the language; in all of my life, I'd never heard my father say so much as *darn*. He just wasn't that kind of guy. I reached out and touched his arm, and we both stopped walking to turn and face each other.

"Why are you talking about this, Emerson?"

He went on, almost as if he hadn't heard the question. "It's why I didn't want children. I didn't want to love anything so much, something that could be taken away in a vicious act of ignorance and fear. I didn't want to ever have to imagine your suffering, the way I imagined hers for all these years. Wondering what she must have felt, the pain and the terror and the sadness, in those last moments before . . ." He shook his head and raised his eyes to look into mine. "I want you to understand, Josie."

"Emerson?" I said, my eyes filling with tears even as my body told me to run. But I didn't run; I kept my pace, walking at his side, hoping against all hope that this wasn't going the way I knew it was going.

Emerson went on. "I want you to know that everything I've done, I've done so you can live in a world where that kind of thing doesn't happen anymore. You need a place where there's magic." He stopped walking, but didn't look me in the eye. "Just . . . everywhere. Just *everyone*. One town. One place where it's safe to let your guard down for a second. That's all I ever wanted, a place where you could live without ever having to see the things I've seen."

"Emerson?" I could hear the tremor in my voice, so I cleared my throat and spoke louder. "Emerson, you're scaring me. What's going on?"

He pulled on a smile, but I could see the sadness in his eyes. "I know you may never speak to me again after this, and I'm really sorry about your fella there, but I did what I had to do, to get you here. To keep you safe."

Another firework went off. Red sparks turned to

white, and then green. My heart jumped in my throat, and I looked toward the picnic benches to find Desmond . . . until I realized that he wasn't talking about Desmond, and the world began to spin around me.

"Oh my god." I stepped back from him and stumbled on my heel. Emerson reached out to steady me, but I pulled my arm away. "You killed Judd?"

"I was running out of time for you to find out who and what he was," Emerson said. "I had to make a call."

"Make a call? Jesus, this isn't fucking football. This is my *life*."

"And he was a bad part of it," Emerson said. "You weren't happy. Hell, I could tell that, and all I saw were pictures of you. Going to the grocery store, fighting with that no-account on the lawn. Wasting your time, your potential. Every day spent in that life was a waste of everything you are. I couldn't watch it anymore."

"No one asked you to watch. *Jesus*." I put my hand to my forehead and tried to process it all. "And Christy McNagle? Did you mean to kill her, too? God, Emerson! What if Seamus had been in that car with them?" Another firework went off with a big explosion, and then tiny white flames shot out into the sky. I was so jumpy that I cried out, but Emerson just looked up into the sky.

Emerson shook his head. "That was unfortunate. But sometimes, collateral damage—"

"Oh my god . . . I can't listen to this . . ." I started to stumble away from him, but he grabbed my elbow in a tight grip and turned me to face him.

"You ran off last time, and I lost you for sixteen years," he said. "If you go again this time, I want you to know that I'm not some monster. I did what I did for my family. I did it for you, Josie. Because I love you and I want you safe. And if you can't understand that . . ." He shook his head and shot me a victimized look. "Well, then, I guess there's nothing I can do about that."

Everything around me slowed down, and I felt every second like grains of sand slowly falling through an hourglass. I could feel my heart pounding, and while I knew it was beating fast, each beat thrummed through me with painful slowness. "Emerson, what did you do?"

He didn't seem to hear me, so I grabbed his arm and yanked until he looked at me.

"What did you do?"

He pulled me by my shoulders and kissed me on the forehead.

And that's when the fireworks went off.

At first, I thought it was strange; the sun wasn't even down yet. Then I looked over, and saw a blue bolt shoot out, but instead of going upward into the sky, it arced straight at me, and time stopped.

I didn't feel it hit. It didn't feel like anything. Sunlight, I guess, a little, but strangely colder. I held out my hands, on instinct, and then looked down at my feet. The light went through me, arcing out of me in a million little pieces, dancing from me to the people around me, then going ever outward. It seemed like an endless blast, circling outward over everyone. I couldn't tell how far it went, but it was well past as far as I could see.

It was a second, maybe even a nanosecond, and then I held my hand up and looked at it as the last of the blue light danced and died over my fingertips.

No one seemed hurt; the crowd roared with delight at fireworks the likes of which they had never seen before.

I turned around, looking for the picnic table where Desmond and everyone was, but I'd lost my sense of space. I twirled around again, and by the time I looked back at where Emerson had been, he was gone. More fireworks were going off as the sun set, and I looked for him in the flashes of light, but he had disappeared.

"Eliot! Eliot!" Desmond was suddenly at my side, one hand on my upper arm, the other running over me, as though checking for injury. "What happened? Are you all right?"

"No," I said, and vomited into the grass.

"So what do we know?" Liv asked, pouring coffee for all of us in her kitchen, as it promised to be a long night. We hadn't woken Peach and Nick; we wanted to wait until we had some idea of what was going on.

"We know that he wants to spread magic," I said. "And that the blue light was the same thing I saw in Lott's Cove when I was a kid. Last time, people became symptomatic within twelve hours, their magic activating immediately or at the next switch between day and night, depending on what kind of magic manifests. And within twenty-four hours . . ." I looked at Desmond, who reached across the Formica table and took my hand, and the room went silent.

"And it'll just be everybody?" Stacy said. "Everyone in town is going to have magical powers now?"

"If it works the same way it did last time," I said, "then at least everyone touched by the light. Everyone who was within the blast zone . . . yes. I would expect that they would. That would make everyone in town magical, and that's what Emerson wanted."

"But what about free will?" Leo asked, glancing from Stacy to Liv and back to me. "Isn't that a thing with magic? Don't things go wrong if you mess with free will?"

"I don't know. Desmond, you want to field that one?" Stacy said in a snarky tone. All eyes turned to her, and she sighed. "Sorry, Des. Old habits."

"It's quite all right," Desmond said, and looked at Leo. "Free will is an ethical consideration. Magic acts the same whether it was used with permission or not."

"The good news is, some of the people with night magic are just going to go to sleep, so there's a good chance things will be quieter tonight than tomorrow morning," Tobias said. "But there's still going to be some panic starting tonight. Even if there aren't any bad side effects this time, getting sudden magical power has a destabilizing effect. It might make sense for us to start canvassing the town, keep an eye out for anything unusual, and try to calm things where we can."

"The thing is, using the power makes it worse, but people who suddenly get power love to use it," I said. "If you see someone using their magic, you have to convince them to stop, then . . . I don't know." I looked at Liv. "Bring them back here?"

"Absolutely," Liv said. "I'll call Addie and Grace and have them hang out here to take in anyone we find. Let's make sure we've got everyone's numbers in our phones before we head out, so we can keep each other informed."

"I think I should look for Emerson," I said. "I don't know if I'll find him, but if I do, I might be able to get more solid information. If he's been running trials, it might be safe. But if not . . ."

I looked at Liv, and the room went quiet.

"What?" Liv said.

"Magicals were affected, too," I said. "This killed my mother, without her even using her power much. I think just having residual power put her at risk. And given that you're unusually powerful . . ."

Liv stared at me for a moment as she processed

what I was saying, then gave a sad smile. "I'm the canary in the coal mine."

Tobias's face went to stone, and he stood up. "But we don't know that it's the same thing this time."

"We don't," I said. "And the symptoms are very similar to Desmond's trials from last year. He has some potions that might put things off for a while."

"But not enough to keep an entire town going for long," Stacy said.

"I'll be in my lab," Desmond said. "Making as much as I can as quickly as I can, but it's not a fast process, and my supplies are limited."

Stacy stood up, all business. "I'll grab what I've got and meet you there. I can double your speed."

"Let's go." Leo stood up and started toward the door, and Desmond and Stacy conferred about what she'd need to grab from her lab. Tobias and Liv looked at each other, fear in both of their eyes, and I walked over to them.

"Don't use your power deliberately," I said to Liv. "If it starts to spark on its own, and you can't control it, call Desmond immediately. If you feel dizzy, call." I looked at Tobias. "Stay by her side. Once it starts, things move pretty fast."

Tobias nodded grimly, and I wanted to tell them how sorry I was, but there wasn't time. I turned and headed out the front door without saying another word to any of them.

I had to find my father.

* * *

He wasn't at his office, of course, and I had no idea
where he lived. I hadn't asked. I hadn't wanted to know.
To find the person who would know, I had to head
straight to Happy Larry's.

The place was packed, and as far as I could see from
a quick look around, no one was using magic. Based
on my experience, the Happy Larry patrons were not
town-event types. Most likely, they'd been in this brick
building all night, which meant there was a chance
they would have been unaffected by the blast. But it
was a Saturday night, and it was crowded, so finding
Amber Dorsey was gonna take a few minutes. I made
my way to the bar and waved Larry over.

"You comin' in to work tonight?" Larry said. "I
gotta tell you, I could use the help."

"No, sorry. Hey, have you seen Amber tonight?"

Larry nodded, then jerked his head over toward the
pool tables. Of course.

I tapped the bar. "Thanks."

I wove through the crowd to find Amber lining up
her shot, surrounded by guys. Pool balls were spread
all over the table, and Amber was working her angle.

"Now how much do I get when I sink this?" she
asked.

"Between us?" One of guys, a young blond kid who
I'd served when he'd turned twenty-one last week, motioned among all of the guys there. "Forty bucks."

"Put your money down," Amber said, and they all
laid their cash on the rim of the table, then went back

to admiring the exposed tattoo on her lower back. I, however, was actually watching her play. She lined up the shot, wiggled her ass a little bit to distract attention, and opened her hand as she moved the stick. Smoky, orange strings of light shot out from her fingers, and a four ball went sailing straight into the corner pocket. The guys all let out pretend jeers as Amber collected their money and stuffed it into her back pocket.

"Pleasure doing business with you, boys," she said. "Who wants to test me again?"

I stepped into view, and Amber smiled when she saw me. "Eliot!" She threw out her bony arms and wrapped them around my neck. I hugged her back for appearances, and was surprised by how frail she felt in my arms.

"I'm gonna take Amber away for a bit, guys," I said, grabbing her hand. "It'll just be a minute."

There was some complaining from the guys, but I pulled Amber by the hand and dragged her outside.

"You already had a four ball on the table," I said. "You should have played a ball you already sank. They might have noticed."

"What, those guys?" Amber said, popping her gum. "Please. They're dumber than the damn pool cues. Besides, all the balls were on the table. I hadn't sunk a one." She laughed and patted her bulging back pocket. "But Momma's on a roll tonight."

"Not anymore, Momma," I said, taking her by the elbow and pulling her toward my car. "You're coming with me."

She yanked her arm out of my grip and said, "The hell I am. I got rent to pay, and your dad canned me today, so I need to go rustle up some green." She turned to go back into the bar, but I raced to block her.

"What? He fired you? Why?"

Amber gave an uncoordinated shrug, and I could tell she'd had a fair amount to drink. "I don't know. Closing up shop. Leaving town. Said he'd done what he came here to do and now he was hitting the road. Whatever. But seeing as I don't have a job anymore, I'm gonna have to hustle for a while, so if you'd be so kind as to let me get back to that shit—"

"Happy Larry will hire you," I said quickly. "You can work here. You're good in the bar, and he's gonna need help, because I'm quitting."

Her eyes narrowed at me. "Yeah? What, you running off with your dad?"

"No. I'm staying, but . . ." I shook my head. "It doesn't matter. I need you to stop using your magic, and I need you to come with me where I can keep an eye on you. The magic's dangerous, and—"

"Oh, *fuck*," Amber said, throwing her arms in the air. "You're gonna give me a hard time about that? I got magical pool balls, and a crowd full of guys happy to give me their money. Exactly why should I listen to you?"

It was then that I noticed that Amber was weaving on her feet. I reached out and grabbed her arm to stabilize her.

"Oh, man," she said, putting a fist to her chest. "I knew I shouldn'ta had that boilermaker."

And with that, she pitched to the side, her eyes rolling back in her head. I caught her before she fell and dragged her into my car, then got in and called Desmond to tell him to meet me at Liv's.

Chapter 14

Frankie Biggs met me at the curb when I got to Liv's. Without a word, he gathered Amber up in his arms and carried her inside. I got out of the car and met Addie on the porch steps. She looked really upset, and my heart jumped in panic.

"Is it Liv?" I said, and Addie shook her head.

"No, she's fine, far as I know." She nibbled her lip and nodded in the direction Frankie had taken Amber. "What's up with Amber?"

"I don't know yet. Is Desmond here?"

Addie stared out into the night sky, as if she hadn't heard me, so I touched her arm.

"Addie?"

"Hmmmm?" She turned to face me. "Um . . . no. Not yet. He should be here soon." Her eyes filled with tears and she said, "Oh, Eliot, I'm so, so sorry."

I led her to the porch swing and we both sat down.

"What's going on?"

"I knew what he was doing," she said. "I helped him."

"What?" The air went out of me.

Addie's eyes filled. "I thought it would be nice. You know? I had magic two years ago, for just one night, and it was amazing. I don't know . . . I guess I just thought . . . the way he talked, he made it sound like we were just giving the whole town ice cream, you know?"

"Yeah," I said sadly. "I know."

"He explained how persecuted magicals are, how dangerous life can be for you all, and I wanted to make a safe place for you, all of you. But it wasn't just that. I wanted . . . I wanted to feel the way I did that one night . . ."

She raised one hand and moved her fingers. Smoky strings of yellow light moved around her fingertips like storm clouds, and a small lace doily fell from her fingertips onto the swing between us.

"Don't do that," I said. "Don't use your power."

"Why not? It's what I traded everyone's life for, right? So *I* could have magic. So *I* could have adventure." She stared out into the street, her expression despondent. "I have a good life. I've got a wonderful wife and we have enough money to live a peaceful life here in this incredible place where I have friends . . . I mean, who could want more than that?"

"Addie, I'm sorry, but do you know where he went? My father? I need to find him."

She shook her head. "No. I'm sorry." She stared out into the night. "He told me no one would get hurt, and I believed him. But even if no one did get hurt, I messed with free will. I smuggled the firework he gave me into the rotation, and set it off on his signal tonight because I am a stupid, foolish old woman." She turned to face me, her eyes full of tears. "I'm so sorry."

I put my arm around her shoulders and rested my head against hers. "My father is a devious man, and he's smart and charming. He knows how to use people to get what he wants from them. You didn't know what you were dealing with. You couldn't have known."

She nodded, but didn't seem comforted at all. "For two years in a row, we've had people coming here and messing with magic. For two years, I sat on the sidelines and watched, wishing it was me. Even when it got dangerous, even when I knew it was hell for Liv, or Stacy . . . I wanted it to be me. I wanted adventure. I wanted some silly little power, so I could feel special. So I could play with the rest of you. And now . . ." She picked up the doily and held it daintily in her fingers. "Now, I've ruined everything, for *this*."

I looked up to see that Desmond pulled up in front of the house. I took Addie's hand in mine and squeezed it.

"You're forgiven," I said. "Whatever you did was his fault, not yours. He lied to you and he made you think things that weren't true, and none of it is your fault, okay? But right now, we need you to be strong and take care of these people inside. And when this is all done, we'll talk more, okay?"

She sniffed, then squared her shoulders and stood up. "Okay." And with that, she took a deep breath and went back inside. I walked over to the steps and met Desmond, throwing my arms around his neck. He hugged me back, but when we released each other, we were all business.

"Amber?" he said, and I led him inside. I had no idea where Amber was, but I figured she'd been taken to a bedroom, which I assumed was upstairs, so that's where we went. Inside, there were maybe ten people milling about, and Addie, playing the hostess along with another woman, tall and striking, with a sharp bob the color of steel wool. I figured it must be Grace, Addie's wife. I looked forward to meeting her, but that would have to wait.

"I found her at Happy Larry's," I told Desmond as we made our way up the stairs. "She'd been using her magic, but she'd also been drinking. She mentioned a boilermaker, which is a full beer with a shot of whisky for a chaser. She's eighty-five pounds dripping wet. That's enough to knock her out. It might not be the magic."

We got to the landing, and could see Frankie sitting next to a bed through an open door, so we went that way. Amber lay passed out on top of the coverlet, which Frankie had pulled up and over her from one side.

"She's still out," Frankie said unnecessarily as we walked in. Desmond moved past him and sat down next to Amber. He took Amber's wrist in his fingers, and my guess was he was feeling for her pulse. Frankie and I watched, tense and silent, as Desmond worked on Amber. After a moment, Amber groaned, and Frankie said, "I know that sound," and ran to grab the trash can. He was there in a shot, and when Amber vomited over the side of the bed, he caught it expertly. It was romantic, kind of, in its own gross way. Desmond stepped back to hang out with me while Frankie cleaned up after Amber.

"I can't be sure if her reaction is to the magic or the alcohol," Desmond said. "I would hesitate to give her anything just yet. One, it could do more damage than good if she's not reacting to the magic. And two, it's likely she'll throw it up anyway, and we've only got so many doses."

"How many?" I asked.

He gave me a grim look. "Not enough. Stacy's back at my lab working, but even if she works fast, we're going to run out of supplies before long."

"Jesus, Amber!" There was a clunk as a pool ball fell to the floor, and Frankie was holding his cheek. "Why you gotta hit me in the face?"

Amber pushed up on her elbows, and had sobered up enough to give Frankie a withering look.

"Amber, I told you not to use your magic," I said.

"I'm not doing it on purpose!" Amber said, and another pool ball shot from her hands, putting a dent in the ceiling before crashing to the floor, then disappearing.

"I feel like fucking hell," Amber whined and fell back onto the pillows.

Desmond touched my arm. "Peppermint tea and crackers. If we're going to keep the potion down her, we're going to need to settle her stomach."

"On it," I said, and headed for the door. I wandered downstairs just as Leo was bringing two teenage girls into the house. I gave him a quick wave and went into the kitchen. I put a kettle on, and started searching the cupboards for crackers. I found some, set them on the counter, and had to wait for the water to boil. Not having something to do was making me crazy, so I pulled my phone out of my pocket and dialed my father's number.

"This is Emerson Streat." His pleasant tones dripped southern sunshine through the voice-mail recording. "I'm busy with somethin' or other at the moment, but if you'll leave a message, I'll call you back as soon as I can."

There was a beep, and I hesitated, because just the sound of his voice broke my heart. "It's me. I just wanted you to know that your little experiment here has gone south, fast. You were in the blast zone this time, so I'm hoping like hell that means it'll all be okay, because I've never known you to be a man to risk his own skin. But let me tell you this; if anyone here dies, and you survive, I will find you, and I'll kill you myself, you son of a bitch."

And with that, I hung up the phone.

By three in the morning, people were splayed all over Liv's house. I stepped over the sleeping bodies as I walked through the darkened living room, looking for magical sparks happening in their sleep; there was nothing. That was a good sign, and Desmond had managed to stabilize Amber with his potion, but two things worried me. One, Liv and Tobias hadn't returned, and when I called Liv's number, all I got was voice mail.

And two, sunrise was coming. Night magic tended to be quieter than day magic, because most people slept during the night. When daylight hit, Nodaway Falls was going to be sparking magic all over the place. Between Stacy and Desmond, we had enough potion to keep maybe half the people well for a couple of days.

Something was going to have to be done. Hell if I knew what, though.

I felt a warm hand at the base of my back and turned to see Desmond behind me. Silently, he took my hand and led me through the hallway, into Liv's kitchen. He settled me down on one of the chairs at the Formica table, and then went about fixing coffee.

"I am enough of a realist to know that asking you to get some sleep will do no good," he said, "so it would make me feel better if I could at least make you something to eat."

"What about you?" I said. "You've got to be just as exhausted as I am."

"I'm British," he shot back dryly. "We don't tire. Toast?"

I wasn't hungry, but I nodded. He seemed to need something to do, and I could take a few bites of toast without throwing up. Probably.

"I keep running it through my head," I said. "What is it about the wild magic that makes me immune? And how can we give that to everyone else?"

Desmond sighed. "It could be anything. Without trials and controls, we can't possibly test for anything." He popped bread in the toaster and went to get a mug from the cabinet. "Cream? Sugar?"

"Black," I said. "To go with my mood."

Desmond put a cup of coffee in front of me, and I rose up and took a sip. My stomach didn't want anything, but I knew he needed to feed me, so I let him. I raised my head and looked at him. "How are you?"

He looked away, and headed toward the toaster. "Me? I'm fine."

I got up and followed him. "It happened? Your magic?"

Desmond's entire body stiffened, and I had the answer to my question. He turned to face me. "You can't worry about me, Eliot."

"Of course I'm going to worry about you, you idiot." I touched my hand to his face. "What kind of magic is it? Creative, perception, source?"

"Perception," he said. "I briefly made Amber's room

look like a forest. It was just for a moment and controlled, and no one else saw, so let's just let it go for now."

"Perception is the best one to have," I said. "It requires the least amount of magical energy. But still. You took a potion, right?"

Desmond didn't respond until the toaster popped, at which point he said, "Oh, look. Toast."

"Desmond—"

"I'm not having any ill effects." Desmond made himself busy with the toast. "I'm not light-headed, nothing has happened out of my control, and I haven't used my magic since the initial event." He picked up the paper plate with the toast on it and guided me back to the kitchen table. "Don't worry. I'm monitoring the situation."

"Yes, but you realize that they all need you, right? It's like that thing on the plane, put the oxygen mask on yourself first? We can't help these people without you."

Desmond shrugged. "Stacy is quite capable—"

I grabbed his hand. "I can't do it without you." I stared down at our hands, fingers intertwined, and my mind went blank with panic. "If anything happens to you, I won't be able to do anything. You're my rock. I'm leaning on you, and if you—"

"Shhhh." He pulled me up into his arms and held me. "I'm fine. I promise you, if I start to show symptoms, I will take a potion. But we have too few to use them indiscriminately. I just need you to trust me." He pulled back and put his hands on either side of my face. "Can you do that?"

Before I could form a verbal answer, I felt it in my bones. *Yes.* And at first, it shocked me. I had loved men before. I loved my father. I had loved Judd. But I'd never trusted anyone, not until now. Not until Desmond. I never even noticed how easy it had been to share everything of myself with him. I'd never had that with Judd, even on our best days.

"Thank you," I said.

He gave me a surprised look. "For what?"

"For telling me that stupid story about your Kentucky upbringing," I said. "For believing me when I told you I wasn't in league with my father. For bringing that stupid picture of Judd back to me. For telling me my dog was deaf. For being . . . I don't know. For being you, you big idiot."

He smiled. "Are we making our touching confessions now? I apologize. I haven't prepared any remarks."

"God, you really do get more British when things get intense, don't you?"

He laughed. Our eyes met, and the world seemed to calm around us. I could hear a gentle breeze, and . . . crickets?

I glanced around, and we were no longer in Liv's kitchen. Well, we were, I knew we were, but it didn't look like Liv's kitchen. Dancing lights zipped around us; not fireflies, but fairies. Below us, the floor appeared to be moss, and above us, the ceiling had turned into a canopy of tree leaves, with twinkling stars peeking through.

"Desmond," I breathed, my heart starting to pound.

"Don't worry. It's not out of control. I feel fine." He held his hand up between us, and I could see orange ropes of smoky light dancing around his fingertips. "I just wanted a moment . . . something special . . . just us . . ."

He took my face in his hands and kissed me, at first soft and sweet, and then with more urgency. We both knew this might be the last moment we had, just the two of us, and even with things left unsaid and half said, it was perfect.

When we pulled back, the kitchen was a kitchen again, with the exception of one tiny little fairy, glowing orange and flying around us, which disappeared a moment later.

I smiled up at Desmond and touched his face. "You're a big idiot."

He kissed my nose, then turned me toward the table and patted my behind. "Eat your toast."

Two hours later, on the brink of sunrise, Tobias carried Liv through the front door. Her arms were draped around his neck, and at first it looked like maybe she had just fallen asleep at the end of what must have been an exhausting night searching the town for wayward magicals, but once I saw the look on Tobias's face, I knew there was more to it than that. The yellow magical sparks that zipped around the tips of Liv's fingers were lazy and sputtering, like a light that's about to go out for good. Desmond and I followed Tobias up the stairs to Liv's room, where he put her on the bed and sat next to her, holding her hand.

"She just collapsed. She wasn't even using her magic. It was so quick."

Desmond and I exchanged looks. It was time.

"I'll go get my bag," Desmond said, rushing out and heading to Amber's room, where all the supplies were at the moment. I touched Tobias's shoulder.

"Desmond has potions that can help," I said, hoping that they would work as well on Liv as they had on Amber, but we hadn't tried it on a natural magical yet, so who the hell knew? "It'll be okay."

"I know what happened in Lott's Cove," Tobias said, his voice monotone as he watched Liv. "Everyone in ASF knew. When your father got here, I received an assignment to keep an eye on him. I wouldn't have left Liv, and ASF wouldn't have taken me out of town, not when they had a sleeper agent right here. I must have found out something—"

"Which is why Emerson kidnapped you." Of course he had. Of *course* he had. And I had known it, deep down, I knew he'd been the one to take Tobias. I just hadn't wanted to believe it, because I wanted my father to be a decent man. So I let my guard down, and now the whole town was paying the price because I wanted my daddy back.

Desmond walked in and sat on the edge of Liv's

bed, all business. He pulled a hypodermic needle from his bag and pulled the plastic cap off.

"She's out," I said to Tobias. "The only way to administer the potion . . ."

"Yeah, I know."

I patted Tobias's arm. He looked pale and sick, but I didn't want to say anything to him. He was obviously so worried about Liv, and until he collapsed, too, there was no point in fretting over him.

I followed Tobias's anxious stare and watched Desmond, who was ably flicking the hypodermic needle, getting the bubbles out to prepare it for injection. It was amazing, how strong he looked, even in the soft blue of the waxing daylight. Most of the people who'd come in had an ashen look to them, which could be attributed to the shock. Suddenly realizing you had magical powers tended to take the wind out of the sails of a normal person. But Desmond looked so strong, his color was good, his . . .

I blinked, really watching Desmond. He had night magic, and he'd used it, twice, with total control, and no ill effects. Given that, and the fact that he'd been up all night, shouldn't he look worse?

"Oh my god," I breathed, my heart racing as the realization hit.

Desmond turned to look at me, worry in his eyes. "Eliot."

"Step back," I said, and moved to Liv's side. Her hands were clammy and cold, despite it being summer, despite the blankets that covered her. Her incredible power had advanced the effects. This was where everyone in town was headed . . . Addie, Grace, Nick and Peach and the baby . . . unless . . .

"Eliot!" Desmond shouted as I threw my magic through Liv, putting everything I had into it, wanting to see how far my power coupled with hers might take us. Blue sparks exploded through the room, as much a result of Liv's power as mine, and my ears sort of hollowed out, and all I could hear was a loud ringing. I felt the impact of a forceful slam into my back before I realized I'd been thrown across the room, and my consciousness dipped to black as my breath flew out of me.

I came to in Desmond's arms, sputtering for air, and he pushed my hair back from my face, gently. I grabbed his hands, needing to get to my feet, and he helped me, holding me up as my wobbly knees tried to stabilize. Tobias was sitting on the bed next to Liv, who was pushing herself up on her elbows. She looked a little stunned, but even in the weak morning light, I could see that her color was better.

"What was that?" she said, putting her hand to her head.

"Wild magic." I looked at Desmond. "You're fine. You've gotten your power, used it twice, had everything under control. Not so much as a wobble. What's different about you?"

His face cleared in understanding. "You ran your magic through me."

"It's got to be some kind of inoculation or something," I said. "Maybe . . . maybe whatever my father's been able to do with the electricity only does half the job. If I run power through everyone . . ."

I laughed with the thrill of realization, but Desmond wasn't smiling.

"What?"

He and Tobias shared a look. "You just ran it through Liv, and you can barely walk."

"Psssht. I'm fine." I waved my hand in the air dismissively, hoping he wouldn't see that it was still shaking. My knees still felt a little wobbly, too, but I didn't care.

There was a knock on the door. We all ignored it, but a moment later it opened anyway, and Amber stumbled in.

"What the fuck just happened in here? There was blue light all over the house." She looked down at the old metal doorknob. "And where the hell did Liv get these doorknobs?"

I glanced at the doorknob. It was shaped like a potion flask. I shot a questioning look at Tobias, and he shrugged.

"The blue light," Desmond said softly. "It was all over the room."

"Liv's magic," I said, looking at Desmond. "It must have . . . amplified it or something."

Amber's color was good, and as tough as her night had been, she seemed strong. I stepped away from Desmond. My knees were still a little wobbly, but they held me up. "Amber, how are you feeling?"

She gave me a wary look. "Fine. But you don't look so good."

"Eliot," I heard Desmond say behind me, but I pushed out into the hallway, using the walls as support as I made my way down the stairs and into the living room. People were up and milling about, most of them looking confused, but all of them with good color, none looking weak and pallid the way that Amber and Liv had, the way that my mother had.

It was the wild magic. I wasn't a danger to this community; I was the only one who could save it.

Desmond stepped down beside me, his hand going protectively around my waist. I glanced at the front doorknob; it was normal.

"I don't think it went much past the house," I said, "but I want to go check on Nick and Peach next door."

"I'll go with you," he said, but I put my hand on his arm to stop him.

"Liv is still weak," I said. "And if anyone else from town starts presenting symptoms now that day magic will be hitting, people are going to need to know where to find you." I smiled up at him and kissed him on the cheek. "I'll just be next door."

He nodded, but I could feel his eyes watching me as I headed toward the door, so I willed my gait to be steady and strong, and only allowed my knees to buckle a bit after I'd shut the door behind me.

Chapter 15

"Oh my god," Peach said as she poured coffee for me and Nick. "I can't believe you fuckers didn't wake us up!"

"Sleeping was safest, for both of you and the baby," I said. "If you both have night magic—and based on the fact that I just gave you both pretty upsetting news and there have been no sparks, that's what I'm guessing—then you shouldn't have any adverse effects until tonight. And I'm hoping that I'll have this whole thing resolved by tonight." I looked at Peach, who was standing with her hand pressed against her lower back. "You okay?"

"Gotta stand," she said, stretching. "If I sit, the kid kneads my bladder like bread dough, and if I pee one more time this morning, I'm gonna have to kill some-one."

"I'm sorry," I said, speaking as much to the tremendous wriggling bulge as to Peach. "I should have trusted my instincts with my father and known he was gonna try this again. I don't know what effect any of this might have on the baby . . ."

"Pffft," Peach said, giving a dismissive wave. "Honey, I've been an obstetrics nurse for ten years. There are women who run every kind of risk known to man. They drink coffee, they don't exercise, they fall from ladders. I mean stupid, stupid stuff. And most of the time, the babies are fine. There are others who do everything right, I mean *everything,* and the baby still doesn't . . ." She gave a sad smile and patted her stomach. "It's all a crapshoot. Life is risk. We do the best we can, we throw back a shot of Jack Daniel's when we need it, and we move forward. It'll be what it'll be."

I smiled up at her, then looked at Nick. "I can see why you fell for this one."

"Yeah," Nick said, looking proudly at his wife. "Most people think it's because she's so pretty. But I would have married this one if she looked like a foot."

I laughed. I really liked these two, and knowing that I was doing what I was doing to save them, and their baby, would make it all a lot easier.

I looked at Peach. "I need your help this morning. I need a list of everyone who's been touched by magic in this town. The longer they've had it in their systems, the better."

Peach nodded, looking at Nick and then back at me. "Yeah. Why?"

"I have something I need to do," I said, "and I'm gonna need . . . amplifiers. Not you, because you're pregnant and . . ."

Peach opened her mouth to talk, so I spoke louder.

". . . and I won't be able to do what I have to do if you're there. You'll distract me. I can't have it."

Peach closed her mouth and gave me a nod of grudging acceptance.

I went on. "Liv is down for the day, and Tobias is doing something else for me. But the rest of them . . ." I looked at Nick. "How quickly can you get them all to the town square? At the same place where the fireworks went off last night?"

Nick shrugged. "I don't know. An hour, maybe. I can round 'em all up in my truck."

Peach eyed Nick again, a worried expression on her face, but when she spoke, she spoke to me. "Why do you need those people?"

"They've all had magic before," I said. "They'll have the most residual power, and I just need a little extra to do what I have to do. That core group will give us the most bang for our buck."

She pulled Nick's hand instinctively over her belly. "Is it gonna hurt them?"

"No," I said, truthfully. "At least, not if things work the way I think they're going to."

She lowered the hand holding Nick's and eyed me. "What about you?"

I smiled and pushed up from the table. "Make the calls, okay? Tell them it's really, really important. Oh, and tell them to remove all of their jewelry. Amber had a piercing this morning that . . ." I sighed. "You know what, just tell them no metal. Safety precaution."

Nick stood up. "I'll bring 'em to the square," he said. "One hour."

"Thanks." I started toward the door, turning back for a quick wave before I left. "It was really nice, you know, meeting you guys."

"Wait." Peach waddled over to me and pulled me into her arms for one last hug, then released me and stuck a warning finger in my face. "Whatever it is you're planning, you better come back or I'm gonna kick your ass from here to Albuquerque."

"Got it," I said, and left.

I couldn't go back to Liv's without making what I was about to do harder on both Desmond and myself, so I headed out into town, walking without really thinking where I was going, keeping an eye on my watch so I'd know when I had to make it back to the town square. I called Liv's house and got Tobias on the phone and asked him to keep Desmond busy, to physically trap him at Liv's if he had to. I couldn't deal with Desmond right now. I couldn't even think about him. I had to stay focused.

So I thought about other things. Nothing important. Nothing that mattered. I didn't have the strength to think about my endangered friends, or my missing

father, or my dead husband. I thought about putting
a raised garden bed in front of the house, resurrecting
my lawn, maybe painting the exterior of my house. I
imagined all the changes I would make, spending
money in my head that I didn't have, but it didn't matter. None of it was going to happen anyway, because
by that afternoon, I figured I would most likely be
dead. The magic I'd run through everyone in Liv's
house had taken a chunk out of me; my hands were still
shaking, and I'd thrown up twice since leaving Peach's
house. I couldn't imagine getting magic through the
whole town, even with all the help Peach was assem-
bling, and living to tell the tale.

Oddly, I wasn't really scared. When I didn't know
what was happening, or what I could do about it, I
was petrified. But knowing what my job was, even
though it would likely kill me, gave me an odd sense
of peace.

I walked down my driveway, and the first thing I
saw was Judd's crappy blue Chevy truck sitting right
where I'd left it when Desmond had come to pick me
up the night before. I'd put Seamus outside before we'd
gone, and had set water and food out for him by his
doghouse, just in case I ended up spending the night
at Desmond's. The thought seemed so funny now, that
I could have just innocently spent the night with my
boyfriend, rather than dealing with the consequences
of my father's single-minded ambitions.

"Seamus!" I called out, knowing he couldn't hear
me, but still. It felt good to say his name. "Seamus!"

I walked around the house to the side yard where I saw Seamus, sleeping half out of his doghouse. It made me tear up to see him there, just snoring away. Part of me wanted to let him sleep, but I couldn't take the chance of not saying good-bye to him, so I gently rubbed the scruff of his neck. He raised his head, then got up and came toward me, tail wagging. I walked him over to the side steps and sat down, patting him as I spoke.

"I'm gonna try to come home, sweetheart," I said. "But if I don't, I'm gonna need you to look after Desmond, okay? He's kind of hopeless. Can you do that for me?"

Seamus wagged his tail and lay down next to me, resting his head on my lap. I sat there, rubbing his neck, enjoying what time I had left.

When my phone rang, I was expecting it to be Desmond, wondering where the hell I was, but instead, the ID text just read, "Unknown Number." I knew who it was, and accepted the call.

"Punkin?" His voice sounded weak, and tired, which was no surprise.

"Emerson," I said, trying to keep my voice calm, even as my hands were shaking. "Where are you?"

I focused on Seamus, petting his head and finding comfort in his presence.

"In a hotel room," he said. "I'll be gone by the time anyone finds me. I just wanted to call so you would know what happened."

I sighed. "Are you in town? I've got a . . . cure.

Everyone here in town is going to be fine. Can you get here?"

There was a long hesitation. "No. I laid my lot with those people there. That's how much I believed it was going to be okay. Our small trials all worked out fine." He let out a long, shaky breath. "It must have been the scale of it that made it go bad."

"Jesus," I breathed. "You've been running trials? Even after Lott's Cove?"

He gave a weak, wheezy laugh. "It's my life's work, punkin." He sounded awful, much worse than anyone else I'd seen so far.

"Emerson, have you been using your magic?"

The line went silent, and I felt a jolt of panic run through me. "Emerson?"

"So, you say you've got a cure brewing? Desmond work up a concoction to save the day?"

I entertained an angry, vengeful thought about telling him the truth for a moment, but only for a moment. Emerson Streat was dying alone in a hotel room somewhere, and it seemed cruel to tell him what was really happening. All the man wanted was a happy ending for me, where I could live openly and magically. As incredibly single-minded and reckless as he'd been about getting there, I just didn't see the point in telling him that he'd killed his only child along with himself. It just seemed mean, and honestly, I didn't have the heart to do it.

"Yeah," I said. "I'm pretty sure everyone's going to be all right."

I felt as much as heard the sigh of relief. "You're a good girl, Josie."

I stayed on the line for a while, listening to him breathe. After a while, I couldn't hear that anymore, even though the line was still open. I disconnected from my end and held my phone in my hands for a moment.

It was time.

I kissed Seamus on the top of his head and stood up. "Gotta get moving, baby. You wanna come inside? It's gonna be a little hot out today, and this shouldn't take too long. Desmond will come and get you in a while."

I stood up and opened the side door, entering through the kitchen, and that's when I saw them.

Gerbera daisies.

Everywhere.

They were left in pretty little piles on the kitchen counter. They covered the dining room table, a handful of them exploding from an old milk pitcher that had been here when I got here, but mostly, they were just . . . everywhere.

I walked through the house, and they lessened as I walked through. A bunch in the living room; a few sticking out of a Mason jar on the bathroom sink where I kept my Q-tips. One last stray pink one sitting on my pillow.

I walked over and sat down, twirling the daisy in my hand. Emerson had day magic. He must have waited for me here last night so he could charm me into forgiving him one last time. By the time morning came, he must have known that his grand experiment had gone south, and he used the last of what magic he had to make all these daisies for me. The upside of that was, maybe he wasn't that far away. If he was still within the blast range, if he wasn't dead yet . . .

I didn't realize I was crying until I saw a drop fall on Seamus's head, which was resting on my knee. I swiped my face and put the magical daisy on my pillow. It would probably be gone by the time I came back, but there wasn't a huge chance I'd ever be coming back, and I wanted to remember it there, pretty and magical, resting on my pillow.

I slid my phone out of my back pocket and took out my earrings and, finally, pulled my wedding set off my left hand for the first time since Judd had put it on my finger in that courthouse eight years ago. I set the pile of items on my bed and looked down at Seamus.

"I gotta go," I said, standing up. "I love you, you little asshole."

And then I left.

It was only eight o'clock when I made my way to the town square to find Nick standing in a group with about twenty people, most of them women. Stacy was there, and Leo. An angry English teacher in her late forties named Dierdre Troudt was still wearing her floral pajama set. A young redheaded girl, Clementine Klosterman, nervously chewed her lip. Grace and Addie were there, and by Stacy's side was a small, elegant, impossibly thin woman dressed all in black, her white-blond hair pulled back into a bun so tight you could bounce a quarter off it. She gave me a look of withering disdain when Stacy introduced us, and before Stacy said a word, I knew; this was the Widow Lillith Easter.

And then, at the edge of the circle, Liv and Betty. I walked over to them and took Liv's hand.

"You have to go," I said. "You're already weak."

"I'm fine," she said, smiling a little too brightly. She was obviously tired, but honestly, she probably looked better than I did at that moment. "You can't turn down my power right now. We need it."

"I'll keep an eye on her," Betty said. I smiled and grasped her hand, too, then looked back to Liv.

"And Desmond?"

Liv's expression darkened. "Tobias is delaying him, but if you don't want him here for this, we don't have much time."

"Okay," I said, releasing a heavy breath. "Let's get started."

I turned around to look at the group.

"I need everyone to join hands, in a circle," I said, "and in a moment, I'm gonna run my magic through you all."

"Wait, run it *through*?" Dierdre Troudt said, looking at Nick. "You didn't tell us about anything running through anything."

Nick shrugged. "My job was to get you here. I did my job."

"Forget it," Dierdre said. "It's bad enough I've got magic that makes little cartoon birds fly in a circle around my head, but now I'm supposed to be some electrical lead in this chick's magical hippie love circle? I don't think so."

"She's legit, Dierdre," Stacy said. "And she's here to save your sorry ass. Shut up, get back in line, and trust her."

I looked up, surprised to see Stacy Easter grabbing her mother's hand at one side, and Nick's at the other.

"Go for it," Stacy said. "Do your thing."

I smiled at her. She didn't smile back, but that was okay, because following her lead, everyone joined hands as well, and no one said another word. I took Nick's hand in mine, and Clementine's in the other, and as soon as the circle connected, I could feel the power zipping through me like a wild charge. It rattled my teeth and made me dizzy. A loud buzzing ripped through my ears, and I saw a concerned look on Stacy's face as she mouthed, "Eliot?" and I knew I didn't have much time.

So I threw my magic outward, and that was it.

It was weird, like a gentle *pop,* not unlike a well-controlled champagne cork. Just *pop* and I was out of my body, floating above the crowd. Time was weird; it was both slowed down and nonexistent. I could see the initial blast of electric blue light, shooting outward, bouncing off everyone in the circle exactly as I'd hoped it would, using them as amplifiers, each one increasing the signal exponentially. The blue lightning zipped over the town at wild speed, looking like a blast radius that moved ever outward, until finally dissipating well after the outskirts of town. I would bet it reached even farther than Emerson's original shot, and while there might be some confused people in Findley Lake with flask-shaped doorknobs that morning, everyone in Nodaway Falls was safe. They were also magical now, and god knew there would be a lot to deal with on that score as things progressed, but they would be safe, and that's all I'd wanted.

It took me a while—hours, days, seconds, I had no idea—to realize that my little magical circle was in a frenzy about something, and when I moved back to focus on our area in town square, I realized that they were in a frenzy about me. I couldn't hear anything, but I could see Stacy by my body, doing CPR. Nick was running through the group, trying to find a phone that still worked so he could call 911. Chances were good, considering my power to alter metal, that there wouldn't be a working phone in the boundaries of Nodaway Falls for at least a few days.

But that was okay. I was gone. I was done. It was over for me, and I was shocked by how incredibly peaceful it felt to know that. No more running. No more hiding. No more lying about who I was . . .

"Feels pretty good, don't it?" a cheerful, Boston-laced voice said from behind me, and I turned to see Judd standing there in a space of white limbo, grinning like an idiot.

"Judd?" I couldn't believe how good it was to see

him. All my anger, all my resentment . . . it was just
gone. I reached out and hugged him, and he put his
arms around me, and it was really him. He was really
there.

Either that, or this was just my dying brain halluci-
nating, but whatever it was, it was good.

"It's kinda weird, isn't it?" Judd said when we pulled
apart and I looked back at my body, where Stacy huddled over me, frantically pounding on my chest. He
nudged me with his elbow. "Wish I had a girl that hot
working on me when I was first gone."

"Shut up," I said, and slapped at him. Then I felt it,
a moment of . . . not so much pain as pressure, a deep
thud within my chest as Stacy hit me, hard.

"Don't worry," Judd said. "The connection will
sever for good in a few minutes, and then we can go.
It just takes a little time. Honestly, for me, I didn't even
know I was dead until it was all over. Christy and I
were still fighting over what we'd been fighting about
when the brakes went. And I still don't get why she was
so mad. She asked me to tell her what she could do better in bed, and I told her, and then she lost her freakin'
mind."

I pulled my attention away from Stacy and her
distress and looked at Judd. "Oh. Yeah. About the accident, Judd—"

He held up his hands and grinned at me. "I know.
It's okay. Your dad had me killed. Honestly, I figured
it'd be a father that did me in eventually. That's a risk
you take, bein' a guy like me."

"Yeah," I said, and laughed. "I guess you do." I motioned toward the vast, empty white space behind him. "So, what do we do now? Go through there?"

Judd glanced over and shrugged. "Beats the hell out of me. I don't know. I've been a little worried about it, honestly. I'm not sure what's waiting for me on the other side."

"So . . . what?" I asked. "You've just been . . . here? All this time?"

"Well," he said, spreading his hands. "Time here isn't exactly like it is there, but . . . yeah. Pretty much. Been hanging out with you."

I stared at him, and it took me a moment to realize what he was saying. "You mean . . . that was really you? You were really there? That whole time?"

Judd shrugged. "Yeah. I didn't want to leave you."

I reached out and hit him, and there was a firm connection of . . . not a physical body, but something. I got a sense of satisfaction from the hit, anyway.

"You let me think I was nuts!" I said.

"No, you listened to that doctor who told you I was all in your imagination," he said. "I just didn't argue about it. And then, after a while, it seemed to make it a little easier on you when I could come through, and you stopped expecting me to answer all your questions, so . . . I maybe fed the idea a little."

He made a "teensy bit" gesture with his thumb and index finger. I was about to hit him again when I felt a sharp pain run throughout my body and I doubled over. Judd caught me, and there was a strange kind of existential dizziness as I felt us being pulled away from the white limbo and back into the town square.

"Oh, Ellie? You don't look so good."

I didn't feel great, either. I tried to get my bearings, but the pain was wild. It was like, in just those few moments of peace I'd had, I had forgotten what pain felt like. But now, it was rippling through me, and it took me a moment to identify it as emotional pain. I felt my feet land on earth, and when I looked up, Judd and I were in the town square, and the white limbo was fading.

And Desmond was walking toward my body. He wasn't rushing. He already knew there was nothing to be done. He knew he was too late.

"Oh," I said simply at the sight of him. There was something about being without a body that made every sensation so powerful and sudden that it rocked you, like being on the bow of a ship in wild swells. There was no anchor strong enough to keep you grounded.

Stacy was kneeling next to me, her knees tucked under her in defeat. Desmond fell to his knees beside her, his face stony. She said something to him, and I could see tears on her face. He didn't look at her, his eyes were focused on me, but he reached out and squeezed her hand. She squeezed back, and another wave of pain and longing and sadness shot through my entire being.

Desmond released Stacy's hand, and slid his arms

under me. I looked like a rag doll in his arms, but he held me close, protectively, despite the fact that there was nothing to protect me from anymore. I wanted to touch him, to comfort him, to tell him everything was all right, that I was okay, but when I reached out, my hand went right through him.

"Yeah," Judd said from behind me, his voice thick. "That's really hard. I was there when the cops came to the door to tell you. I was with you after they left. Took you a while to see me there. I had to really work for it."

I didn't respond to Judd. I didn't care. All I wanted was to be with Desmond again. The pain of separation was unbearable, and yet, I couldn't leave him. I knelt beside him as he held me in his arms.

"Ellie?" Judd said. "Maybe you don't want to do this. You're not gonna make him feel any better, and you're only going to make yourself feel worse. Maybe we should just go back."

Nodaway Falls was in chaos; people coming out of their houses, wandering in the street, trying and failing to start their cars. Magic everywhere. Somewhere not far from where Desmond sat next to my body, a child made snow in summer, and laughed. For all the temporary destruction I had wrought to mechanical and electrical items, the people were okay, and there was a town where magic was out and open and normal.

But none of that mattered to me. I'd given my life for it, but all I could see, and feel, and know, was

Desmond. He held me in his arms and his face was still a mask of stone, but I could feel the storm inside him. Not having a body to process emotion for me meant that every emotion hit at full force, even other people's. I felt Desmond's despair, his grief, his guilt, his devastation. His love. Some of it was mine, too. The idea of leaving him, of *ever* leaving him, was unthinkable. I would stay here, by his side, until . . . until . . .

"Hey, Ellie," Judd said behind me, his tone tense. "We really need to go."

Desmond smoothed my hair away from my face and kissed my forehead. "My dear little girl."

"Oh!" I said, and turned to Judd. "I heard him! I can hear him! Can he hear me?" I waved my hands around him, trying to touch him and failing. "Desmond! Desmond!"

And that's when a pain, white hot and terrifying, ran through me, and I crumpled down, falling to the ground. I could hear the grass crunch under me, and Desmond glanced my way quickly, but saw nothing, and then turned his attention back to my body.

"What's happening?" I asked, looking up at Judd.

"Yeah." He sighed and ran a hand through his hair, rumpling it. "There's a thing you should probably know." He hesitated while I watched him, panting under the pain.

"What?" I asked.

"You can go back, if you want to," Judd said finally.

Elation ran through me, followed by hot spasms of wild pain.

"It's gonna hurt," Judd said. "It's gonna hurt a lot. But if he's worth it to you—"

Pop.

I wanted to scream, but I couldn't. My body felt like it was lying on spikes that were slowly sinking into me, ripping me apart from within. My lungs burned as I gasped for air, and the world spun around me, pulling me into darkness.

"Eliot?" Desmond's frantic voice called to me, anchoring me, and I pulled up from the darkness. I opened my eyes a tiny bit, allowing a small shaft of light in, and shards of pain shot through my head. I pulled in another breath, and my lungs burned with a fury.

"Stacy! Nick! Someone! Help!" Desmond laid me on the grass gently and tipped my head back to open my air passages. I took in another ragged breath and coughed.

Fuck, I thought. *This hurts.* But I couldn't say anything. I was too weak to say anything. All the peace that I'd felt in that space between life and death had gone. I was inside this body which suddenly felt unreasonably heavy and gross. Every inch of me seared with pain like I'd never felt before and yet . . . I was happy.

I stretched out my fingers, a tiny movement that took almost all my strength. Immediately, Desmond's hand was holding mine. I felt him kiss my knuckles, not raising my hand to his lips, but rather lowering himself to me. Then he gently kissed my forehead, and I felt his breath shoot against my skin as a sob overtook him.

I opened my eyes again, and withstood the pain of the light as my sight adjusted. Finally, I was able to see Desmond looking down at me, the sky bright white and blinding behind him.

"Help is coming," he said. "You're going to be all right."

He pulled me into his arms again. I rested my head on his shoulder and looked into the white sky, where Judd looked back down at me. His mouth moved, but I couldn't hear him. After a moment, he threw me a kiss, gave a short wave, and walked away into the whiteness.

And then, everything went black.

The walls of my room were pink.

The natural light was dim in the room, so it was either dawn or dusk, but I had no idea which. It wasn't a hospital room, but when I moved my hand, I felt something pulling on the back of my hand, and when I looked down, there was an IV taped on, and a plastic tube running up to what looked like a saline bag. A door opened, and a short, pudgy redheaded woman I'd never seen before stepped in wearing pink scrubs. She walked over to my bag, checked it, and then looked down at me. A look of pleasant surprise washed over her face, and she smiled at me.

"Well, hello there," she said. "How are you feeling, sweetheart?"

"Um . . ." My voice was hoarse and my throat was scratchy. The nurse rushed to the nightstand and poured some water from a plastic hospital pitcher into a plastic hospital cup. I drank gratefully and tried again.

"Where am I?" I asked.

"Olivia Kiskey's house," she said. "My name is Beverly. I live down on Jefferson, by the old laundromat?"

"Oh. Right," I said. "Yeah, I go there."

"It's a good place. Anyway, I work with Peach at the hospital. I smuggled in the equipment." She winked at me. "Apparently, treating magical injuries at the hospital can make things worse, so we've had that British doctor managing your care."

My heart started to race at the mention of what I presumed to be Desmond, but Beverly didn't seem to notice.

"Anyway, you've been out for about fifteen hours, but everything is going to be just fine. We've set up a triage here for magical injuries, and that guy has been running around like a chicken with his head cut off."

"You mean . . . you mean Desmond, right?"

She waved a hand in the air and laughed. "Is that his name? I came in and he started barking orders at me and I just took to calling him Doc. We were never really introduced." She sat down on the edge of my bed. "So . . . this magic thing. That's a pip, huh?"

"Yeah," I said, looking at her. "You live in town? Do you . . . ?"

Her expression remained friendly, but I could see a hint of freaked-out in her eyes. "Night magic. I do a thing with my hands, there's a whole bunch of weird green sparks, and then *poof*! *Watermelon*." She laughed. "It's the damnedest thing. 'What's your magic?' is the new pickup line at Happy Larry's. It's crazy." She patted the bed and sat up. "Well, honey, it's still early. Maybe you should go back to sleep."

"Um . . . the doctor . . . ? Is he . . . ?"

"He's sleeping," she said. "Finally. They said something like he hadn't slept since the fireworks, poor guy. Are you all right? Did you want me to wake him?"

"Oh." *Yes. Yes. Yes.* "No. Let him sleep. I'll see him later. I'm fine."

"All right, honey." Beverly started for the door, then stopped and turned around. "We're not supposed to talk to you about it. The doc says not to upset you or anything, but . . ." She took in a deep breath, and her chin quivered a bit. "I've got a small boy. He's twelve years old. The magic hit and he was so excited. We didn't know it would hurt him to use it, so we let him play and then . . ." She let out a sharp sigh and swiped at her eyes. "Well, you know. I was scared to death, and then all of a sudden, this blue spark whips over town and our TV set stops working and he just hops out of bed and asks for Fruit Loops." She laughed. "We're not supposed to say anything to you, but I just can't leave this room without saying thank you for saving my little boy."

Her eyes filled with tears and she rushed over and gave me a quick hug.

"Don't tell the doc I said anything, okay? He'll skewer me with a fire poker if he finds out I defied his direct orders."

I smiled. "I won't say anything."

"Good. We'll keep it just between us girls, then." She headed back toward the door. "You sure there's nothing I can get for you, Ms. Parker?"

"No, thank you," I said. "And you can call me Eliot."

"Okay, Eliot. If you need anything, there's a little wireless button on your nightstand there that will ring a bell downstairs." She laughed. "We had to go get 'em at the Home Depot out in Buffalo. Nothing in this town works anymore!"

And with that, she slipped out and shut the door behind her. In the hallway, I heard the tone of her voice talking to someone, and a moment later, the door opened slowly, and Desmond walked in.

He stood there by the door for a while, just watching me. Unlike Beverly, Desmond wasn't dressed for the job, and he looked like hell. His face was sporting a patchy layer of scruff, his tie was gone, his shirt unbuttoned at the collar and half sticking out of his trousers, which were wrinkled and still had grass stains on the knees.

"Wow," I said. "You clean up good."

He let out a short laugh and looked down at himself, and it seemed as if this was the first thought he'd given to his appearance in days.

"Yes. Well." He walked over to me and pulled a chair up next to my bed, but didn't say anything, just stared at me with an expression I couldn't quite read, except to tell that it wasn't happy. He picked up a notebook that was sitting on the edge of my bed; I guessed that was my medical chart. "It looks like your vitals are improving."

"I'm sorry I didn't tell you where I was going," I said. "You would have tried to stop me."

"You're right." His eyes landed heavily on mine. "I would have. It was stupid and reckless and it might not even have worked—"

"But it did," I nudged.

"But it might *not* have." His face was stony calm, much as it had been when he'd been sitting over my dead body. He lowered his eyes, going back to the notebook. "I would like to keep you under observation here for another twenty-four hours at least."

"I'm sorry," I said again. "I know that was hard on you."

"You can't *begin* to know . . ." He trailed off, his eyes still on the notebook, but I could tell he wasn't focused on the writing.

"I know," I said. "I was there. I was watching."

He looked up at that, his dark eyes wild. "No. *I* was there. I held your body."

"I know," I said, but then he looked up with dark fury in his eyes and said, "You *don't* know!"

I went quiet and waited for him to talk again. It took a while, but he did.

"I apologize for speaking harshly to you. I don't mean to. You did what you thought was best, and you were triumphant. You saved an entire town full of people, and given the choice to do it again, you would do it again. It's who you are, and it's why I—"

He stopped short, gathered himself, then started again.

"It's why I think so highly of you," he said, very carefully, as if each word was a struggle. I would have felt elated at the confession, except I knew what was coming next. I could see it on his face.

"For years, I felt nothing. And then, one day, I felt *everything*. It was like stepping into the sun after being in a dark room for too long. It blinded me, and it was excruciating. So I moved back into the shadows and stayed there. I maintained a distance between myself and others. It was working out rather well. Until I met you."

I felt tears pushing at the sides of my eyes, so I clenched a fist to keep control. He had been so strong for me. Now it was my turn.

"You were so charming, so intelligent, so breathtakingly beautiful—"

I snorted, unable to stop myself, and he smiled sadly at me.

"So tragically incapable of graciously accepting a compliment."

"I mean . . . thank you," I said, trying to lighten things a bit.

"Well done," he said softly, and visibly steeled himself for the rest of it. "Everything happened so quickly, and under such intense circumstances . . . had we simply met and gotten to know each other like normal people . . . maybe . . ." He stared out the window for a moment, then shook his head. "But . . . probably not. Every emotion is overwhelming for me. Happiness at seeing a friend. Sadness at a television commercial . . ."

"Oh," I said. "The one with the puppies and the grandma?"

He smiled. "It's why I gave up my television. It's why I keep myself at a remove from people. I just snapped at you for being foolish and reckless, but that's exactly what I've been. It was so careless of me to allow any of this to happen, and I apologize, Eliot. I shouldn't have allowed it to go as far as it did." He looked at me, his expression tormented and tired. "Finding you in the town square yesterday, I felt . . . shattered. I don't know how else to describe it, and the word falls woefully short of the experience. Every part of me now is a ragged piece, and when I feel emotions, they all cut into me. And when I look at you, I feel . . . emotion." He sank back into the chair, dropped his eyes, and spoke so quietly I almost didn't hear him. "Do you understand?"

He seemed almost like a little boy. So lost, so vulnerable. And of course, I knew exactly what he was talking about. For those moments, I felt it. Before shooting back into my body, that excruciating pain I'd felt hadn't been mine. It had been his. And if being with me was going to make him feel like that, how could I possibly ask it of him?

It was at that moment, of course, that I broke down. My chin quivered and my eyes filled and tears fell down my cheeks and the poor guy . . . he just looked wrecked.

"It's okay," I said. "I'm okay, but you have to go." I reached over and hit the button by the bed, and Desmond stood up, moving closer.

"Are you all right? Is there anything you need? Are you in pain?"

"I'm fine. I'm fine." I reached out and grabbed his hand, holding it tight and trying to show in my face that I wasn't angry, that I didn't blame him, that it was okay. "It'll take me a couple of weeks, but I can go back to Massachusetts, or maybe . . . Emerson's gone now. He's probably left me an estate or something." I let out a laugh that turned into a sob. "I'm probably rich."

"Eliot, it's not necessary for you to leave—"

"No, I should. I mean, we can't risk bumping into each other on the street. If I cause you pain when you see me—"

"There will be no risk," he said. "I'm leaving, to-morrow."

I blinked up at him, stunned. "But . . . they're going to need a special doctor, someone who understands . . ."

"They will," he said, his face stony. "I have a friend from Niagara Falls, who is both a magical and a physician. He'll be setting up a practice in town. You're well enough that you no longer need me, and everyone should be fine under Beverly's care until he gets here."

"And now that Emerson is gone, there's no reason for you to stay," I said, finishing his thought. "And every reason for you to leave."

We went silent for a bit, my hand clutching his as I tried not to cry and failed miserably, knowing this was probably the last time I'd ever see him. He reached out and touched my face and when I looked up at him, he looked like hell. His face was stony, but his eyes were hot with pain, and it hurt me just to see it. I couldn't imagine what he was feeling, how terrifying it must be to know that if you felt anything, even happiness, it would sear through you like a hot poker.

There was a gentle knock on the door, and we released our hands. Beverly walked in, saying, "Sorry that took me so long, honey, but I had a kid got knocked in the head with his own magical baseball bat and we have to heal the stupid just the same as the smart." She saw my expression then, and her eyes shot up to Desmond. "Doc? Everything okay?"

Desmond kept his head lowered. "She's on track for

a full recovery. She should remain on observation until tomorrow, and then she can go home."

With that, he handed the notebook to Beverly and walked out the door. Beverly glanced down at the notebook, a look of confusion on her face, but jerked her head back up when I broke out into unrelenting sobs.

"Oh, honey." She walked around and sat down on the bed next to me, pulling me into her arms. "Oh, shhhh. I know it's scary being all cooped up. You should have seen me after my C-section. I cried for three days straight, and the nurses were . . ."

She kept talking, running her hand over my hair and getting me tissues, just talking endlessly, somehow understanding on instinct that what I needed at the moment was to think about anything other than my own consuming sadness.

Chapter 16

"Well, that's the stupidest line of bullcrap I've ever heard," Stacy said, stabbing a hot dog off the grill and stuffing it into her bun. We were at Liv and Tobias's, celebrating a return to what passed for normalcy in Nodaway Falls with a barbecue. Liv handed out margaritas while Tobias manned the grill; apparently, Stacy's job that day was to be pissed off at Desmond.

"Asshole just got me to like him again, then he just takes off and leaves town, abandoning you?" Stacy rolled her eyes and sat down on the Adirondack chair next to mine. "I'm telling you, if I had any idea where that limey butthole went, I'd hunt him down and beat the hell out of him."

"It's weird," Liv said, taking a sip of her margarita. "You hating him isn't that much different from you forgiving him."

"Stacy is a complicated woman," Leo said, taking a bite of his burger. "It's why I love her so much."

"Look, it's okay," I said. "We weren't even really a thing. We were—"

"If you say 'just friends' I'll smack you," Stacy said. "And it's not okay for him to leave you like that. If he'd just allow himself to feel *something,* if he'd sit down and get it all out with a good cry like Leo does, he'd be fine."

Tobias snorted, and Leo shot Stacy a look. "Hey."

Stacy patted his knee. "It doesn't take away from your masculinity, honey. It takes strength to cry, and feel your feelings, and deal with whatever's bugging you. That makes you manlier than any of these other guys."

At this, Tobias's posture straightened. "Hey."

"All I'm saying," Stacy went on, "is that Desmond's problem isn't from the potions. It's from being Desmond. Hell, when he saw Eliot, the woman he *loves,* lying on the ground, dead as a doornail, he didn't even cry. Seriously, what the fuck?"

"He didn't love me," I said. "It never got that far. We were just—"

"Don't say it," Stacy warned. "I'll have to kill you and I'm starting to like you a little bit." She went quiet for a moment, then shook her head and said, "I don't care what you say, that man loves you. Maybe he didn't cry, but I saw the look on his face, and it wasn't the look of a man who had just lost his favorite piece of ass."

"Stace," Liv said, warning in her voice, and when I looked up, she was shooting a worried expression my way. I smiled at her, as much as I could.

"It's okay," I said. "Really, I love reliving this whole thing. Can we do it some more?"

"Sorry." Stacy patted me on the knee so I would watch as she stuffed her hot dog in her mouth, shutting herself up. She smiled around a mouthful of food, and everyone groaned and laughed.

"You are disgusting," I said.

"I'm adorable," she taunted back, mouth still full.

And I had to admit it; she was.

It had only been a week since the magical world had broken open at Nodaway Falls, and somehow, most things were oddly normal. Amber had taken over my job at Happy Larry's and it was a perfect fit. She was mean to the patrons and made an absolute ton in tips, without having to be constantly corrected by my father. She did show up at my place with flowers when the news came that his body had been found in a hotel room in Buffalo, which I thought was nice, and some evidence that he'd had a good influence on her, at least a little.

Meanwhile, a lawyer had been in touch with me, and while I was still living off my Happy Larry's tips at the moment, it did appear that Emerson's life insurance and estate were going to keep me in lights and dog kibble for the rest of my life. I was in no rush for it, though; I didn't have any big plans.

I hadn't seen Judd since the day I died, and that was

okay. I missed him, sometimes, a little, but I was glad he'd finally gone toward the light. Maybe he and Emerson were out there on the other side, having the dead-guy equivalent of a beer. I had no idea if that was even possible, but the idea made me happy.

"Watch out, everybody. The party is *here*!"

I looked up to see Peach, Nick, and baby Josie coming through the back gate. Peach looked amazing; five days past giving birth, and she was already moving faster than I was. She had dragged me out at five in the morning that day to go on a training run.

"It'll be mostly walking," she'd said. "Hardly any running at all. I'm still getting back into shape."

I almost died. She didn't break a sweat.

"Here she is," Peach said as we all gathered around her, admiring the baby. Only Peach and I knew that Josie was sort of named for me, which was fine by me. I'd had enough of people making a big deal over me during the past week. Between saving the town, being abandoned by Desmond, and my father's body being found, people had been very attentive, and it was making me a little tense. I was glad to shower some attention on baby Josie and have it not be all about me, for once.

"There's the woman of the hour!" Nick said, and came over to give me a quick peck on the cheek. "We were really sorry to hear about your dad, and . . . well . . . everything."

"Thanks, Nick." I wanted to throw the attention back on baby Josie, but Liv was giving me an expectant look, and it was time to get something over with. "But now that I've got your attention."

Liv walked over to stand next to me. We had talked about this earlier, and she had been the one to encourage me to do it with everyone there as support. Still, it felt a little weird, but then again, it had been a long time since I'd had family. It would take some getting used to.

"I came here, just a few weeks ago, an unemployed widow, dead broke, my magic gone, with nothing to my name but a broken-down shack, a crappy truck, and a deaf dog." I glanced over in the corner of the yard, where Seamus was happily chewing on the rawhide bone I'd given him to keep him busy while we ate. "Now I'm . . . well, I'm still unemployed . . ."

"Yeah, cry me a river, heiress," Stacy said.

". . . and I'm still *widowed*," I said, punctuating the word to humble Stacy. From the shameless way she grinned up at me, it didn't work. "But now I have friends, and I don't need to define myself by what I've lost anymore."

"Oh!" Peach put her hand to her mouth and teared up. I smiled at her as I reached into my front pocket and pulled out my wedding set.

"Liv came up with an idea for me, and I think it's a good one. So if you'll just . . ." I set down my margarita and held the ring set with my fingertips, so everyone could see. I willed the magic through me, to the metal, bending and twisting it easily, until the two thin, gold bands wrapped around each other at the middle and formed the shape of two butterfly wings on either side, with the tiny cubic zirconia (which Judd had always insisted was a real diamond) accenting the tip of one wing.

"Oh, wow!" Peach said. "That's so cool how you've got the wings hinged together like that!"

Liv smiled at me and held out her hand. I put the little butterfly into her palm and watched as she closed her hand around it. Little sparks of yellow danced over her fingers, and when she opened her palm, the butterfly took flight, bouncing around the backyard for a moment before zooming into the sky.

"Oh, Jesus, you guys, what the hell is wrong with you two?" Stacy dabbed at the edge of her eye with a napkin.

"Yeah, and *I'm* the one who cries all the time," Leo said, nuzzling her as she leaned her back against his chest.

Liv put her arm around my shoulder and rested her head against mine as we watched the last glint of the butterfly disappear into the sky. I picked up my empty margarita glass and said, "Someone's got to fill this for me, now."

And someone did.

"You know that dog's not supposed to be in here," Larry said as he stopped by the corner booth. In the past few weeks, it had become my booth. I would come in and sit there to read or think, order a drink and not drink it, then leave a hell of a tip. I could afford big tips now, and that's why Larry complained about Seamus coming in with me, but never actually threw us out.

"What are you reading?" he asked, leaning against the wall.

"Don't you have to work?"

He motioned toward the bar, where Amber was arguing with a patron. "She's got it under control."

I closed my book and showed him.

"Witness to My Life." He picked it up and read the cover. *"The Letters of Jean-Paul Sartre to Simone de Beauvoir."*

"Yeah," I said, and went quiet. Desmond, being the guy that he was, had returned his copy before leaving town. Me, being the girl I was, took it out, claimed I lost it, and bought the library a replacement copy while keeping that one.

Larry slapped the book back on the table. "Yeah, I'm more of a Kant guy myself."

"Larry!" I stared up at him, laughing. "Are you seriously kidding me with this?"

"I went to Brown. Biology major, philosophy minor," he said, his voice just as gruff as ever. "I was gonna go premed, but my dad passed and left me his bar and well . . . what are you gonna do, right?"

"No way!" I said, slapping my hand down on the table. "This bar was named for your dad? So it's not ironic, then? There actually *was* a Happy Larry?"

"Eh," Larry said, and shrugged. "I don't know if I'd go so far as to say *happy* . . ."

A shaft of light came into the bar as the front door opened. I couldn't see who had come in, but based on Amber's expression, it was Someone. Since the big magical explosion, agency guys had been poking around, trying to get a foothold in the power structure here. Between my RIAS connections and Tobias's ASF ones, we'd managed to keep them out of our hair, but every so often, another one would show up and give it a try. I sighed and pushed up from the booth.

"Time for business," I said, and then froze.

He looked just as he always had. Tall, lean, clean shaven, well groomed. Shirt, tie, and trousers, all pressed and perfect. I watched as he walked to the bar and ordered. Amber nodded and pulled a beer for him, shooting a quick look at me as she slid it across the bar to Desmond.

He looked over and our eyes locked.

He smiled.

I smiled back.

"Beat it, Larry," I whispered, and Larry disappeared like a mensch, without another word.

Desmond took his beer from the bar and walked over to me.

"Hello." He sounded amazing. God, I loved that accent.

"Hi," I said.

"Do you mind if I join you? I used to come here quite a lot, and this is where I would usually sit."

"Sure." I motioned toward the booth. "Take a load off."

He started to sit when Seamus saw him, stood up
and barked, wagging his tail. Desmond put his beer
down and ruffled Seamus's neck, looking genuinely
joyful to see the stupid mutt. My heart started to race,
and as I sat down across from Desmond and watched
him love up on my dog, my limbs felt shaky from the
hope shooting through my veins. I was too stupid to
protect myself from it; if he broke my heart again, fine.
But I wasn't going to shut down to the pure happiness
it gave me to see him again.

Seamus calmed down and sat by Desmond's side
and Desmond looked at me first, then down at the
book. When he looked back up at me and met my
eye, he smiled warmly and took a sip of his beer.

"I thought you didn't drink during the day," I said.

"I didn't," he replied, then added on an amused huff,
"I do now."

I resisted the temptation to follow that up with
some kind of snappy repartee. Whatever was going
on here, I didn't want it to be snappy. I wasn't going to
hide behind clever bullshit anymore. Desmond Lamb
wasn't the only one to engage in emotional growth.

"You look well." He smiled at me. "Beautiful,
actually."

"Thank you. You, too. Really great. You look . . ."
I wasn't sure what word to use. Happy? Peaceful? They
seemed like strange things to say, and yet, it was the
truth. Which could really only mean one of two things;
either he was over me, and I didn't cause him to feel

anything anymore, or he'd somehow fixed it, and had returned to win me back.

Under the table, I crossed my fingers, hoping it was the second option.

"Well, I was planning on sitting here for a bit to gather my thoughts before seeing you, but I guess we're both here, so now's the time . . ." He paused, then laughed a little to himself. "I don't quite know how to start."

"That's fine," I said, leaning back. "I'm unemployed. I have loads of time."

"All right. Well . . . this is going to sound exceedingly stupid, but . . . recently, I reactivated my phone number. My phone, like all the rest in town, had of course ceased to function, and I'd just left it behind. I didn't want to be reachable, at first. I felt it was . . . best."

"Yeah, that makes sense. You didn't want a bunch of ranty voice mails from your ex bogging you down."

For the first time since our eyes had met, his smile faltered, and I was okay with that. I was glad to see him and everything, and I still cared about him and would work hard to fix it all if he still wanted me, but he hadn't been the only one to suffer from this whole thing, and I didn't mind making that clear.

"It turned out, my ex hadn't tried to get in touch with me at all," he said, "which, I'll admit, I found more a disappointment than a relief."

"She was respecting your space," I said, a little edge working into my voice. "Honoring your request."

"I know she was. *You* were. Thank you." He reached out and touched my hand, meeting my eyes. "Thank you."

"You're welcome." The warmth of his hand on mine was excruciating. *Get to the point, buddy,* I thought, *or you're gonna kill me here.*

He pulled his hand back, but kept his eyes locked with mine.

"I did, however, find a number of . . . to borrow your terminology . . . ranty voice mails, e-mails, and texts from a mutual friend."

I smiled with instant knowing. "Stacy Easter."

He let out a short laugh. "As it turns out, she had a theory about my . . . well, *problem* . . . which, once I sorted through all the profanity and name-calling—"

"Oh, oh!" I bounced a little in my seat. "What was the best one?"

He glanced upward, retrieving the memory. "I think 'fucking limey shithead bastard' was my personal favorite. What it lacked in eloquence it more than made up for in passion. I saved that voice mail. I can play it for you later, if you'd like."

"Oh, I'd like that very much," I said, my heart full of wild love for Stacy Easter.

"Anyway," Desmond continued, "her theory, to paraphrase, was that I should be a man, strap on a pair, and just . . . have a good cry."

His face flushed a bit as he spoke, but he held my gaze.

"So," he said, "that's what I did."

He went silent at that point, and I waited as long as I could before saying, "Well? What happened?"

"Oh, it was dismal," he said. "I was staying in a hotel in Surrey—"

"You went back to England?"

"Yes," he said. "I had this thought that going home again would be a good idea. It wasn't."

"A good idea?"

He looked at me. "It wasn't home."

I felt myself flush, all over, as he looked at me and was grateful when he finally looked away.

"It was a pathetic affair," he said. "I wept openly for three days straight. My eyes were raw. I was dehydrated. I went through an unconscionable number of tissues."

"Wait," I said. "What about the handkerchiefs?"

"Ran out, day one," he said. "It was a tragic display, and the most alarming discovery came at the end of it. It turned out, against all expectation, Stacy Easter was right."

I gasped and put my hand to my mouth. "No!"

"Are you making light of my emotional breakdown?" he said, but there was a glint of humor in his eyes.

"Sorry. Carry on."

He gave me a playful look of admonishment. "Anyway, at the end of it all, I felt better. I felt . . . free. I felt happy, and nothing hurt. Well, nothing except how horribly I missed . . . well . . . you."

There was a long silence.

"That's it?" I said after a while.

"I'm sorry. Is that not enough?"

"No, it's not enough," I said. "You have to tell me that you still want me."

"Oh. Is that how this goes?"

"That's how it goes, you big idiot," I said. "Look, I'm glad you've worked out your emotional issues and everything, but I'm not just going to jump in your lap because you said you missed me."

He raised one brow at me. "Oh? And what are the magic words that would get you to jump into my lap?"

I pointed an accusatory finger at him. "Don't get cute with me. You loved me and left me, you can't just waltz back in here and—" I stopped suddenly, realizing what I'd said. "I mean, you didn't . . . I meant *love* like, you know, had sex with, not—"

"I loved you," he said, his voice low.

We both went silent, and the funny bit we'd been improvising didn't seem that funny to me anymore.

"You . . . you . . . you did?" I said quietly, stammering pathetically, not sure when the moment was that I'd lost control of this ship. My heart was suddenly racing and I felt a little faint, so I grabbed his beer and took a deep drink.

"I thought you didn't drink during the day," he said, with a teasing tone.

"I do now," I said, and took another gulp before setting it on the table between us.

"Eliot, you are the best friend . . . the *only* friend,

that I've had in a long time. I don't want to come here and make confessions and mess it all up. I don't know how to do this properly, I just know I don't want to lose you." He raised his eyes to mine. "I never want to do that again."

"Oh, god. This is just painful." I shot up out of my seat and moved over to his side, nudging him over, and then I angled my body to face him.

"Let me simple this up for both of us. Just say this: 'I love you. I need you. I want you.' That's all you have to do, and I'm yours."

He smiled wider than I'd ever seen him smile.

He reached up and touched my face. "I love you, Eliot Parker." His eyes shifted up as he moved his fingers through my hair. "I need you." His gaze dropped down to my lips. "I want you."

"See?" I said, breathless. "That's all you needed to say."

His eyes met mine again. "And you?"

I gave him a blank look, teasing. "What about me?"

"Now you're being willfully cruel," he said, "but it's all right. I deserve it. But now you must tell me. Have I buggered this all beyond repair or do I have a chance to win you back?"

I smiled and nodded, blinking away the tears. "You're a hot mess, Desmond Lamb, but god help me, I love you, too."

I threw my arms around his neck and hugged him to me, feeling dizzy with how good it was to touch him again. We held each other tight for a moment, and

when he pulled back to look down at me, the
tear at the corner of his eye.

"Holy cow," I said, wiping it away with my finger-
tip. "You weren't kidding, were you?"

"Do shut up, Ms. Parker."

He kissed me then, and everything else in the world
disappeared. Even Amber's hooting and hollering from
the bar was a distant note from some faraway universe.
Desmond was back, and he was mine, and as he kissed
me on that Wednesday afternoon in the grungiest dive
in upstate New York, I finally knew what it felt like
to be truly home.